PENGUIN CLASSICS

THE SATYRICON

TITUS PETRONIUS ARBITER is reputedly the author of the *Satyricon*. Historical and literary evidence strongly suggests that he is the same Petronius whose character and strange death in AD 66 are so graphically described in Tacitus' *Annals*. As governor of Bithynia and as consul Petronius showed vigour and ability, but his chief talent lay in the pursuit of pleasures, in which he displayed such exquisite refinement that he earned the unofficial title of the Emperor Nero's 'style expert' (*arbiter elegantiae*). Court rivalry and jealousy contrived to cast on Petronius the suspicion that he was conspiring against the emperor, and he was ordered to commit suicide. He gradually bled to death, opening his veins, binding and reopening them, passing his last hours in social amusement and the composition of a catalogue of Nero's debaucheries.

J. P. SULLIVAN was Professor of Classics at the University of California at Santa Barbara when he died in 1993. He previously held posts at the universities of Oxford, Cambridge, Texas, Buffalo, Minnesota and Hawaii. He was the author of many works, including *The Satyricon of Petronius: A Literary Study* and *Literature and Politics in the Age of Nero*.

HELEN MORALES is Associate Professor of Classics at the University of California at Santa Barbara. She is co-editor of the journal *Ramus: Critical Studies in Greek and Latin Literature*, author of *Vision and Narrative in Achilles Tatius' 'Leucippe and Clitophon'* and *Classical Mythology: A Very Short Introduction*, and editor of the Penguin Classic *Greek Fiction*.

PETRONIUS

The Satyricon

Revised edition

Translated by
J. P. SULLIVAN
Introduction and Notes by
HELEN MORALES

PENGUIN BOOKS

PENGUIN CLASSICS

Published by the Penguin Group
Penguin Books Ltd, 80 Strand, London WC2R ORL, England
Penguin Group (USA) Inc., 375 Hudson Street, New York, New York 10014, USA
Penguin Group (Canada), 90 Eglinton Avenue East, Suite 700, Toronto, Ontario,
Canada M4P 2Y3 (a division of Pearson Penguin Canada Inc.)
Penguin Ireland, 25 St Stephen's Green, Dublin 2, Ireland (a division of Penguin Books Ltd)
Penguin Group (Australia), 250 Camberwell Road, Camberwell, Victoria 3124, Australia
(a division of Pearson Australia Group Pty Ltd)
Penguin Books India Pvt Ltd, 11 Community Centre, Panchsheel Park, New Delhi – 110 017, India
Penguin Group (NZ), 67 Apollo Drive, Rosedale, Auckland 0632, New Zealand
(a division of Pearson New Zealand Ltd)
Penguin Books (South Africa) (Pty) Ltd, 24 Sturdee Avenue, Rosebank, Johannesburg 2196, South Africa

Penguin Books Ltd, Registered Offices: 80 Strand, London WC2R ORL, England

www.penguin.com

This translation first published 1965
Reprinted with revisions 1969
Reprinted with revisions 1974
Reprinted with *The Apocolocyntosis* 1977
First published in Penguin Classics 1986
This edition, including new editorial matter, first published in Penguin Classics 2011

004

Translation copyright © J. P. Sullivan, 1965, 1969, 1974, 1977, 1986
Editorial material copyright © Helen Morales, 2011
All rights reserved

The moral right of the editor has been asserted

Set in 10.25/12.25pt PostScript Adobe Sabon
Typeset by Jouve (UK), Milton Keynes
Printed in Great Britain by Clays Ltd, St Ives plc

ISBN: 978-0-140-44805-4

www.greenpenguin.co.uk

Contents

The Satyricon

Acknowledgements

I would like to express my general scholarly debts to Dr Konrad Müller, P. T. Eden and Gareth Schmeling; their help in various ways was invaluable. Allan Kershaw kindly read the proofs. Elizabeth Frech worked wonders in processing a complicated and much corrected original and saved me from many mechanical errors.

To the late Betty Radice, once editor of this series, I am deeply indebted for her constant encouragement, advice and friendship.

In Memoriam Betty Radice

JPS, 1986

Thanks are due to Peter Carson, wise and patient editor, and to the Universities of Cambridge and California, Santa Barbara, for intellectual and financial support. Thanks also to John Henderson who first taught me to think hard about Petronius, and, above all, to Tony Boyle, John Sullivan's friend and my partner, for daily debate about literature, politics, and pleasure.

For A. J. Boyle

HLM, 2010

Preface on J. P. Sullivan

Petronius' *Satyricon* is the most controversial work in the classical literary canon. It now enjoys a wide readership and is regularly taught in schools and universities worldwide, but its risqué sexual scenes and subversive style meant that this has not always been the case. More than anyone, it was John Sullivan who was responsible for rehabilitating the *Satyricon*, both through his groundbreaking scholarship on the novel and through this acclaimed translation.

Sullivan, who died in 1993, came from working-class roots in Liverpool, England. He won a scholarship to study Classics at St John's College, Cambridge in 1948 (and among the many lifelong friends he made there was the writer Frederic Raphael, who was later to translate the *Satyricon* for the Folio Society in 2003). He then went on to Oxford University, first as a Junior Research Fellow in Ancient Philosophy at Queen's College, and then as University Lecturer at Lincoln College. During his years at Oxford, Sullivan became fascinated by the tradition of translating the classics, and the intellectual problems involved in translation, and gave a new, bold, series of lectures on 'Creative Translation: Ben Jonson to Ezra Pound'. His long critical reflection on translation, realized when Sullivan translated Petronius, is one of the ingredients that make this translation a truly great one.

He left Oxford in 1963 at the behest of William Arrowsmith (another translator of *Satyricon*, for Mentor Classics in 1959), and took up a post at the University of Texas at Austin. Sullivan's *Satyricon* was first published two years into his time there, and two years before the hippy-euphoria of the Summer of Love, in the middle of the Swinging Sixties. It is very much a product of that decade. 1960 saw the most notorious case in Great Britain ever brought under the Obscene Publications Act, when Penguin Books was prosecuted for publishing D. H. Lawrence's *Lady Chatterley's Lover*. Penguin was acquitted and, in the subsequent more-relaxed climate, it became possible for the first time in modern publishing to publish the *Satyricon* without censoring its more explicit sexual scenes. In the same year as Sullivan's translation was published by Penguin, Holloway House Publishing Company published a translation by Paul Gillette. The front cover announces: '*Satyricon*: Memoirs of a Lusty Roman. First complete and uncensored reconstruction of the Petronius classic novel depicting the full moral depravity and decadence of imperial age Rome', and the author's biography assures us that 'Dr. Gillette is well-known to magazine readers in the United States and on the Continent. Segments of his *Satyricon* reconstruction, along with other translations from classic French, Spanish, Italian and Polish works, have appeared in *Playboy*, *Knight*, *Cavalier* and many other magazines.' Penguin's marketing was more sober, but Sullivan's translation is as unrestrained as its time. Arguably, the in-your-face machismo that marks some of the translation is as much a product of Sixties chauvinism as it is the effective rendering of Petronian style and tone.

The Sixties were also a time of great fascination in scholarship with narrative: with how stories are told and with the different forms narrative can take. Narratology, a systematic theory of narrative, was first launched. In classics, Sullivan was at the forefront of these new developments in literary criticism. He co-founded the (then) radical literary journal *Arion*, and dedicated a special issue of the journal to Petronius (1966). His book *The Satyricon of Petronius: A Literary Study* came out two years later, and, even though certain aspects of it seem dated now, it remains one of the best critical studies of *Satyricon*.

Sullivan's 'golden age' (as he described it) at Texas came to an end in 1969 when he took up professorships at SUNY

Buffalo and, later, at the University of California at Santa Barbara. Sullivan was a man of contradictions. This self-description in 1990 (the tenses now changed) is appropriately Petronian:

> His favourite exercise was jumping to conclusions; his favourite food, *chorizo* and red peppers; favourite drink, dry Plymouth gin martini up with a twist; and he was fond of blondes and brunettes who gave him a lot of lip. Most people regarded him as sane, but there was a substantial minority who wished to see him committed, at least during the summer months and at Xmas. He was almost never convicted of rape or wife-beating or marketing junk-bonds. His favourite recreations were reading eighteenth century pornography and ensnaring housewives in logical dilemmas. His list of victims was quite small. Height, taller than Napoleon but shorter than Julius Caesar or President Bush. Complexion, sub-choleric; voice, sinister and menacing; ears, scarcely noticeable; eyes, uncrossed pools of panic. Blood type O with extra large platelets.[1]

No political correctness here, but Sullivan in fact worked hard to support women in the profession. He helped found, in 1972, the Women's Classical Caucus of the American Philological Association and edited (1971–5) *Arethusa*, a Classics journal that champions theoretical approaches to literature, including feminism.

Sullivan died in 1993 of throat cancer. It is quite a responsibility to revise the work of another scholar. I have not altered the translation itself (but see the Note on the Text and Translation), which has become a classic in its own right. I have, however, completely rewritten the Introduction and Notes, and added a section on recommended reading. Sullivan revised his translation in 1986 and for this used the 3rd edition of the Latin text by Konrad Müller (*Petronius Satyrica*, Munich, 1983). Where he disagreed with Müller about the text, he has listed the changes (see Textual Changes, pp. xxxviii–xxxix). The student who is reading the translation against Müller's Latin text is advised to keep the Textual Changes bookmarked; if the translation strays far from the text, it is worth checking to see if Sullivan has accepted a different textual reading. Where the translation differs from the text because it is impossible to render jokes and puns literally, I have discussed it in the Notes.

NOTE

1. JPS on 'JPS', quoted in A. J. Boyle's tribute to Sullivan, in A. J. Boyle, ed., *Roman Literature and Ideology: Ramus Essays for J. P. Sullivan* (Bendigo, Victoria, Australia: 1995), pp. 6–23. Boyle's essay contains extensive information about Sullivan and provides a bibliography of all his works.

Introduction

Petronius and his Neronian context

The *Satyricon* is generally agreed to have been written by a courtier of the Emperor Nero, his 'style expert' or *arbiter elegantiae*. The best introduction to him is that given by the Roman historian Tacitus, who describes Petronius' downfall and death during Nero's reign of terror (*Annals* 17.18–19):

18. Petronius deserves a brief obituary. He spent his days sleeping, his nights working and enjoying himself. Others achieve fame by energy, Petronius by laziness. Yet he was not, like others who waste their resources, regarded as dissipated or extravagant, but as a refined voluptuary. People liked the apparent freshness of his unconventional and unselfconscious sayings and doings. Nevertheless, as governor of Bithynia and later as consul, he had displayed a capacity for business.

Then, reverting to a vicious or ostensibly vicious way of life, he had been admitted into the small circle of Nero's intimates, as Arbiter of Taste: to the blasé emperor nothing was smart and elegant unless Petronius had given it his approval. So Tigellinus, loathing him as a rival and a more expert hedonist, denounced him on the grounds of his friendship with Flavius Scaevinus. This appealed to the emperor's outstanding passion – his cruelty. A slave was bribed to incriminate Petronius. No defence was heard. Indeed, most of his household were under arrest.

19. The emperor happened to be in Campania. Petronius too had reached Cumae; and there he was arrested. Delay, with its hopes and fears, he refused to endure. He severed his own veins. Then, having bound them up again when the fancy took him, he

talked with his friends – but not seriously, or so as to gain a name for fortitude. And he listened to them reciting, not discourses about the immortality of the soul or philosophy, but light lyrics and frivolous poems. Some slaves received presents – others beatings. He appeared at dinner, and dozed, so that his death, even if compulsory, might look natural.

Even his will deviated from the routine death-bed flatteries of Nero, Tigellinus, and other leaders. Petronius wrote out a list of Nero's sensualities – giving names of each male and female bedfellow and details of every lubricious novelty – and sent it under seal to Nero. Then Petronius broke his signet-ring, to prevent its subsequent employment to incriminate others.

(Tacitus, *The Annals of Imperial Rome*,
trans. Michael Grant (Penguin: 1956, revised edition 1996))

Tacitus refers here to C. (i.e. Gaius) Petronius, while most manuscripts of the *Satyricon* refer to the author as Petronius Arbiter, or simply Petronius; and Plutarch and Pliny mention a Titus Petronius. This confusion over his name, and Tacitus' failure even to mention the *Satyricon*, have caused scholars some anxiety about identifying the author with Nero's courtier, but the arguments for strongly outweigh those against. Language and style, as well as historical and economic references, all point to a first century AD date. If we agree on identifying Tacitus' Petronius with the author of the *Satyricon*, we can date the novel with some precision to between AD 63 and 65. Of course, Tacitus' account is biased, and might be no more accurate a portrait of the real Petronius than Leo Genn's performance in the 1951 movie *Quo Vadis*, in which the hounding to death of the noble courtier by Peter Ustinov's sinister Nero recalled and criticized the ongoing McCarthy witch-hunts against Hollywood. Nonetheless, it is irresistibly attractive to read Tacitus' Petronius in light of the *Satyricon*, and vice versa, and for us to ask: for this author, to what extent did art imitate life?

Certainly, Tacitus' Petronius conveys several characteristics of the *Satyricon*, and of its characters. In Tacitus' description, Petronius is not what he at first appears to be, just like all the

major characters in the novel; *Satyricon* is full of fakes and
impostors. Petronius makes judgements on style and taste; style
and taste (literary and social) are preoccupations of *Satyricon*.
A year before Petronius died, the philosopher and playwright
Seneca, who had been tutor and adviser to Nero, also killed
himself, as did his nephew, the poet Lucan. Seneca's death is
described by Tacitus as a heroic death, reminiscent of that of
the philosopher Socrates (as described in Plato's *Phaedo*), while
Petronius, in choosing to listen to 'light lyrics' and 'frivolous
poems', to sleep and eat rather than philosophize, effectively
parodies this tradition. Parody and death are two recurrent
concerns of the *Satyricon*. These striking similarities prompt
further questions, ones that take us to the heart of the difficul-
ties involved in interpreting this novel. Is it a coded critique of
Neronian society? To what extent is there an agenda – political,
ideological, philosophical – to the *Satyricon*?

Satyr tales in fragments

Haphazard manuscript transmission has left us with a tattered
text, so full of gaps that questions of interpretation are hard.
Astonishingly, we possess perhaps less than a tenth of the ori-
ginal work. It was divided into books, possibly 24 in number,
and we think that the bulk of the surviving text comes from
Books 16–18 of the original. The description of Trimalchio's
dinner party is the only fragment that offers some sense of con-
tinuity. One effect of this is that the dinner party takes pride of
place; whether the episode would have been as central to the
original we cannot say. Reconstructing the novel is a Mission
Impossible: we simply have too few pieces of a giant jigsaw
puzzle to do more than guess at what the larger picture might
once have been. Of course, it is precisely this sense of frustra-
tion and possibility, and the lure of detective work, that is part
of the *Satyricon*'s continuing appeal.

What we have are glimpses into the adventures of three free-
loaders: the narrator Encolpius (whose name means 'In-crotch'),
the teenager he is in love with called Giton ('Mate'), and a rival

for Giton's affections Ascyltus ('Unshagged-out'). They travel around Italy – with what aim or purpose we do not know – and encounter various losers, eccentrics and bullies along the way, including the brothel-keeper Quartilla; Lichas, a ship captain who is in angry pursuit of Encolpius for some reason; the pretentious ex-slave-turned-millionaire Trimalchio; and the poet and con man Eumolpus. (In the translation I have provided glosses to help guide the reader through the narrative, but should stress that these, and the chapter headings, are of my own devising.)

We might be helped in our efforts to reconstruct the *Satyricon* if we could be guided by generic expectation, but it is far from clear to which genre, if any, the work belongs. The title is *Satyricon* (genitive plural from the Greek adjective *satyrikos*, 'about satyrs', with *libri*, 'books', understood) or *Satyrica*, and means 'books about satyrs' or 'satyr tales'. Satyrs were mythical creatures, half-human, half-goat, who are represented on many a Greek vase drinking too much, attempting (but failing) to rape maenads and nymphs, and brandishing their enormous penises. The title *Satyricon* thus conjures up a world of appetite and lechery. Indeed, Encolpius, Giton and Ascyltus have all manner of sexual adventures and show little self-restraint. The ruling deity in this licentious world is not Poseidon (as in Homer's epic poem, the *Odyssey*), but Priapus, the god who sported a huge erection and was associated with lust, humour and aggression (statues of Priapus stood in Roman gardens where they threatened potential intruders with punishment by penetration). Encolpius repeatedly encounters Priapus, or images of Priapus, and appears to have done something to have angered the god.

The sexual licence of the *Satyricon*, and the fact that male–male liaisons are as frequent as male–female ones, has led to the novel's becoming, in the modern world, a classic of gay fiction. It is listed in *The Advocate*'s *100 Best Lesbian and Gay Novels* (22 June 1999) alongside Thomas Mann's *Death in Venice* and James Baldwin's *Giovanni's Room*. An early twentieth-century translation of *Satyricon*, in fact one of the best in English, was attributed to 'Sebastian Melmoth', a pseudonym used by Oscar Wilde, the playwright who was a classical scholar talented

enough to have done such a translation, and knew his Petron-
ius, as a reference in *The Picture of Dorian Gray* makes clear.
Wilde died in 1900, two years before the publication of the
translation, in impoverished circumstances after his imprison-
ment for 'the love that dare not speak its name'. The translation
is now generally agreed to be a literary hoax, designed to trade
on Wilde's notoriety for sexual impropriety. However, it was
an intelligent hoax, and one that invited comparisons between
the two artists. In the preface to *The Trial of Oscar Wilde*, by
the same publisher that published the Sebastian Melmoth
translation, Charles Grolleau compares the writers and the per-
secutions they suffered: '. . . we are suddenly called upon to
witness the heart-rending spectacle of the slow death-agony of
a haughty, talented poet, a Petronius self-poisoned through fear
of Caesar or a Wilde whom a vicious and over-wrought Public
had only half-assassinated, raising his poor, glazed eyes towards
the marvellous Light of Truth'.

However, the reader who anticipates that the *Satyricon* will
be titillating is likely to be disappointed. It is far from the cele-
bration of male sexuality that its status as a gay classic might
suggest. 'She tried to excite me, but the thing was cold with the
chill of a thousand deaths,' laments Encolpius of one of his
many episodes of impotence (ch. 20). Sex in *Satyricon* is frus-
trated or interrupted more often than it is enjoyed.

Poetry, prose and questions of genre

The *Satyricon* (as it has come down to us) begins with a heated
discussion between Encolpius and Agamemnon, a professor of
rhetoric. The two criticize the rhetorical training that the
Roman youth receive in schools (Encolpius blames the teach-
ers, Agamemnon the pupils' parents). 'All they get,' gripes
Encolpius of the literature used in the classroom, 'is pirates
standing on the beach, dangling manacles, tyrants writing
orders for sons to cut off their fathers' heads, oracles advising
the sacrifice of three or more virgins during a plague – a mass
of cloying verbiage: every word, every move just so much
poppycock' (ch. 1). It is not like the good old days, continues

Encolpius, when they had Homer, Pindar, Plato, Sophocles, Demosthenes and other great works of 'intrinsic beauty' rather than the school exercises in declamation that break 'the rules' and are the worse for it. These complaints are actually rather hackneyed (we find similar criticisms in Seneca the Elder, Quintilian and Tacitus); the critics, as well as the literature they are criticizing, are Petronius' targets here. However, they operate, as do many similar passages in the novel, to prompt the reader to think about what is good rhetoric and what makes a great work of literature. Does Petronius follow the rules, or is his book too 'just so much poppycock'?

Why this question is so difficult to answer is because it is hard to know what the rules are; by which standards we are to judge the *Satyricon*. A crucial aspect of interpreting and evaluating any work is the reader's generic expectations. What makes a good romance novel is different from what makes a good pantomime or horror film, car advert or newspaper obituary, and genre was fundamental in organizing a reader's engagement with the written word no less in the ancient world than in the modern one. The *Satyricon* does not 'fit' into any generic category. It is a highly allusive and self-conscious work that plays upon many genres including epic, especially Virgil's *Aeneid* and Homer's *Odyssey* (the characters Circe, Agamemnon and Menelaus obviously evoke their famous Homeric counterparts, and Polyaenus, the pseudonym used by Encolpius at Croton, is one of Homer's epithets for Odysseus), Senecan tragedy, ancient mime and Latin love poetry.

I have called the *Satyricon* a 'novel' because that is the term we now typically use to refer to an extended work of prose fiction. 'Novel' is, however, a modern generic term, not an ancient one. There were ancient 'novels': prose works of fiction written in Greek and Latin largely in the first two centuries AD. Some of the Greek novels display a common pattern: girl and boy fall in love, become separated, and endure horrid trials and tribulations (involving pirates, oracles, tyrants and virgin sacrifice) until their eventual reunion and marriage. Several had similar titles: *Ethiopian Tales*, *Ephesian Tales*, *Babylonian Tales*. So the title *Satyr-tales* casts Petronius' work as a comic take on the Greek novels, whether or not it was an *intentional* parody. The fickle promiscuity of Encolpius, Ascyltus and Giton, and the disconnected meandering of the narrative, are in sharp and humorous contrast to the constancy of the lovers and strong narrative teleology of many of the Greek novels. Nor does *Satyricon* have much in common with the Latin novels, Apuleius' *Metamorphoses* and the anonymous *Apollonius, King of Tyre*.

Another clue offered by the title is the similarity in sound between *Satyricon* and *satura*, the Latin word for satire. The two words are in fact unrelated, but their similarity creates a punning association that draws attention to the satiric content of the novel. A particular branch of satire has often been said to be the key to understanding the *Satyricon*: Menippean satire. In fact, this is a largely bogus category. A modern term used to identify writing that mixes prose and verse (also known as prosimetric writing), Menippean satire takes its name from Menippus of Gadara (third century BC) who wrote Cynic parodies, none of which survives. With its mixture of prose and poetry, *Satyricon* qualifies to be called Menippean satire, but this classification does little genuinely to illuminate the work and its literary context. Indeed, knowing what to make of its poems is perhaps the most frustrating conundrum posed by the *Satyricon*.

The two longest poems are both recited by Eumolpus, who takes centre stage in the second half of the novel as we know it. The first of these is the 'Troiae Halosis' or 'The Fall of Troy' (ch. 89): a poem on the familiar subject of the fall of the city at the end of the Trojan War, which Eumolpus performs in the course of discussing the exhibits in the art gallery. The second is an epic account of the 'Civil War' (chs 119–24, 'Bellum Civile') between Julius Caesar and Pompey (though Pompey is not explicitly named), which ended with the defeat of Pompey in 48 BC at the Battle of Pharsalus. Both poems are prefaced with Eumolpus' views on how poetry should be written: hackneyed opinions delivered in a terribly pompous manner. Both poems are also incomplete and end abruptly, possibly reflecting the form of the original *Satyricon*. They are not good poems: they are repetitive and uncontrolled, in some places trite and in others overblown. They function to characterize Eumolpus as a pretentious mediocrity: part of the *Satyricon*'s aggressive satirizing of (so-called) educated men. When Eumolpus has finished reciting the 'Fall of Troy', his audience pelts him with stones: the typical response, he says, to his recitals. Eumolpus, whose name means 'Good Singer', is anything but. Bad poets were favourite targets of Roman satirists: Juvenal and Persius (a contemporary of Petronius) both attack them (Juvenal, *Satires* 1, and Persius, *Satires* 5).

But the 'Fall of Troy' and 'Civil War' do more than simply function to caricature Eumolpus. They respond to other poems, though which ones and the exact nature of the responses remain unclear. The 'Fall of Troy' is written in metre and diction reminiscent of Seneca's tragedies, but its subject matter strongly recalls the first part of Book 2 of Virgil's *Aeneid*. Nero wrote a poem on the fall of Troy; rumour had it that this was the poem he sang as Rome burned. Perhaps Petronius was satirizing this, or Seneca's accounts of the same theme in his *Agamemnon* and *Trojan Women*, or a version by the poet Lucan called *Iliacon*, or Virgil's treatment, or all of these. Eumolpus' 'Civil War' is some kind of response to an epic poem by Lucan on the same subject, also known as 'Bellum Civile', or 'Pharsalia'. Initially Lucan was a favourite of Nero's, but the relationship deteriorated (different explanations are conjectured) and in 65 BC Lucan joined the conspiracy of Gaius Calpurnius Piso against Nero. When his treason was exposed, Lucan was forced to commit suicide. He died, aged 25, a year before Petronius. Eumolpus' 'Civil War', like his 'Fall of Troy', concerns acts of deception (a major theme of the *Satyricon*), and both poems square up to literary rivals and tackle Rome's relationship with its past. Quite how the politics and the parody played out, however, are unrecoverable.

As the generic frames of the *Satyricon* shift and slide, so do the reader's emotional and intellectual expectations of the work. This is disorientating: a hall of mirrors in Petronius' anarchic carnival.

Trimalchio's feast

Trimalchio's feast (also known as *Cena Trimalchionis*) is the longest surviving episode (chs 28–79) in the novel. It is an outrageous extravaganza of which it is undoubtedly more pleasurable to be a reader than a guest. Trimalchio is a freedman (an ex-slave) who, since being granted his freedom, has made vast amounts of money. The name 'Trimalchio' is thought to mean something like 'Three Times the Master'; he is certainly a character both larger than life and very much aware of his own power.

A gap in the manuscripts means that we do not know the circumstances in which Encolpius and his party have been invited to the feast. However, even before they reach the dining-room, the companions are surprised and shocked as their first sight of their host is of a bald old man playing a ball game in the grounds of his house with eccentric rules (the player scores each time a ball is dropped rather than successfully returned). Trimalchio then pisses in a chamber pot while he is still playing and wipes his hands afterwards on the head of a young slave. After more excesses in the baths, they make their way to the entrance of Trimalchio's mansion where a notice on the door announces: 'ANY SLAVE LEAVING THE HOUSE WITH-OUT HIS MASTER'S PERMISSION WILL RECEIVE ONE HUNDRED LASHES' (ch. 28). As he is trying to take all this in, Encolpius is terrified by what he thinks is an enormous dog. Much to the amusement of the others it turns out only to be a painting of a dog on the wall under the motto 'BEWARE OF THE DOG' (ch. 29). There are other wall paintings: one depicts Trimalchio's life story, another scenes from Homer's *Iliad* and *Odyssey* alongside those of a gladiatorial contest (a strange combination). No wonder Encolpius and his companions find themselves 'choking with amazement' and 'gaping' (chs 28, 29).

This prelude to the feast highlights the definitive characteristics of the *Cena*: topsy-turvy rules, the odd juxtaposition of refinement and vulgarity, the emphasis on bodily functions, an acute awareness of social status, the threat of violence, the display of erudition but not quite getting it right, and appearances being deceptive. Throughout it all Petronius creates an overwhelming sense of rush, of breathlessness and things happening all too quickly, and of guests' reactions being those of anxiety and amazement, rather than of pleasure.

Encolpius' encounter with the *trompe l'œil* dog is one of many examples that expose his character's gullibility. There is a crucial difference between Encolpius the adventurer, who is an often naïve protagonist, and Encolpius the narrator, who relates his adventures with melodramatic flourish. However, we need always to be conscious of where we as readers stand in relation to him. Given that Encolpius has so often and so easily been duped, and that *any* first-person narrator gives a partial account, we should recognize that he is an unreliable narrator.

The *trompe l'œil* dog is the first of many instances where things are not what they seem. The entire *Cena* is an assault course of surprises. The reader learns (well before Encolpius catches on) that the food dishes are designed to deceive the guests. What look like ordinary hens' eggs turn out to have marinated figpeckers inside their shells (ch. 33). During dessert, when anyone helps themself to the delicious cakes and fruit, he or she is squirted in the face with saffron juice from the phallus of a confectionery Priapus (ch. 60). All of this is quite ingenious; there is nothing straightforward or without conceit. Even the stories that the diners tell, like those of the werewolf and the changeling boy (chs 62, 63), are about disguise and changes of identity. There is an essential instability to things and people in the feast episode; as soon as you think you have grasped something – a person or an object – it changes. This is true of the *Satyricon* as a whole; it is a world of fabrication and flux.

The unpredictability of events in the feast creates a sense of lurking menace and imminent violence. Sometimes the violence is feigned. On one occasion Trimalchio threatens to have the chef flogged for not gutting a pig before roasting and serving it. This turns out to be a staged conceit: the chef is spared and reveals that he has, in fact, cooked sausages and black pudding inside the pig (ch. 49). At other times, the violence is real. Trimalchio assaults his wife, Fortunata, by throwing a glass at her face (ch. 74), and his hunting dogs, brought in as part of another culinary spectacle, turn on each other (ch. 64). All of this adds to the atmosphere of chaos and anxiety.

The *Cena* is often praised for its realism. It is undoubtedly true that from the description of the *trompe l'œil* dog, an image strikingly like real wall paintings that survive from Pompeii and other places, to the freedmen's speech, distinguished from those of the elite by its poor Latin, Petronius paints his world with breathtaking vividness and attention to detail. The *Cena* is brought alive through acutely observed sights, smells and sounds. However, what distinguishes the *Satyricon* is not realism per se, but the juxtaposition of the realistic with other registers, of the familiar with the strange. A realistic description of a dessert, for example, is followed by the abrupt entrance of a character, Habinnas, whose interruption is designed to recall the entrance of Alcibiades in Plato's *Symposium* (ch. 65), the celebrated philosophical feast that provided a model for all Greek and Roman accounts of feasts written thereafter. The philosophical allusion transports the reader to quite a different register and a different interpretative frame.

The extravagance of Trimalchio's feast is part of his conspicuous display of wealth. We are repeatedly reminded of his status as a freedman. Freedmen were in the uneasy position of having the liberty to do business and perhaps amass, as in Trimalchio's case, considerable wealth, but never quite to gain the respect and social standing of the freeborn elite. Every age finds something ridiculous about social climbers; the ridicule of Trimalchio is not so different from the British twenty-first century behaviour of mocking 'chavs' (white, working-class people who wear designer labels and aspire to a better lifestyle than they were born into). This comparison (while not appropriate in every respect) is useful in that it serves to highlight the conservatism of the *Satyricon*. Its politics are not as radical as its literary form. Ridiculing the social climber is one way of keeping the lower classes in their place and protecting the superiority of the elite.

Ex-slaves were widely disparaged in Latin literature. 'He had a freedman's mentality,' wrote Seneca of one former slave,

Calvisius Sabinus, 'and I never saw a man use his wealth more disgustingly' (*Letters* 20). Like Calvisius Sabinus, Trimalchio shows off his knowledge of Greek mythology, only to get the stories embarrassingly muddled. Like Pacuvius, another freedman satirized by Seneca, Trimalchio morbidly celebrates his own funeral. Trimalchio also recalls the vulgar Nasidienus, in the satirist Horace's *Cena Nasiendi*: both freedmen stuff their guests with course upon course of lavish yet indigestible food, and both unwittingly give their guests a moment's relief when they leave the table to urinate. Other of Trimalchio's features resonate with those depicted in Theophrastus' *Characters*, a collection of short character sketches written in the fourth century BC. Like Theophrastus' Garrulous Man, Trimalchio effusively praises his wife in public; like the Disgusting Man, Trimalchio discusses the remedy for constipation (pomegranate rind and pinewood dipped in vinegar, apparently).

These vulgarities make it all the more outrageous – and funny – that Trimalchio is also characterized as a parodic version of the Emperor Nero. The most striking parallels are that Trimalchio wears a golden bracelet on his arm, as Nero was said to have done; he keeps the shavings of his first beard in a golden casket, as Nero was said to have done; he has a ceiling whose panels open up to shower the guests with gifts, as did Nero, and an acrobat falls on him during a feast (chs 32, 29, 60, 53), as one was said to have done with Nero. Moreover, in Trimalchio we are invited to see the theatricality, infantile power play and caprice of the emperor. It would be a mistake to reduce Trimalchio to a parody of Nero, but equally erroneous to ignore the political dimension of his characterization.

If Trimalchio was partly created through previous literary caricatures, he in turn became the literary prototype for the decadent nouveau-riche character of Jay Gatsby in F. Scott Fitzgerald's Great American Novel, *The Great Gatsby*. It was first published in 1925 (the same year as T. S. Eliot's *The Waste Land*), but letters to his publishers show that Fitzgerald dithered over the title of his novel, also considering *Trimalchio at West Egg* (Gatsby's mansion was situated at West Egg in Long Island) and finally – but too late – deciding on *Trimalchio*. Like

Trimalchio, Jay Gatsby ostentatiously paraded his great wealth; we are struck by 'the colossal vitality of his illusion', and he retreats into fantasy. Like Trimalchio, Gatsby is both part of, and marginal to, high society (Gatsby has made his money through gangster activities). Unlike Trimalchio, Gatsby dies a *real* death at the end of his novel: 'the lights in his house failed to go on one Saturday night – and, as obscurely as it had begun, his career as Trimalchio was over'. Ultimately Fitzgerald's portrayal of Gatsby is more sympathetic than Petronius' of Trimalchio. An early draft of *The Great Gatsby*, called simply *Trimalchio*, was edited and published in its own right in 2000 by James L. W. West. It presents a different Gatsby, more shadowy and enigmatic, and, ironically, rather less like his Petronian model than was his later incarnation.

Perhaps the most notorious lines of the *Cena* are those spoken by Trimalchio at the dinner table: 'In fact, I actually saw with my own eyes the Sibyl at Cumae dangling in a bottle, and when the children asked her in Greek: "What do you want, Sibyl?" she used to answer: "I want to die"' (ch. 48). Eliot quotes this as the preface to *The Waste Land*, and Ezra Pound also quotes it in his *Canto 64*. Eliot's poem evokes the *Satyricon* throughout and his allusions and this quotation serve to suggest that the world is barren, desolate: a spiritual void. Sometimes critics have injected Eliot's nihilism back into Petronius. But the *Satyricon* is no Waste Land. Indeed, if we look more closely at the context of Trimalchio's remark, we can see it serves many functions, not one of which is to engender hopelessness. It forms part of Trimalchio's muddled mythology (it comes immediately after mention of stories from Homer, yet is neither Homer, nor the version of the hero Aeneas' encounter with the Sibyl told in Virgil's *Aeneid*). It also suggests that we see Trimalchio as a kind of Aeneas (which is in itself funny), about to descend into the Underworld (Cumae is where, with the Sibyl's help, Aeneas went down to the Underworld). This is all part of Trimalchio's confusion of categories: he even gets life and death muddled up. It is also a metaphor for Trimalchio's status as a freedman: he is suspended between two worlds, in a kind of no man's land. But this is an altogether more light-hearted, raucous and energetic world than that portrayed by Eliot. Trimalchio is, at least, the life and soul of his (hellish) party.

Fellini-Satyricon

While John Sullivan was translating *Satyricon* in America, the innovative director Federico Fellini was in Italy, in the initial stages of preparing to turn the novel into a film. His *Fellini-Satyricon* is an imaginative take on Petronius' novel and a masterpiece of its era. Released in 1970, the film was nominated for an Academy Award for Best Foreign Film and Fellini for Best Director. The film was called *Fellini-Satyricon* because another film of the novel, a pornographic movie directed by Gian Luigi Polidoro and released a year before Fellini's, competed for the title *Satyricon* and won. But the prefix also acknowledges that the film is not so much a 'version' of *Satyricon*, and even less an authentic rendition of it, than an original creation (written by Fellini and Bernardino Zapponi) inspired, but not limited, by the novel.

Fellini explained:

> What interests me is . . . to work as an archaeologist does, when he assembles a few potsherds or pieces of masonry and reconstructs not an amphora or a temple, but an artefact in which the object is implied . . . [T]his artefact suggests more of the original reality, in that it adds an indefinable and resolved amount to its fascination by demanding the participation of the spectator.
>
> Are not the ruins of a temple more fascinating than the temple itself?
>
> (*Fellini's Satyricon*, ed. Dario Zanelli and trans. Eugene Walter and John Matthews (New York: 1970), p. 4)

This metaphor implies that the lacunae in Petronius' novel are as fascinating as the fragments that survive, as Fellini elsewhere confirmed: 'the missing parts; that is, the blanks between one episode and the next . . . [t]hat business of fragments really fascinated me' (Giovanni Grazzini, *Federico Fellini: Comments on Film*, trans. Joseph Henry (Fresno, CA: 1988), pp. 171–2).

What Fellini kept from *Satyricon* was the relationship between Encolpius, Ascyltus and Giton; Trimalchio's feast; the story of the widow of Ephesus (ch. 108; told by a guest at the feast, not, as in *Satyricon*, on board Lichas' ship); and the Lichas episode. He added several original scenes: a theatre episode with a sadistic actor Vernacchio, a brothel episode in the Suburra (a red-light district with apartment buildings), the collapse of the Suburra, the assassination of the emperor, the Villa of the Suicides episode, the theft and death of the hermaphrodite, and the Festival of Laughter (which contrarily evokes the other Latin novel, Apuleius' *Metamorphoses*, whose second book features a Festival of Laughter).

Fellini designed his work to be 'a film outside of time, an atemporal film' (Costanzo Constantini, ed., *Conversations with Fellini*, trans. Sohrab Sorooshian (San Diego: 1975), p. 75). The emperor who is killed is not identifiable as any one specific emperor. However, certain scenes have political bite. When a dejected Encolpius is forced to marry the ship's captain Lichas, the episode does not allude to anything in Petronius, rather to the prurient accounts that the Roman historians give of Nero's marriages (to his boy slave and to his freedmen). The Villa of the Suicides episode, dramatizing the dignified deaths of a man and his wife, is one of the few emotionally affecting scenes in the film. It is reminiscent of many suicides under Nero's reign, but one in particular must stand out. As Fellini put it: 'Petronius himself appears in *Satyricon*. He is the wealthy freedman who commits suicide with his wife after he has freed his slaves' (Charlotte Chandler, *I, Fellini* (New York: 2001), p. 173). These scenes are vignettes of the cruelty and coercion of (the myth of) Nero's reign, and forge a sympathetic bond between filmmaker and novelist.

But *Fellini-Satyricon* is as much about the decadent hedonism of the Sixties as it is about ancient Rome. Fellini said:

[I]t was impossible for me not to see that the world described by Petronius bore a remarkable similarity to the one in which we live, me included. Petronius's characters are prey to the same devouring existential anxieties as people today. Trimalchio made

me think of Onassis: a gloomy, immobile Onassis with the stony
glare of a mummy. The other characters reminded me of hippies.
(Constantini, *Conversations with Fellini*, p. 75)

Indeed, the film's definitive features: the dream-like quality of
the episodes, the shots of faces staring impassively into nothing,
the vivid, unreal colours, the sumptuous visual freak-show of
physical grotesques, the sexual excess, the eerie atonal electronic
music, and the way the voices do not synchronize with the speak-
ers' lips, evoke both the hallucinatory, spaced-out world of a
Sixties druggie and the essence of Petronius' oneiric and elusive
text. There is a strong sense of dislocation and defamiliarization.
In capturing so acutely the atmosphere of the *Satyricon*, Fellini's
film is absolutely true to Petronius.

The sense of dislocation and strange juxtaposition appealed
to other artists in the early seventies who also turned to the
Satyricon. Bruno Maderna's opera *Satyricon* (1973) created its
soundscape from snatches of conversation in different lan-
guages together with jazz, classical and atonal music. Another
Italian filmmaker, Pier Paolo Pasolini, spent the final years of
his life working on a novel entitled *Petrolio*. He envisaged this
as purposefully unfinished and containing drafts of itself, as
well as letters from its author and commentators, a metaliter-
ary work that demands its reader to reconstruct it. Pasolini
wrote: '*Petrolio* as a whole (from the second draft) should be
read as a critical edition of an unpublished text (considered as
a monumental work, a modern-day *Satyricon*)' (quoted in Mas-
simo Fusillo, 'Modernity and Post-modernity', in T. Whitmarsh,
ed., *The Cambridge Companion to the Greek and Roman Novel*
(Cambridge/New York: 2008), p. 333). Pasolini was murdered
before he could finish his novel – a cruel irony that the staged
incompleteness of his novel became a genuine incompletion.
Fellini-Satyricon, together with these other works, imaginatively
reworks Petronius in different media for different audiences. In
so doing, they confirm and perpetuate the status of *Satyricon* as
the iconic experimental, elusive and (what we would now call)
postmodern novel.

Further Reading

This list is intended for students and other interested readers. For a fuller bibliography including works in languages other than English, the online journal *Ancient Narrative* (www. ancientnarrative.com) is invaluable.

Connors, C., *Petronius the Poet: Verse and Literary Tradition in the Satyricon* (Cambridge: 1998)

Conte, G. B., *The Hidden Author: An Interpretation of Petronius' Satyricon* (Berkeley: 1996)

Elsner, J., 'Seductions of Art: Encolpius and Eumolpus in a Neronian picture gallery', *Proceedings of the Cambridge Philological Society* 39 (1993), pp. 30–47

Fellini, F., *Fellini's Satyricon*, ed. Dario Zanelli and trans. Eugene Walter and John Matthews (New York: 1970). Screenplay and essays.

Fitzgerald, W., *Slavery and the Roman Literary Imagination* (Cambridge: 2000)

Harrison, S. J., ed., *Oxford Readings in the Roman Novel* (Oxford: 1999)

Hofmann, H., ed., *Latin Fiction: The Latin Novel in Context* (London and New York: 1998)

Konstan, D., *Sexual Symmetry: Love in the Ancient Novel and Related Genres* (Princeton: 1993)

Panayotakis, C., *Theatrum Arbitri: Theatrical Elements in the Satyrica of Petronius* (Leiden/New York/Cologne: 1995)

Prag, J. and I. Repath, eds., *Petronius: A Handbook* (Chichester: 2009)

Rimell, V., *Petronius and the Anatomy of Fiction* (Cambridge: 2002)

Rudich, V., *Political Dissidence under Nero: The Price of Rhetoricisation* (London and New York: 1997)

Schmeling, G. L., ed., *The Novel in the Ancient World*, rev. edn (Leiden: 2003)

Slater, N. W., *Reading Petronius* (Baltimore: 1990)

Sullivan, J. P., 'Petronius, Seneca and Lucan: A Neronian Literary Feud?', *Transactions of the American Philological Association* 99 (1968), pp. 453–67

——, *The Satyricon of Petronius: A Literary Study* (London: 1968)

——, *Literature and Politics in the Age of Nero* (Ithaca, NY: 1985)

——, 'The Social Ambience of Petronius' Satyricon and Fellini Satyricon', in *Classical Myth and Culture in the Cinema*, ed. M. Winkler (Oxford: 2001), pp. 258–71

Walsh, P. G., *The Roman Novel: The 'Satyricon' of Petronius and the 'Metamorphoses' of Apuleius* (1970; reprinted Bristol: 1995)

Whitmarsh, T., ed., *The Cambridge Companion to the Greek and Roman Novel* (Cambridge/New York: 2008)

Zeitlin, F. I., 'Petronius as Paradox: Anarchy and Artistic Integrity', *Transactions of the American Philological Association* 102 (1971), pp. 631–84. Reprinted in Harrison, *Oxford Readings*, pp. 1–49.

——, '*Romanus Petronius*: A Study of the *Troiae Halosis* and the *Bellum Civile*', *Latomus* 30 (1971), pp. 56–82

Note on the Text
and Translation

The surviving text of Petronius is regrettably fragmented and mutilated. Edifying snippets were preserved in *florilegia*; sections, words and phrases are quoted by high-minded authors such as Fulgentius and John of Salisbury, or by metricians and grammarians. But the larger narrative comes down to us in three forms. The *Cena Trimalchionis*, more or less intact, survives for posterity in a single manuscript, the *Traguriensis*. Now in Paris, it was written in 1423, but rediscovered only about 1652 in Trau (now Trogir in Croatia); this is our sole witness to the *H*-tradition. The *L*-tradition is a collection of longer extracts from the work, which survives in several manuscripts, the most noted being a much-edited copy made by Joseph Scaliger in Leiden in 1571, the *Leidensis* (*l*). Finally we have the shorter excerpts (*O*), represented by three early manuscripts from the ninth and twelfth centuries (*B*, *R*, *P*) and a number of later manuscripts and early editions. These three sources and the *florilegia* overlap.[1] But the text that results from their amalgamation would be more unsatisfactory than it is were it not for the painstaking work of generations of scholars such as Scaliger, Pithoeus, Heinsius, Jacobs, Bücheler and Müller. An important task of the editor – and therefore of the translator – of Petronius is deciding on the plausibility of competing emendations.

In this revised translation I have generally followed the latest text, Konrad Müller's third edition in *Petronius Satyrica, Schelmengeschichte* (Munich: Artemis Verlag, 1983). I record here my indebtedness in general to his work on the many difficulties presented by the manuscripts. I have ventured to disagree with his readings in a few places, sometimes because of the exigencies of any translator, who must find some sense even where the truth is difficult to discern. The more significant differences and changes from Müller's text are listed below in Textual Changes.

The Fragments attributed by editors to Petronius, with greater or lesser confidence, present further problems. Bücheler in his 1862 edition printed 53; Müller's latest edition has reduced these to 28, all of which have been directly connected, in one source or another, to Petronius. Whatever the number, some of these clearly need a context such as the *Satyricon* to make sense; others, however, might well be self-sufficient poems which may have come from some separate collection of Petronius' poetry.

In any case, I have decided to err on the side of generosity and I have translated almost all of the short verse pieces which have the remotest claim, at least in some editors' thinking, to Petronian authorship.[2] Of the poems with some claim to authenticity, Poems XXXI–XXXII, XXVII, XXXIII–XLIV and XXVI are found in this order in a ninth-century manuscript (Vossianus L. Q. 86). They are not attributed there to Petronius, but follow a number of epigrams specified as the work of Seneca. Two of this set of poems are quoted by Fulgentius as from Petronius (Fragments XVII and XXVIII) and, with XXVI, also quoted, are accepted as such by Müller. The rest, however, were also attributed to Petronius by Scaliger, who was impressed by their general resemblance to Petronius' style in the *Satyricon*. These offer a reasonable claim to inclusion.

Poems XLV–LVI were found in a lost manuscript once at Beauvais. The contents of this Codex Bellacovensis were published in 1579 by Claude Binetus. XLV–LVI were attributed to Petronius in the manuscript, according to the editor; LV and LVI were not, although they impressed Binetus as Petronian in style. Six further poems which followed in the manuscript were given to Petronius by Baehrens (*Poetae Latini Minores* iv. 103–8), although neither style nor content indicates Petronian authorship. These are not translated here.

Another two poems (Fragments XXIX and XXX) are found

in the ninth century in Codex Vossianus L. F. III under Petronius' name, and following the poems found in chs 14 and 83 of the *Satyricon*. Stylistically, they have much in common with Petronius' other verse writings.[3]

For the convenience of the reader who may wish to consult the Latin, I have followed the sequence of the fragments as edited by Müller and then the order used by H. E. Butler in the Loeb Library, *Petronius, Seneca* (London and Cambridge, MS: 1951, 1969).

The translation of such a highly original and artistic work as the *Satyricon*, written in a mixture of prose and verse, offers special problems also.[4] The amount of imitation and parody of other authors is considerable; the style moves from serious and elaborate discussion of literature to the humorous vernacular conversations of Trimalchio and his circle. And these are set within the basic narrative framework which is the generally terse, swift-moving Latinity of Encolpius. The complex problem of the prose style thus takes us to the very heart of the work.

Before discussing this major obstacle for the translator, it might be well to turn at once to the question of Petronius' verse insertions.

The verse of the *Satyricon* is of course dramatic *vers d'occasion* and, as such, subject to the exigencies of his plot. As a result, one cannot expect too much – nor does one get it. Petronius, on the evidence of the verse insertions and certain fragments, is not a great poet, despite the claims occasionally made for him. The few poems of merit sometimes included in the Fragments (e.g. LIII and LV) are not necessarily by Petronius. Some of the discredit must go to his somewhat reactionary critical principles in poetry. Petronius set himself against the mainstream of Latin verse, which was moving towards the wit of Martial and the pointed rhetoric of Juvenal, and is already well established in Latin literature by Nero's time in the works of Lucan. Whatever criticisms may be made of this, a mere traditionalism based on Virgil and Horace would be powerless to deflect or revolutionize contemporary poetic diction. Petronius' metrical virtuosity is, however, clear: he employs a variety of metres – choliambics, elegiacs, dactylic hexameters, hende-casyllables, etc. This, too, has to be taken into account by the translator, if only to the extent of trying to reproduce this *variety* of verse forms. Patently it is impossible to offer readable versions which reproduce these metres in English and so, like most translators, I have chosen whatever type of verse seemed suitable for the subject. It is, of course, an easy matter to ensure that the verse is bad where the Latin verse was intended to be bad. For the most part, I have attempted to be readable and therefore I have felt free to use modern methods of verse translation, notably *vers libre*, modern rhythm and diction, and pastiche. In various ways, like so many translators, I am indebted to Ezra Pound, and most notably to his *Homage to Sextus Propertius*, although this translation is in no way intended to be a 'creative translation' like that work. Pound's own epic, like Lucan's, is unfinished; and I have adopted the *Cantos* as my model for translating the long poem on the Civil War (chs 119–24). The original was meant to be a rehandling of the *Pharsalia* of Lucan, a sort of epic parody. There is no contemporary verse translation of Lucan to play host to the parasite, as the first three books of Lucan played host to Petronius' poem; in any case, the whole rationale of the exercise is too remote to us, so I have concentrated on making this strange fragment of an epic comprehensible to the modern reader by retaining the subject matter and making the style reminiscent at least of the style of the *Cantos*. With the poem on the Capture of Troy in ch. 89, written in iambic *senarii* and reminiscent in other ways of the basic metre of Seneca's tragedies, I found the language too jejune to resort to Elizabethan iambic pen-tameters and so I tried to bring out its alliterative qualities by borrowing something from translations of Anglo-Saxon material, such as Pound's *The Seafarer*.

This opportunistic method of translation, however, will not serve for the prose sections. It would be gratifying if the translator, like Matthew Arnold with Homer, could simply point to a limited number of qualities in the original which he had tried to bring out in the translation. But this is difficult to do except sketchily: in the main, Petronius is deliberately and deceptively simple over large stretches of his work; there is, furthermore, a pervasive irony which leaves the reader often in some doubt as to the author's intentions at certain points (how serious, for example, is the opening discussion of contemporary rhetoric?). Above all, there is the constant auctorial sophistication which makes itself felt through the pretentious or unsuccessful sophistication which the narrator Encolpius tries to adopt. In few works do we have such a separation of the author and his narrative vehicle.

As I stated earlier, Petronius strikes us as peculiarly modern. As T. S. Eliot said of Donne:

> There are two ways in which we may find a poet [or writer] to be modern: he may have made a statement which is true everywhere and for all time ... or there may be an accidental relationship between his mind and our own.[5]

That 'accidental relationship' may only be partial, even if it accounts for the unexpected popularity in certain ages of a particular classic (as with the epigrammatist Martial in the Elizabethan and Jacobean periods). But there are certain indisputably Roman qualities of humour and fantasy, particularly in the episodes at Croton, which leave behind the cynical and sophisticated realism of the *Cena Trimalchionis*, with which we feel completely at home.

These qualities are difficult to reproduce and, indeed, their interplay and local appearance in the work are sometimes hard to pin down exactly. I have tried in the preceding section to lay out my critical estimate of the work as a whole, but sometimes the particular intentions of a given section are problematic and it would be a dangerous optimism to force too blatant or crude an interpretation simply for the sake of brightness in translation. In Petronius above all the tone is of supreme importance, more important even than the range and flexibility of his style and subject matter, for it is through the tone that the objectivity and irony of the author make themselves apparent.

NOTES

1. For a full and recent account, see K. Müller, *Petronius Satyrica,
    Schelmengeschichte* (Munich: 1983), pp. 381–448. For an admir-
    ably succinct account in English, see M. D. Reeve, in L. D. Reynolds
    (ed.), *Texts and Transmission: A Survey of the Latin Classics*
    (Oxford: 1983), pp. 295ff. For individual discussions of textual
    points and for earlier editions of the text see G. L. Schmeling and
    J. H. Stuckey, *A Bibliography of Petronius* (Leiden: 1977).

2. Even the last little poem on Hermaphroditus, interesting but
    hardly Petronian, was included in Maurice Rat's edition of the
    Satyricon (Paris: 1934).

3. For a general discussion of the manuscripts, see A. Wegner, 'The
    Sources of the Petronius Poems in the *Catalecta* of Scaliger',
    Transactions of the American Philological Association 64 (1933),
    pp. 67ff.

4. For a lengthier discussion of the problems and of other transla-
    tions of Petronius in English, see J. P. Sullivan, 'On Translating
    Petronius', in D. R. Dudley, ed., *Neronians and Flavians: Silver
    Latin*, I (London: 1972), pp. 155ff.

5. *Nation and Athenaeum* 33 (1923), p. 331.

JPS

*

It is quite a responsibility to revise the work of another scholar.
The translation has become a classic in its own right, so I have
left the text as John Sullivan had it. The book titles are modern
insertions, as are the chapter divisions within them. I have relo-
cated and changed Sullivan's titles to emphasize the events
taking place more than their geographical location (not least
because the latter is not always certain). Attempts at recon-
structing the beginnings and ends of the books are not helped
by the aleatory character of the narrative.

It is useful to reprint Sullivan's original Note on the Text and
Translation (with a few minor changes), as well as his list of
Textual Changes. The text of Petronius is so frequently uncer-
tain that all modern translators make changes to the Latin text
of the Müller edition. If the translation seems to differ wildly
from the original, it is worth looking at the Textual Changes to
see if Sullivan altered the Latin text, either emending it himself

or accepting the emendations of other scholars (the editor's name is found in brackets after the Latin).

I have, however, completely rewritten the Introduction and the Notes, and added some suggestions for further reading. Where the translation differs from the Latin text because it is impossible to render jokes and puns literally, I have discussed this in the Notes.

HLM

TEXTUAL CHANGES

2.7 *regula eloquentia* (Haase) for *eloquentiae regula . . .*; 2.8 *ad
summam, quis postea* (Scriverius); 4.2 *propellunt* (*L*); 4.3 *artifici*
(Müller) for *Attico*; 5.v.16 *vox Romana* (Sullivan) for *exonerata*;
6.1 *mutus* (Nisbet) for *motus*; 7.2 *<subsequi coepi>*; 7.3 *inter
vetulas* (Sullivan) for *inter titulos*; 9.9 *meridiana* (Walsh) for *de
ruina*; 14.3 *quo cicer lupinosque* (Gronovius) for [*sicel*] (*quo*)
lupinos[*que quibus*]; 14.5 *operto* (Wouweren) *capite quae . . .
steterat* for *aperto capite* [*quae . . . steterat*]; 14.7 *nostram* [*scili-
cet*] *uno ore deridebant* (Ehlers) for *nostram scilicet de more
ridebant*; 14.8 *repente* (Müller) for +*pene*+ ; 15.5 *constitutum
<diem>* (Sullivan); 21.2 *<cerasino>* (Sullivan); 24.3 *num* (Rose)
for *nostram*; 26.7 [*id . . . cenae*] (Bücheler); 28.4 [*Trimalchione*]
(Bücheler); 30.1 *multa iam* (Sullivan) for +*multaciam*+ ; 30.9
[*dextros*] (Fraenkel); 34.4 *habere* (Braswell) for *esse*; 35.4 *<scor-
pionem> marinum* (Sullivan); [*pisciculum*] (Gaselee); *oculatam*
(Sullivan) for *oclopetam*; 37.7 *vides tantum auri* (Sullivan) for
t.a.v.; 38.12 *liberti sceleratique* (Sullivan) for *liberti scelerati,
qui*; *aves <aeno> coctos* (Sullivan) *pisces lepores* (Reiske) for
aves . . . cocos pistores; 40.5 [*qui altilia laceraverat*] (Sullivan);
41.9 *invitare <nos ipsi ad bibendum>* [*convivarum sermones*]
(Fuchs) for *invitare . . . convivarum sermones*; 41.10 *pateram
acinae* (Walsh) for +*pataracina*+ ; 42.2 [*cotidie*] (Rose); 42.4
<illae> (Ernout) for *<muscae>* (Heinsius); 44.5 *si simila siligine
inferior esset* (Sullivan) for *similia sicilia interiores et*; 44.9 *assi* [*a
dis*] (Gurlitt) for *assi a dis* (Burman); 48.7 *<oculum> pollice* (Sul-
livan) for *pollicem poricino*; 52.2 *mihi patronus meus* (*patav.*,
Bücheler) for *patrono <meo> rex Minos*; 54.1 *<in lectum>* (Sul-
livan); 57.1 [*is ipse . . . discumbebat*] (Fraenkel); 58.7 *nenias*
(Scheffer) for *menias*; 61.2 *suavis* for *suavius* (*H*); 62.4 *stelas*
(Reiske) . . . *stellas* (*H*) for *stellas* (*H*) . . . *stelas* (Bücheler); 62.9
matutinas (Heinsius) for +*matavitatau*+ ; 62.10 *in larem* (Sullivan)
for *in larvam*; 62.14 *viderint qui de hoc aliae opinionis sint* (Sul-
livan) for *viderint alii quid de hoc exopinissent* (Bücheler); 66.7
[*catillum concacatum*] (Sullivan) *tum pax! pelamides* (Heinsius)
for *pax Palamedes* (*H*); 67.7 *babaecalae* (Heinsius) for *barcalae*

(*H*); 72.7 [<*et*> *qui etiam pictum timueram canem*] (Müller);
73.5 [*quod Trimalchioni* <*tem*> *perabatur*] (Sullivan); 74.13 *non
meminit, sed de machina* (Bücheler) for *non meminit?* [*se*] *de
machina*; 76.10 *libertos* for <*per*> *libertos*; 77.4 *casa adhuc*
(*patav.*, Corbett) for +*cusuc*+ ; *sursum* (Sullivan) for *susum*;
[*hospitium hospites* <*C*> *capit*] (Sullivan); 79.6 *tabernarius*
[*Trimalchionis*] (Delz) for *tabellarius Trimalchionis*; 79.7 *ex
vehiculis* (Sullivan) *rediens* (Müller) for +*vehiculis dives*+ ; *per
eandem fenestram* (Sullivan) for +*per eandem . . . terram*+ ; 83.4
[*etiam pictorum*] (Fraenkel); 83.5 [*fabulae quoque*] (Fraenkel);
87.1 [*id est ut pateretur satis fieri sibi*] (Haley); 88.7 *cultissima*
(*R*) for +*consultissima*+ ; 89.1.31 *mari* (Tollius) for *minor*; 90.1
<*quidam*> (Sullivan); 94.10 *ante* <*me*> (Nodot); 99.5 *properan-
dum* (*t*^m) for +*propudium*+ ; 100.6 [*subter constratum*] (Fraenkel);
100.7 [*exulem*] (Müller); 101.7 <*nos*> *naufragio imponimus*
(Sullivan) for *naufragium imponimus*; 102.15 [*quod . . . infig-
itur*] (Stephanie West); 104.4 *ut . . . expiaret* (Nisbet) for *ut . . .
expiavit*; 111.2 [*Graeco more*] (Fraenkel); 114.3 *volturnus fla-
bat* (Sullivan) for +. . . *ventus dabat*+ ; 114.3 (*vis maris*) *manifesta*
(Sullivan) for ˚*manifesta*; 117.1 *divitationis* (Gruterus) for *divi-
nationis*; 118.3 *inanitatem* (Sullivan) for *vanitatem; fabulas
sententiarum tormento* (Sullivan) for *fabulosum sententiarum*
+*tormentum*+ ; 119 l.9 *Ephyreiacum* (Heinsius) for *Ephyre*
+*cum*+ ; l.11 *crustas* (Scaliger) for +*accusatius*+ ;l.79 *magistra*
(Sullivan from *CLE* 255.3); ll.110, 113 (Bouchier) for 110, 115
(Suringar); ll.220–237 for ll.220, 223–237, 221–232 (Ehlers);
124.3 [*exaggerata verborum volubilitate*] (Stöcker); 125.1 *sae-
pius* (Bücheler) for +*suis*+ ; 126.15 *curvaturam* (Fraenkel) for
+*scripturam*+ ; 133.3 1.4 *septifluus* (*L*); 134 <*peream*> *nisi* (Sul-
livan) for . . . *nisi*; 134.12 ll.11–16 (del. Wehle, def. Sullivan);
135.4 *clavum* <*ligneum*> . . . *camella* [*lignea*] (Sullivan); 136.12
pensationem (Bücheler) for *pensionem*; 137.10 [*sine medulla*]
ventosas . . . plenas [*integro fructu*]; 135.8 l.17 *Battiadae vatis*
(Pius) *miranda tradidit arte* (Müller) for +*Bachineas veteres
mirando*+ *tradidit aevo*; 139.4 [*querellam*] (Fraenkel); 140.2
<*coepit, cui soli posset*> *credere* (Sullivan); 140.5 *pygica* (Sullivan)
for *Aphrodisiaca* (Bücheler) or *pigiciaca* (MSS).

JPS

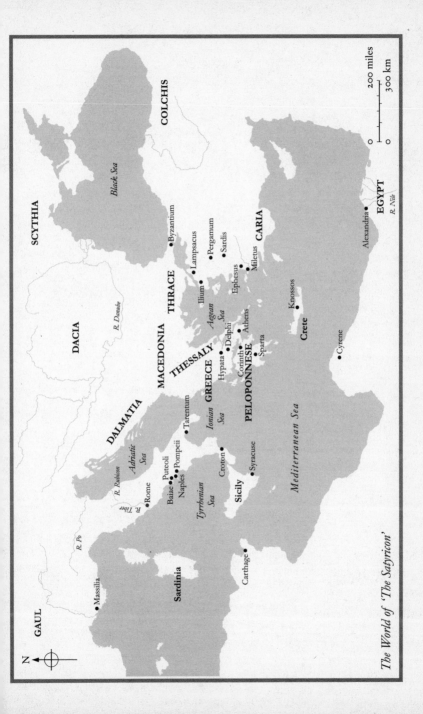

The World of 'The Satyricon'

The Satyricon

AT THE SCHOOL OF RHETORIC

1. [*Encolpius*] . . . 'Our professors of rhetoric are hag-ridden in the same way, surely, when they shout "I got these wounds fighting for your freedom![1] This eye I lost for you. Give me a hand to lead me to my children. I am hamstrung, my legs can't support me." We could put up with even this stuff if it were a royal road to eloquence. But the only result of these pompous subjects and this empty thunder of platitudes,[2] is that when young speakers first enter public life they think they have been landed on another planet. I'm sure the reason such young nit-wits are produced in our schools is because they have no contact with anything of any use in everyday life. All they get is pirates standing on the beach, dangling manacles, tyrants writing orders for sons to cut off their fathers' heads, oracles advising the sacrifice of three or more virgins during a plague[3] – a mass of cloying verbiage: every word, every move just so much poppycock.[4]

2. 'People fed on this kind of thing have as much chance of learning sense as dishwashers have of smelling clean. If you'll pardon my saying so, you are mainly responsible for ruining good speaking. Your smooth and empty sound effects provided a few laughs, and as a result you took the guts out of real oratory, and that was the end of it. Young men were not tied down to rhetorical exercises when it was Sophocles or Euripides who developed the proper language for them. Academic pedants had not addled their wits when Pindar and the nine lyric poets shrank away from the Homeric style. And apart from the poets I can cite, I certainly cannot see Plato or Demosthenes[5] going in for this sort of training. The elevated, what one might call the

pure style, is not full of purple patches and bombast: it is lifted up by its intrinsic beauty. It is not so long since that long-winded spouting of yours travelled from Asia to Athens[6] and its foul pestilential breath infected every youthful ambition. Once the rules go, eloquence loses vigour and voice. In short, who since then has equalled Thucydides or Hyperides[7] in their reputation? Why, not even poetry has shown a spark of life. All forms of literature have been faced with the same diet and lost their chance of a ripe old age. Even the great art of painting has met the same fate since the unscrupulous Egyptians[8] invented short cuts for painters.'

3. Agamemnon, after his own sweat in the classroom, did not allow me to hold forth in the colonnade for longer than himself.

'Young man,' he said, 'your opinions show extraordinary good taste and you have that extremely rare quality – a love for intellectual merit. So I shall not baffle you with any expertise. *Of course* teachers are making immoral concessions with these exercises – they *have* to humour the madmen. If the speeches they make do not win the approval of their young pupils, as Cicero says, "they will be the only ones in their schools".[9] When spongers in drama[10] are trying to get a dinner out of their rich friends, their main object is to find out what they would most like to hear. The only way they will get what they are after is by captivating their audience. It is the same with a tutor of rhetoric. Like a fisherman he has to bait his hook with what he knows the little fishes will rise for; otherwise he's left on the rocks without a hope of their biting.

4. 'What's the answer? It's the parents you should blame. They won't allow their children to be properly controlled. In the first place they sacrifice everything, even their hopes, to their ambition. Then in their over-eagerness they direct these immature intellects into public life. They will tell you that there is no mightier power than oratory and they dress up their boys as orators while they are still drawing their first breath. If only parents would not rush them through their studies! Then young men who are prepared to work would cultivate their minds with solid reading, mould their characters with sensible advice,

and prune their words with a stylish pen. They would wait and listen before they tried themselves and they would realize that an adolescent taste is quite worthless. Then the noble art of oratory would have its true weight and dignity. Boys today are frivolous in school; young men are laughing-stocks in public life; and, the greatest shame of all, even when they are old they refuse to give up the mistakes they learnt earlier.

'But just to show you how I am not above a bit of low-level improvisation in the manner of Lucilius,[11] I'll throw you off a few lines expressing my feelings:

5.   'Ambition to fulfil the austere demands of Art,
      The mind moving to mighty themes,
      Demands discipline, simplicity –
      The heart like a mirror.
      Disdain the haughty seats of the mighty,
      Humiliating invitations to drunken dinners,[12]
      The addictions, the low pleasures,
      The mental spark guttering out with the wine.
      Refuse theatre seats,
      Refuse to sell applause
      To the actor's empty mouthings.

      'Under smiling battlements of martial Athens,
      In Lacedaemonian colony,[13]
      By the home of the Sirens[14] even,
      No matter:
      Verse for your early education,
      Deep joyful draughts from Homeric springs
      Then full of the Socratic circle,
      Let your reins ride loose,
      Rattle the great sword of Demosthenes.
      Now our Roman squadrons swirl round you like a flood,
      Roman voices mixed with Greek music,
      Changing their savour.
      Then leave the forum behind
      And let your reading advance
      Till the power of Fortune

Makes itself heard in History,
Clearly and distinctly
          in running cadences.
War's epic sounds should feast your ears;
Shudder at the mighty orotundities
Of Cicero,
          who never lost a cause.
This is the right armour of genius –
"Drink deep or taste not the Pierian spring."[15]
Only then pour out your heart.'

ADVENTURES WITH
ASCYLTUS AND GITON

6. As I was listening carefully to him, I did not notice Ascyltus slipping away . . . and while I paced about silenced by this flood of ideas, a huge crowd of students entered the colonnade. Apparently they had been listening to an extempore declamation by whoever it was who had followed Agamemnon on the speaker's platform. While the young men were laughing at the points he made and picking to pieces the arrangement of the whole speech, I took the opportunity to slip away and started off hastily after Ascyltus. But I was not paying much attention to the way I went, and I had no idea where our lodging was.[1] Whichever direction I took, I came back to the same spot. Finally, worn out with running and dripping with sweat, I went up to an old woman selling fresh vegetables.

7. 'Excuse me, mother,' I began, 'I don't suppose you know where I'm staying, do you?'

She was amused by my naïve politeness.

'Why shouldn't I know?' she said. She got to her feet and set off in front of me. I thought she was uncanny, and followed her. And then, as we reached an out of the way place, the kind old lady threw back a patchwork curtain and said to me:

'This is where you must be staying.'

I was just telling her I did not recognize the place, when I caught sight of some naked old prostitutes and some customers furtively prowling up and down in the middle of them. Slowly, in fact too late, I realized I had been taken to a brothel. Cursing the old woman's tricks I covered my face and began hurrying right through the whorehouse to the other side. At the very door who should bump into me but Ascyltus. Like me he was worn out and practically dead. It looked as though he had been brought there by the same little old woman. Greeting him with a smile, I asked what he was doing in this dreadful place.

8. He wiped away the sweat with his hands and said:

'If only you knew what has been happening to me!'

'What happened?' I said.

'I wandered through the whole town,' he began faintly, 'and I couldn't find where I'd left our lodgings. Then a respectable-looking gentleman came up and very kindly offered to show me the way. He went down various pitch-dark turnings and brought me to this place. Then he offered me money and began making improper suggestions. The woman had already got her money for the cubicle and he had his hand on me. If I'd not been stronger than he was, I should have been in a bad way.'

*

In fact, everyone all around seemed to have been drinking aphrodisiac[2]. . .

*

Our combined forces made short work of the nuisance.

*

9. As though through a fog I caught sight of Giton standing at the side of the street. I rushed to the spot . . .

*

I asked my little friend[3] if he'd prepared anything for supper. At this the boy sat down on the bed and wiped away a stream of tears with his thumb. I was deeply shocked at the dear boy's state and urged him to tell me what had happened. Slowly and reluctantly – in fact I had to plead and threaten alternately – he told me:

'It was your dear friend, the fellow you go round with, anyway. Just a few minutes ago he ran into my room and began wanting to rape me. When I shouted for help, he took out his big knife and said: "If you're playing Lucretia, I'm your Tarquin."'[4]

When I heard this, I shook my fist in front of Ascyltus's face: 'What have you to say, you round-heeled tart! Your very breath stinks from your dirty ways!'

Ascyltus pretended to be horrified. Then he made an even braver show with his own fists and shouted far more loudly than I had: 'Shut up, you dirty gladiator! You could even perform for the noonday crowd. Shut up, you stab-in-the-dark! Even when you were at your best, you never managed to lay a decent woman. I was very close to you in the park, wasn't I? Just the way the boy is now in the hotel.'

'Didn't you slip away,' I said, 'when we were talking to the professor?'

10. 'Well, you fool, what did you expect me to do, when I was dying of hunger? I should have been listening to his rubbishy platitudes, I suppose! They're not worth a row of broken bottles – he'd be interpreting his dreams next! *You* are a hell of a sight worse – I didn't praise his poetry to cadge a dinner.' ... So our mortifying quarrel collapsed in roars of laughter, and we turned peaceably to other things ...

*

But his treachery stuck in my mind, so I said: 'Look, Ascyltus, I see it is impossible for us to get along together. I suggest we divide our belongings and try to make a living by ourselves. You've got an education and so have I. I don't want to interfere with your earnings, so I'll offer some other line. Otherwise every day hundreds of different things will set us at each other's throat, and get us talked about all over town.'

Ascyltus had no objection. He merely said: 'Look, at the moment we've accepted an invitation to dinner as teachers – don't let us waste the evening. Tomorrow, if this is the way you want it, I'll find myself lodgings and someone else to live with.'

'It's just wasting time,' I pointed out, 'why put off our pleasures?' My desires were responsible for the suddenness of this split. For some time now I had been wanting to be rid of my troublesome chaperon and be back on my old footing with dear little Giton.

*

11. I looked everywhere in the town before going back to our little room. At last I enjoyed his kisses without looking for excuses. I held the boy in my arms as though I'd never let him go. I had what I wanted and anyone would have envied me my luck. But we were still in the middle of this when Ascyltus came quietly to the door, forcibly shattered the bolts, and found me playing

around with Giton. He filled the little room with laughter and
applause. He rolled me out of the cloak I was lying in and said:

'What *were* you up to, my pious old friend? What's this? Are
you just setting up house under the blanket?'

And he did not limit himself to words, but taking the strap
from his bag he began to lay into me in earnest, punctuating it
with insolent remarks like – 'So, that's your idea of fair shares,
is it?'

*

12. It was[5] getting dark when we came into the square. We
noticed a lot of things on sale, none of them of any great worth –
in fact, the sort of things whose dubious origin is best concealed
in the dim light of evening. As we ourselves had brought along
the cloak we had stolen we decided to take advantage of this
excellent opportunity by unfolding just the edge of it in a corner.
Our hope was that the high-quality cloth would attract some
chance buyer. It was not long before a countryman, who looked
familiar to me, approached with a young woman companion
and started examining the garment very closely. Ascyltus in turn
shot a keen glance at the tunic dangling over the shoulders of
the country customer. Suddenly he almost fainted and couldn't
open his mouth. Even I lost some of my composure when I
looked at the man. He appeared to be the very person who had
found our tunic in the wilds. Clearly it was the same man.
Ascyltus however was afraid to trust his eyes in case he did
something rash. So he began by moving closer like a customer,
then he pulled the edge of it from his shoulders and ran his fin-
gers carefully over it.

13. What a marvellous stroke of luck! The countryman's
prying hands so far hadn't even tried the stitches. He was sell-
ing it like something a tramp had picked up and wanted to be
rid of. As soon as Ascyltus realized our hoard was intact and
the man selling it was a person of no account, he took me a
little way out of the crowd and said: 'Do you know, dearie, the
loot I was so cross about has returned to us. That's our tunic
and it looks as if it's still stuffed with the money – it hasn't been
touched. Now what are we going to do? How are we going to
claim our property?'

I was delighted not only because I saw the loot but because I was now fortunately free of that loathsome suspicion.[6] I opposed anything underhand: legal methods were clearly our best line of attack. If he would not hand someone else's property over to its rightful owner, then it would come to a court-order.

14. Ascyltus on the other hand was afraid of the law. 'Who knows us in this place?' he said. 'And who is going to believe what we say? I'm all for buying it now we have spotted it, even though it is our own. I would rather lay out a small sum to recover valuable property than go to court, where the outcome is very uncertain.

> 'What use are laws where money is king,
> Where poverty's helpless and can't win a thing?
> Even Cynics[7] who sneer are rarely averse
> To selling their scruples to fill up their purse.
> There's no justice at law – it's the bidding that counts
> And the job of the judge is to fix the amounts.'

However, apart from a solitary coin which we had intended to spend on chickpeas and lupines, we had no ready money. So in case the loot should slip from our fingers in the meantime, we decided to knock down the price of the cloak and take a small loss for the sake of the greater gain. As soon as we unwrapped our merchandise, the woman standing by the countryman with her head uncovered carefully examined the marks on it, grabbed the edge with both hands and screamed at the top of her voice: 'Stop the thieves!' As for us, we became panicky in case we looked at a loss, so we began hanging on to the torn and shabby tunic, and shouting just as indignantly that they had *our* property. But the two sides were in a very different position, and the dealers who had come milling round at the noise unanimously ridiculed our malicious charge. For they saw one side demanding back an extremely valuable cloak, while the other side was after a tattered old thing, which it would be a waste to use good patches on. Then Ascyltus suddenly managed to quieten their laughter and get himself heard:

15. 'Everyone obviously likes his own things best. Let them

give us back our tunic and take back their cloak.' Although the countryman and the woman were in favour of this exchange, the night watchmen however had been summoned and they insisted that both articles should be deposited with them, so that a magistrate could look into the matter the next day. It was not merely the articles themselves that were at stake, but there was the quite different question that both parties were suspected of theft. It was agreed that persons to take charge of them should be appointed, and one of the dealers, a bald-headed man with a very knobbly forehead, who sometimes handled court cases too, had pounced on the cloak and was swearing that the exhibit would appear next day. Of course it was obvious what he was after: once the cloak was left with him it could be sat on by these thieves, and we would be too afraid of the legal proceedings to turn up at the appointed time. This was clearly what we wanted too, and by a piece of luck both sides got what they were after. The countryman, infuriated by our claim that this patched old thing was an exhibit, threw the tunic into Ascyltus' face. So much for our particular charge – the cloak was the only thing in dispute and we were told to hand it over into custody . . .

The prize was ours again, we thought, and we went hastily back to our lodgings. Once behind locked doors we began ridiculing the sharp wits of our accusers and the dealers equally – it was very smart of them to give us our money back.

> Anything on which I'm set
> Should be hard to get;
> A ready-made victory
> Never appeals to me.

*

QUARTILLA'S BROTHEL

16. But we had only just filled ourselves up with the supper Giton had kindly prepared, when there came a knock, bold enough to make the door rattle. We turned pale and asked who it was. 'Open up and you'll find out!' came the answer. As we were speaking, the bolt gave way of its own accord and fell to the floor: the door was suddenly thrown open to admit the caller. It was a woman, however, with her head covered.

'Did you think you could make a fool out of me?' she said. 'I am Quartilla's personal maid and it was her religious service you burst into at the entrance to the grotto. And now she is on her way to the inn and she wants to talk to you. Don't get upset. She won't blame you or punish you for your mistake. She is really wondering what in heaven brought such charming young men to her part of the world.'

17. We had not yet said a word nor had we agreed one way or the other, when the lady herself entered with one young girl in attendance. She sat on my bed and cried for a long time. Not even this drew comment from us: in complete amazement we waited for this tearful show of grief to end. When the calculated storm of tears subsided, she uncovered her haughty head and wrung her hands till the joints cracked.

'What monstrous conduct is this?' she said. 'Where did you pick up such unimaginably criminal ways? Heaven knows, I'm deeply sorry for you. You see, it's absolutely forbidden – no one has ever seen it without being punished. Especially as our part of the world is so full of watchful powers that it's easier to run across a god than a man. And don't think I have come here for vengeance. I am more worried about your youth than my own injuries. Through sheer ignorance – I still believe this – you have committed an unforgivable sin. That very night I was full of unrest: I shivered with such a deadly chill I was afraid it was an attack of fever. And so I looked for a cure in my dreams and I was instructed to get hold of you and alleviate the onset of the attack by a subtle method which was revealed to me. But it is not the remedy I am so greatly concerned about; there is a deeper pain raging in my heart, which has brought me almost to death's door – I am afraid that in your youthful recklessness you will be driven to make public what you saw in the shrine of Priapus[1] and let out to all and sundry the workings of the divine mind. So I throw myself at your feet and I solemnly beg you not to make our nocturnal rites into a laughing-stock, and not to spread abroad the secrets of centuries – secrets which hardly three people know about.'

18. After this moving plea, she again burst into tears; shaking with great sobs, she pressed her face and bosom to my bed. I was torn between sympathy and fear. I told her not to be upset and not to worry on either score. No one would spread abroad her holy mysteries; and if the god had revealed to her some further cure for her fever, then we were ready to assist the divine providence, no matter what the risk to us.

This promise made her more cheerful; she covered me with kisses, her tears turned to laughter, and she slowly smoothed the hair falling over my ears.

'I'll make a truce with you,' she said. 'I withdraw my charges. Though if you had not been amenable about this medicine I'm after, there was a mob waiting for tomorrow to avenge my injuries and vindicate my honour.

> 'Scorn only scoundrels; Pride makes its own laws:
> My passion is to go as I please.
> Even the wise man fights when offended,
> And the victor is merciful, when the fight's ended.'

Then she clapped her hands and suddenly burst into such a peal of laughter that she frightened us. The maid who had arrived before her did the same, and so did the little girl who had come in with her.

19. The whole place rang with their theatrical laughter,[2] while we were still wondering why this sudden change of mood and looking now at each other, now at the women.[3]

*

'Therefore, I have given orders that not a living soul is to be allowed into this inn today, so I can get from you the remedy for my fever without any interruption.'

As Quartilla said this, Ascyltus looked stupefied for a moment. I personally went colder than winter in Gaul, and I couldn't get a word out. But our numbers banished any fears I felt of worse to come. After all, they were three weak women, if they wanted to try anything; on the other side, we, if nothing else, were of the male sex, but, in addition, we were certainly less hampered by clothes. In fact, I had already decided how we were to be matched, so that if it came to a fight, I would face Quartilla myself, Ascyltus the maid, and Giton the girl.

*

Then all our courage absolutely vanished. Our surprise was complete. Our eyes began to close at the prospect of certain death.

*

20. 'Please lady,' I said, 'if you have anything worse in store for us, get it over quickly. Surely we have not committed such a great crime that we deserve to be tortured before we die.'

*

The maid, whose name was Psyche, carefully spread a blanket on the hard floor.

*

She tried to excite me, but the thing was cold with the chill of a thousand deaths.

*

Ascyltus had pulled his cloak over his head; obviously he had been warned it was dangerous to pry into other people's secrets.

*

The maid produced two thongs from her pocket and tied our hands and feet with them.

*

Our amusing conversation was just tailing off, when Ascyltus asked: 'Hey, don't I deserve a drink?' Summoned by my laughter, the maid clapped her hands and said: 'I did put it down near you, young man. But have you drunk all that medicine by yourself?' 'Really?' said Quartilla. 'Has Encolpius drunk all the aphrodisiac there was?'

*

Her sides shook with her charming laughter.

*

In the end even Giton joined in the joke, particularly when the little girl threw her arms round his neck and kissed him an incredible number of times without any struggle.

*

21. In our desperation we wanted to shout for help, but there was no one to come to our aid. Besides, whenever I wanted to call for assistance from outside, Psyche stuck a hairpin into my cheeks. Meanwhile the girl was stifling Ascyltus with a cosmetic brush which she had soaked in aphrodisiac.

Finally, up came a male prostitute, dressed in myrtle-green shaggy felt, which was tucked up under a cherry-red belt. He pulled the cheeks of our bottoms apart and banged us, then he slobbered vile, greasy kisses on us, until Quartilla, carrying a whalebone rod, with her skirts up round her, ordered an end to our torments.

*

Both of us swore a solemn oath that such a dreadful secret would die with us.

*

Some training attendants came in, who rubbed us with the appropriate oil and made us feel better. Somehow or other we threw off our weariness, put on dinner clothes again and were taken into the next room. There were three couches ready and every other refinement of gracious living magnificently laid out. We took our places as we were told, and beginning with some wonderful hors d'oeuvres we were then practically swimming in Falernian wine. After helping ourselves to a long series of dishes, we were beginning to fall asleep, when Quartilla said, 'Do you actually intend to go to sleep when you know the whole night has to be a vigil in honour of our guardian Priapus?'

*

22. Ascyltus, overcome by all he had gone through, was dropping off to sleep, so the maid he had rudely rejected took some soot and rubbed it all down his face and, without his feeling it in his drunken stupor, she painted his sides and shoulders with wine lees. I was also worn out, and I had already dropped into the lightest possible doze. In fact, the whole household, indoors and out, had done the same. Some were lying here and there round the feet of the guests, others were propped up against the walls, a number stayed in the doorway with their heads together. The lamps were running out of oil too, and were casting only a dim dying light, when two Syrians on the prowl entered the dining-room. They began quarrelling greedily among the silver and smashed a decanter they'd taken. Over went the table, silver and all, and a cup which was knocked off from quite a height cracked the maid's skull as she drooped over the couch. The blow made her scream and she gave the thieves away, as well as waking up some of the drunken guests. The would-be thieves, realizing they were trapped, dropped side by side next to a couch – you'd have thought it was pre-arranged – and began snoring as though they had been asleep for hours.

By now the butler likewise was awake and poured oil into the guttering lamps. The slaves, after rubbing their eyes a bit, had returned to their duties, and a girl with cymbals entered and the clash of brass woke everyone up.

23. The party began again and Quartilla called us back to drinking, the songs of the girl with the cymbals adding to the conviviality.

*

In comes a male prostitute,[4] a low creature and just what you would expect in that house. Cracking his fingers with a groan, he blurted out some verses of this sort:

> 'Pansy boys, come out to play,[5]
> You've been cropped the Delian way:[6]
> Young or old, there's room for you

And room for roaming fingers too!
Hips and bottoms, waggle away,
Pansy boys, come out to play.'

Once his lines were finished, he slobbered a filthy kiss on me.
Then he even came on the couch and tried with all his strength
to pull my clothes off. He kept working away fruitlessly at my
crotch. Trickles of acacia-pomade ran down his sweaty fore-
head and there was so much powder in the wrinkles on his
cheeks that he looked like a peeling wall in a thunderstorm.

24. I couldn't keep my tears back any longer, I was in the
depths of misery.

'Please lady,' I said, 'surely you ordered me a night-cap.'[7]
She clapped her hands daintily and said: 'Oh, you clever man.
You're bubbling over with native wit. Well now, hadn't you
discovered that a pansy could be a night-cap?'

Then in case my comrade-in-arms should get off too lightly,
I said: 'Be fair. Is Ascyltus the only one at the table to have a
holiday?'

'Really,' said Quartilla, 'let Ascyltus have a night-cap too.'

Thereupon the prostitute swapped horses and after making
the changeover to my companion, pounded him with his but-
tocks and kisses.

Giton was standing there while all this went on and splitting
his sides laughing. And Quartilla, catching sight of him, asked
with great interest whose was the boy. I replied that he was my
boy-friend.

'Then why hasn't he given me a kiss?' said Quartilla. And
calling him to her, she pressed her lips to his. Then she slipped
her hand into his clothes and felt his immature little tool.
'Tomorrow this will serve nicely as hors d'oeuvre to tempt my
appetite,' she said. 'For the present, I don't want any ordinary
stuffing after such a nice cod-piece.'

25. As she said this, Psyche came and laughingly whispered
something in her ear:

'Yes, yes,' said Quartilla, 'thanks for reminding me. It's such
an excellent opportunity, why shouldn't our little Pannychis
lose her virginity?'

The girl was brought forward immediately – quite a pretty thing who appeared no more than seven years old. Everyone applauded and called for a wedding. I was quite taken aback by this and insisted that Giton, who was a very nice boy, was not up to this loose behaviour, nor was the girl old enough to take on the heavy duties of womanhood.

'Really?' said Quartilla. 'Is she any younger than I was when I had my first man? Juno's curse on me, if I can even remember being a virgin. When I was a child I played dirty games with boys of the same age, then as the years went by, I turned to bigger boys till I reached maturity. I even think this is the origin of the proverb – if you carry the calf, you can carry the bull.'

So in case my little friend should suffer worse treatment out of my sight, I got up to help with the ceremony.[8]

26. Psyche had already put a veil round the girl's head and old Night-cap was leading the way with a torch. The tipsy women, still clapping, had formed a long line and had fixed up a bridal chamber with draperies in the appropriate sacrilegious way. Then Quartilla, highly excited by all this playful obscenity, rose to her feet herself, seized Giton, and dragged him into the chamber.

It was obvious the boy had not struggled and even the girl had not been dismayed or scared by the mention of marriage. And so, when they were shut in and lying down, we sat round the chamber doorway, and Quartilla was one of the first to put an inquisitive eye to a crack she had naughtily opened, and spy on their childish play with prurient eagerness. Her insistent hand pulled me down also to have a similar look, and since our faces were pressed together as we watched, whenever she could spare a moment, she would move her lips close to mine in passing and bruise me with sly kisses.

*

We threw ourselves on our beds and spent the rest of the night without fear.

The next day but one finally arrived[, and that meant the prospect of a free dinner]. But we were so knocked about that we wanted to run rather than rest. We were mournfully discussing how to avoid the approaching storm, when one of Agamemnon's slaves broke in on our frantic debate.

'Here,' said he, 'don't you know who's your host today? It's Trimalchio – he's terribly elegant ... He has a clock in the dining-room and a trumpeter all dressed up to tell him how much longer he's got to live.'

This made us forget all our troubles. We dressed carefully and told Giton, who was very kindly acting as our servant, to attend us at the baths.

27. We did not take our clothes off but began wandering around, or rather exchanging jokes while circulating among the little groups. Suddenly we saw a bald old man in a reddish shirt, playing ball with some long-haired boys. It was not so much the boys that made us watch, although they alone were worth the trouble, but the old gentleman himself. He was taking his exercise in slippers and throwing a green ball around. But he didn't pick it up if it touched the ground; instead there was a slave holding a bagful, and he supplied them to the players. We noticed other novelties. Two eunuchs stood around at different points: one of them carried a silver pissing bottle, the other counted the balls, not those flying from hand to hand according to the rules, but those that fell to the ground. We were still admiring these elegant arrangements when Menelaus hurried up to us.

'This is the man you'll be dining with,' he said. 'In fact, you are now watching the beginning of the dinner.'

No sooner had Menelaus spoken than Trimalchio snapped his fingers. At the signal the eunuch brought up the pissing bottle for him, while he went on playing. With the weight off his bladder, he demanded water for his hands, splashed a few drops on his fingers and wiped them on a boy's head.

TRIMALCHIO'S FEAST

28. It would take too long to pick out isolated incidents. Anyway, we entered the baths where we began sweating at once and we went immediately into the cold water. Trimalchio had been smothered in perfume and was already being rubbed down, not with linen towels, but with bath-robes of the finest wool. As this was going on, three masseurs sat drinking Falernian in front of him. Through quarrelling they spilled most of it and Trimalchio said they were drinking his health.[1] Wrapped in thick scarlet felt he was put into a litter. Four couriers with lots of medals[2] went in front, as well as a go-kart in which his favourite boy was riding – a wizened, bleary-eyed youngster, uglier than his master. As he was carried off, a musician with a tiny set of pipes took his place by Trimalchio's head and whispered a tune in his ear the whole way.

We followed on, choking with amazement by now, and arrived at the door with Agamemnon at our side. On the door-post a notice was fastened which read:

ANY SLAVE LEAVING THE HOUSE WITHOUT
HIS MASTER'S PERMISSION WILL RECEIVE
ONE HUNDRED LASHES

Just at the entrance stood the hall-porter, dressed in a green uniform with a belt of cherry red. He was shelling peas into a silver basin. Over the doorway hung – of all things – a golden cage from which a spotted magpie greeted visitors.

29. As I was gaping at all this, I almost fell over backwards and broke a leg. There, on the left as one entered, not far from the porter's cubbyhole, was a huge dog with a chain round its

neck. It was painted on the wall[3] and over it, in big capitals, was written:

BEWARE OF THE DOG

My colleagues laughed at me, but when I got my breath back I went on to examine the whole wall. There was a mural[4] of a slave market, price-tags and all. Then Trimalchio himself, holding a wand of Mercury and being led into Rome by Minerva. After this a picture of how he learned accounting and, finally, how he became a steward. The painstaking artist had drawn it all in great detail with descriptions underneath. Just where the colonnade ended Mercury hauled him up by the chin and rushed him to a high platform. Fortune with her horn of plenty and the three Fates spinning their golden threads were there in attendance.

I also noticed in the colonnade a company of runners practising with their trainer. In one corner was a large cabinet, which served as a shrine for some silver statues of the household deities with a marble figure of Venus and an impressive gold casket in which, they told me, the master's first beard was preserved.[5]

I began asking the porter what were the pictures they had in the middle.

'The Iliad, the Odyssey,' he said, 'and the gladiatorial show given by Laenas.'[6]

30. Time did not allow us to look at many things there . . . by now we had reached the dining-room, at the entrance to which sat a treasurer going over the accounts. There was one feature I particularly admired: on the door-posts were fixed rods and axes[7] tapering off at their lowest point into something like the bronze beak of a ship. On it was the inscription:

PRESENTED TO C. POMPEIUS TRIMALCHIO[8]
PRIEST OF THE AUGUSTAN COLLEGE[9]
BY HIS STEWARD CINNAMUS

Beneath this same inscription a fixture with twin lamps dangled from the ceiling and two notices, one on each door-post. One of them, if my memory is correct, had written on it:

30 AND 31 DECEMBER
OUR GAIUS
IS OUT TO DINNER[10]

The other displayed representations of the moon's phases and the seven heavenly bodies. Lucky and unlucky days were marked with different coloured studs.

Having had enough of these interesting things, we attempted to go in, but one of the slaves shouted: 'Right foot first!'[11] Naturally we hesitated a moment in case one of us should cross the threshold the wrong way. But just as we were all stepping forward, a slave with his back bare flung himself at our feet and began pleading with us to get him off a flogging. He was in trouble for nothing very serious, he told us – the steward's clothes, hardly worth ten sesterces, had been stolen from him at the baths. Back went our feet, and we appealed to the steward, who was counting out gold pieces in the office, to let the man off.

He lifted his head haughtily: 'It is not so much the actual loss that annoys me,' he said, 'it's the wretch's carelessness. They were my dinner clothes he lost. A client had presented them to me on my birthday – genuine Tyrian purple, of course; however they had been laundered once. So what does it matter? He's all yours.'

31. We were very much obliged to him for this favour; and when we did enter the dining-room, that same slave whose cause we had pleaded ran up to us and, to our utter confusion, covered us with kisses and thanked us for our kindness.

'And what's more,' he said, 'you'll know right away who it is you have been so kind to. "The master's wine is the waiter's gift."'

Finally we took our places.[12] Boys from Alexandria poured iced water over our hands. Others followed them and attended to our feet, removing any hangnails with great skill. But they were not quiet even during this troublesome operation: they sang away at their work. I wanted to find out if the whole staff were singers, so I asked for a drink. In a flash a boy was there, singing in a shrill voice while he attended to me – and anyone else who was asked for something did the same. It was more like a musical comedy[13] than a respectable dinner party.

Some extremely elegant hors d'oeuvres were served at this point – by now everyone had taken his place with the exception of Trimalchio, for whom, strangely enough, the place at the top was reserved. The dishes for the first course included an ass of Corinthian bronze with two panniers, white olives on one side and black on the other. Over the ass were two pieces of plate, with Trimalchio's name and the weight of the silver inscribed on the rims. There were some small iron frames shaped like bridges supporting dormice sprinkled with honey and poppy seed. There were steaming hot sausages too, on a silver grid-iron with damsons and pomegranate seeds underneath.

32. We were in the middle of these elegant dishes when Trimalchio himself was carried in to the sound of music and set down on a pile of tightly stuffed cushions. The sight of him drew an astonished laugh[14] from the guests. His cropped head stuck out from a scarlet coat; his neck was well muffled up and he had put round it a napkin with a broad purple stripe and tassels dangling here and there. On the little finger of his left hand he wore a heavy gilt ring and a smaller one on the last joint of the next finger. This I thought was solid gold, but actually it was studded with little iron stars. And to show off even more of his jewellery, he had his right arm bare and set off by a gold armlet and an ivory circlet fastened with a gleaming metal plate.

33. After picking his teeth with a silver toothpick, he began: 'My friends, I wasn't keen to come into the dining-room yet. But if I stayed away any more, I would have kept you back, so I've deprived myself of all my little pleasures for you. However, you'll allow me to finish my game.'[15]

A boy was at his heels with a board of terebinth wood with glass squares, and I noticed the very last word in luxury – instead of white and black pieces he had gold and silver coins. While he was swearing away like a trooper over his game and we were still on the hors d'oeuvres, a tray was brought in with a basket on it. There sat a wooden hen, its wings spread round it the way hens are when they are broody. Two slaves hurried up and as the orchestra played a tune they began searching through the straw and dug out peahens' eggs, which they distributed to the guests.

Trimalchio turned to look at this little scene and said: 'My friends, I gave orders for that bird to sit on some peahens' eggs. I hope to goodness they are not starting to hatch. However, let's try them and see if they are still soft.'

We took up our spoons (weighing at least half a pound each) and cracked the eggs, which were made of rich pastry. To tell the truth, I nearly threw away my share, as the chicken seemed already formed. But I heard a guest who was an old hand say: 'There should be something good here.' So I searched the shell with my fingers and found the plumpest little figpecker, all covered with yolk and seasoned with pepper.

34. At this point Trimalchio became tired of his game and demanded that all the previous dishes be brought to him. He gave permission in a loud voice for any of us to have another glass of mead if we wanted it. Suddenly there was a crash from the orchestra and a troop of waiters – still singing – snatched away the hors d'oeuvres. However in the confusion one of the side-dishes happened to fall and a slave picked it up from the floor. Trimalchio noticed this, had the boy's ears boxed and told him to throw it down again. A cleaner came in with a broom and began to sweep up the silver plate along with the rest of the rubbish. Two long-haired Ethiopians followed him, carrying small skin bags like those used by the men who scatter the sand in the amphitheatre, and they poured wine over our hands – no one ever offered us water.

Our host was complimented on these elegant arrangements. 'Mars loves a fair fight,' he replied. 'That is why I gave orders for each guest to have his own table. At the same time these smelly slaves won't crowd so.'

Carefully sealed wine bottles were immediately brought, their necks labelled:

FALERNIAN
CONSUL OPIMIUS[16]
ONE HUNDRED YEARS OLD

While we were examining the labels, Trimalchio clapped his hands and said with a sigh:

'Wine has a longer life than us poor folks. So let's wet our whistles. Wine is life. I'm giving you real Opimian. I didn't put out such good stuff yesterday, though the company was much better class.'

Naturally we drank and missed no opportunity of admiring his elegant hospitality. In the middle of this a slave brought in a silver skeleton,[17] put together in such a way that its joints and backbone could be pulled out and twisted in all directions. After he had flung it about on the table once or twice, its flexible joints falling into various postures, Trimalchio recited:

> 'O woe, woe, man is only a dot:
> Hell drags us off and that is the lot;
> So let us live a little space,
> At least while we can feed our face.'

35. After our applause the next course was brought in. Actually it was not as grand as we expected, but it was so novel that everyone stared. It was a deep circular tray with the twelve signs of the Zodiac arranged round the edge. Over each of them the chef had placed some appropriate dainty[18] suggested by the subject. Over Aries the Ram, chickpeas; over Taurus the Bull, a beefsteak; over the Heavenly Twins, testicles and kidneys; over Cancer the Crab, a garland; over Leo the Lion, an African fig; over Virgo the Virgin, a young sow's udder; over Libra the Scales, a balance with a cheesecake in one pan and a pastry in the other; over Scorpio, a sea scorpion; over Sagittarius the Archer, a sea bream with eyespots; over Capricorn, a lobster; over Aquarius the Water-Carrier, a goose; over Pisces the Fishes, two mullets. In the centre was a piece of grassy turf bearing a honeycomb. A young Egyptian slave carried around bread in a silver oven . . . and in a sickening voice he mangled a song from the show *The Asafoetida Man*.[19]

36. As we started rather reluctantly on this inferior fare, Trimalchio said:

'Let's eat, if you don't mind. This is the sauce of all order.'[20] As he spoke, four dancers hurtled forward in time to the music and removed the upper part of the great dish, revealing underneath plump fowls, sows' udders, and a hare with wings fixed to his middle to look like Pegasus. We also noticed four figures of Marsyas[21] with little skin bottles, which let a peppery fish-sauce go running over some fish, which seemed to be swimming in a little channel. We all joined in the servants' applause and amid some laughter we helped ourselves to these quite exquisite things.

Trimalchio was every bit as happy as we were with this sort of trick: 'Carve 'er!' he cried. Up came the man with the carving knife and, with his hands moving in time to the orchestra, he sliced up the victuals like a charioteer battling to the sound of organ music. And still Trimalchio went on saying insistently: 'Carve 'er, Carver!'[22]

I suspected this repetition was connected with some witticism, and I went so far as to ask the man on my left what it meant. He had watched this sort of game quite often and said:

'You see the fellow doing the carving – he's called Carver. So whenever he says "Carver!" he's calling out his name and his orders.'

37. I couldn't face any more food. Instead I turned to this man to find out as much as I could. I began pestering him for gossip and information – who was the woman running round the place?

'Trimalchio's wife,' he told me, 'Fortunata is her name and she counts her money by the sackful. And before, before, what was she? You'll pardon me saying so, but you wouldn't of touched a bit of bread from her hand. Nowadays – and who knows how or why – she's in heaven, and she's absolutely everything to Trimalchio. In fact, if she tells him at high noon it's dark, he'll believe her. He doesn't know himself how much he's got, he's so loaded – but this bitch looks after everything; she's even in places you wouldn't think of. She's dry, sober and full of ideas – you see all that gold! – but she's got a rough tongue and she's a real magpie when she gets her feet up. If she likes you, she likes you – if she doesn't like you, she doesn't like you.

'The old boy himself now, he's got estates it'd take a kite to fly over – he's worth millions of millions. There's more silver plate lying in his porter's cubbyhole than any other man owns

altogether. As for his servants – boy, oh boy! I honestly don't
think there's one in ten knows his own master. In fact he could
knock any of these smart boys into a cocked hat.

38. 'And don't you think he buys anything, either. Every-
thing is home-grown: wool, citrus, pepper. If you ask for hen's
milk, you'll get it. In fact, there was a time when the wool he'd
got wasn't good enough for him, so he brought some rams
from Tarentum and banged them into his sheep. To get home-
grown Attic honey, he ordered some bees from Athens – the
Greek strain improved his own bees a bit at the same time.

'And here's something more – this last few days he wrote off
for mushroom spores from India. Why, he hasn't a single mule
that wasn't sired by a wild ass. You see all these cushions –
every one of them has either purple or scarlet stuffing. There's
happiness for you!

'But mind you, don't look down on the other freedmen here.
They're dripping with the stuff. You see that man on the very
bottom couch. At present he's got eight hundred thousand of
his own. He started out with nothing. It's not long since he was
humping wood on his own back. They say – I don't know
myself, I've heard it – they say he stole a hobgoblin's cap and
found its treasure. I don't begrudge anyone what God has given
him. Besides, he can still feel his master's slap and wants to give
himself a good time. For instance, the other day he put up a
notice which said:

GAIUS POMPEIUS DIOGENES
IS MOVING TO HIS HOUSE AND
WILL LET THE ROOM OVER
HIS SHOP FROM 1 JULY

'Now that fellow in the freedman's place – look how well off
he was once! I'm not blaming him – he had a million in his
hands, but he slipped badly. I don't think he can call his hair his
own. Yet I'd swear it wasn't his fault: there's not a better man
alive. Some freedmen and crooks pocketed everything he had.
One thing you can be sure of – you have partners and your pot
never boils, and once things take a turn for the worse, friends
get out from underneath. What a respectable business he had

and look at him now! He was an undertaker. He used to eat like a king – boars roasted in their skins, elaborate pastry, braised game birds, as well as fish and hares. More wine was spilt under the table than another man keeps in his cellar. He wasn't a man, he was an absolute dream! When things were looking black, he didn't want his creditors to think he was bankrupt, so he put up notice of an auction like this:

'GAIUS JULIUS PROCULUS
AUCTION OF SURPLUS STOCK'

Trimalchio interrupted these pleasant reminiscences. The dish had already been removed and the convivial guests had begun to concentrate on the drink and general conversation. Leaning on his elbow, Trimalchio said:

39. 'Now you're supposed to be enjoying the wine. Fishes have to swim. I ask you, do you think I'm just content with that course you saw in the bottom of the dish? "Is this like the Ulysses you know?"[23] Well then, we've got to display some culture[24] at our dinner. My patron – God rest his bones! – wanted me to hold up my head in any company. There's nothing new to me, as that there dish proves. Look now, these here heavens, as there are twelve gods[25] living in 'em, changes into that many shapes. First it becomes the Ram. So whoever is born under that sign has a lot of herds, a lot of wool, a hard head as well, a brassy front and a sharp horn. Most scholars are born under this sign, and most muttonheads as well.'

We applauded the wit of our astrologer and he went on: 'Then the whole heavens turns into the little old Bull. So bullheaded folk are born then, and cow-herds and those who find their own feed. Under the Heavenly Twins on the other hand – pairs-in-hand, yokes of oxen, people with big ballocks and people who do it both ways. I was born under the Crab, so I have a lot of legs to stand on and a lot of property on land and sea, because the Crab takes both in his stride. And that's why I put nothing over him earlier, so as not to upset my horoscope. Under Leo are born greedy and bossy people. Under the Virgin, effeminates, runaways and candidates for the chain-gang.[26] Under the Scales, butchers, perfume-sellers and anyone who weighs things up. Under Scorpio poisoners and murderers. Under Sagittarius are born cross-eyed people who look at the vegetables and take the bacon. Under Capricorn, people in trouble who sprout horns through their worries. Under the Water-Carrier, bartenders and jugheads. Under the Fishes, fish-fryers and people who spout in public.

'So the starry sky turns round like a millstone, always bringing some trouble, and men being born or dying.

'Now as for what you see in the middle, the piece of grass and on the grass the honeycomb, I don't do anything without a reason – it's Mother Earth in the middle, round like an egg, with all good things inside her like a honeycomb.'

40. 'Oh, clever!' we all cried, raising our hands to the ceiling and swearing that Hipparchus and Aratus[27] couldn't compete with *him*.

Then the servants came up and laid across the couches embroidered coverlets showing nets, hunters carrying broad spears, and all the paraphernalia of hunting. We were still wondering which way to look when a tremendous clamour arose outside the dining-room, and – surprise! – Spartan hounds began dashing everywhere, even round the table. Behind them came a great dish and on it lay a wild boar of the largest possible size, and, what is more, wearing a freedman's cap on its head. From its tusks dangled two baskets woven from palm leaves, one full of fresh Syrian dates, the other of dried Theban dates. Little piglets made of cake were all round as though at its dugs, suggesting it was a brood sow now being served. These were actually gifts to take home. Surprisingly the man who took his place to cut up the boar was not our old friend Carver but a huge bearded fellow, wearing leggings and a damask hunting coat. He pulled out a hunting knife and made a great stab at the boar's side and, as he struck, out flew a flock of thrushes. But there were fowlers all ready with their limed reeds, who caught them as soon as they began flying round the room.

Trimalchio gave orders for each guest to have his own bird, then added: 'And have a look at the delicious acorns our pig in the wood has been eating.'

Young slaves promptly went to the baskets and gave the guests their share of the two kinds of date.

41. As this was going on, I kept quiet, turning over a lot of ideas as to why the boar had come in with a freedman's cap on it. After working through all sorts of wild fancies, I ventured to put to my experienced neighbour the question I was racking my brains with. He of course replied:

'Even the man waiting on you could explain this obvious point – it's not puzzling at all, it's quite simple. The boar here was pressed into service for the last course yesterday, but the guests let it go. So today it returns to the feast as a freedman.'

I damned my own stupidity and asked no more questions in case I looked like someone who had never dined in decent company.

As we were talking, a handsome youth with a garland of vine-leaves and ivy round his head, pretending to be Bacchus the Reveller, then Bacchus the Deliverer and Bacchus the Inspirer, carried grapes round in a basket, all the time giving us a recital of his master's lyrics in a high-pitched voice. At the sound, Trimalchio called out, 'Dionysus, now be Bacchus the Liberat . . .'

The lad pulled the freedman's cap off the boar and stuck it on his head. Then Trimalchio commented:

'Now you won't deny my claim to be the liberated sort.'[28] We applauded his joke and kissed the boy hard as he went round.

After this course Trimalchio got up and went to the toilet. Free of his domineering presence, we began to help ourselves to more drinks. Dama started off by calling for a cup of the grape.

'The day's nothin',' he said. 'It's night 'fore y'can turn around. So the best thing's get out of bed and go straight to dinner. Lovely cold weather we've had too. M'bath hardly thawed me out. Still, a hot drink's as good as an overcoat. I've been throwin' it back neat, and you can see I'm tight – the wine's gone to m'head.'

Seleucus took up the ball in the conversation:

42. 'Me now,' he said, 'I don't have a bath every day. It's like

getting rubbed with fuller's earth, havin' a bath. The water
bites into you, and your heart begins to melt. But when I've
knocked back a hot glass of wine and honey, "Go fuck your-
self," I say to the cold weather. Mind you, I couldn't have a
bath – I was at a funeral today. Poor old Chrysanthus has just
given up the ghost – nice man he was! It was only the other day
he stopped me in the street. I still seem to hear his voice. Dear,
dear! We're just so many walking bags of wind. We're worse
than flies – at least they have got some strength in them, but
we're no more than empty bubbles.

'And yet he had been on an extremely strict diet? For five
days he didn't take a drop of water or a crumb of bread into his
mouth. But he's gone to join the majority. The doctors finished
him – well, hard luck, more like. After all, a doctor is just to
put your mind at rest. Still, he got a good send-off – he had a
bier, and all beautifully draped. His mourners – several of his
slaves were left their freedom – did him proud, even though his
widow was a bit mean with her tears. And yet he had been
extremely good to her! But women as a sex are real vultures.
It's no good doing them a favour, you might as well throw it
down a well. An old passion is just an ulcer.'

43. He was being a bore and Phileros said loudly:

'Let's think of the living. He's got what he deserved. He lived
an honest life and he died an honest death. What has he got to
complain about? He started out in life with just a penny and he
was ready to pick up less than that from a muck-heap, even if
he had to use his teeth. So whatever he put a finger to swelled
up like a honeycomb. I honestly think he left a solid hundred
thousand and he had the lot in hard cash. But I'll be honest
about it, since I'm a bit of a cynic: he had a foul mouth and too
much lip. He wasn't a man, he was just trouble.

'Now his brother was a brave lad, a real friend to his friends,
always ready with a helping hand or a decent meal.

'Chrysanthus had bad luck at first, but the first vintage set
him on his feet. He fixed his own price when he sold the wine.
And what properly kept his head above water was a legacy he
came in for, when he pocketed more than was left to him. And
the blockhead, when he had a quarrel with his brother, cut him

out of his will in favour of some sod we've never heard of. You're leaving a lot behind when you leave your own flesh and blood. But he kept listening to his slaves and they really fixed him. It's never right to believe all you're told, especially for a businessman. But it's true he enjoyed himself while he lived. You got it, you keep it. He was certainly Fortune's favourite – lead turned to gold in his hand. Mind you, it's easy when everything runs smoothly.

'And how old do you think he was? Seventy or more! But he was hard as a horn and carried his age well. His hair was black as a raven's wing. I knew the man for ages and ages and he was still an old lecher. I honestly don't think he left the dog alone. What's more, he liked little boys – he could turn his hand to anything. Well, I don't blame him – after all, he couldn't take anything else with him.'

44. This was Phileros, then Ganymedes said:

'You're all talking about things that don't concern heaven or earth. Meanwhile, no one gives a damn the way we're hit by the corn situation. Honest to god, I couldn't get hold of a mouthful of bread today. And look how there's still no rain. It's been absolute starvation for a whole year now. To hell with the food officers! They're in with the bakers – "You be nice to me and I'll be nice to you." So the little man suffers, while those grinders of the poor never stop celebrating. Oh, if only we still had the sort of men I found here when I first arrived from Asia. Like lions they were. That was the life! Come one, come all! If plain flour was inferior to the very finest, they'd thrash those bogeymen till they thought God Almighty was after them.

'I remember Safinius – he used to live by the old arch then; I was a boy at the time. He wasn't a man, he was all pepper. He used to scorch the ground wherever he went. But he was dead straight – don't let him down and he wouldn't let you down. You'd be ready to play *morra*[29] with him in the dark. But on the city council, how he used to wade into some of them – no beating about the bush, straight from the shoulder! And when he was in court, his voice got louder and louder like a trumpet. He never sweated or spat – I think he'd been through the oven all right. And very affable he was when you met him, calling

everyone by name just like one of us. Naturally at the time corn
was dirt cheap. You could buy a penny loaf that two of you
couldn't get through. Today – I've seen bigger bull's-eyes.

'Ah me! It's getting worse every day. This place is going
down like a calf's tail. But why do we have a third-rate food
officer who wouldn't lose a penny to save our lives? He sits at
home laughing and rakes in more money a day than anyone
else's whole fortune. I happen to know he's just made a thou-
sand in gold. But if we had any balls at all, he wouldn't be
feeling so pleased with himself. People today are lions at home
and foxes outside.

'Take me. I've already sold the rags off my back for food and
if this shortage continues I'll be selling my bit of a house.
What's going to happen to this place if neither god nor man
will help us? As I hope to go home tonight, I'm sure all this is
heaven's doing.

'Nobody believes in heaven, see, nobody fasts, nobody gives
a damn for the Almighty. No, people only bow their heads to
count their money. In the old days high-class ladies used to
climb up the hill barefoot, their hair loose and their hearts
pure, and ask God for rain. And he'd send it down in bucket-
fuls right away – it was then or never – and everyone went
home like drowned rats. Since we've given up religion the gods
nowadays keep their feet wrapped up in wool. The fields just
lie . . .'

45. 'Please, please,' broke in Echion the rag-merchant, 'be a
bit more cheerful. "First it's one thing, then another," as the
yokel said when he lost his spotted pig. What we haven't got
today, we'll have tomorrow. That's the way life goes. Believe
me, you couldn't name a better country, if it had the people. As
things are, I admit, it's having a hard time, but it isn't the only
place. We mustn't be soft. The sky don't get no nearer wherever
you are. If you were somewhere else, you'd be talking about
the pigs walking round ready-roasted back here.

'And another thing, we'll be having a holiday with a three-
day show that's the best ever – and not just a hack troupe of
gladiators but freedmen for the most part. My old friend Titus
has a big heart and a hot head. Maybe this, maybe that, but

something at all events. I'm a close friend of his and he's no way wishy-washy. He'll give us cold steel, no quarter and the slaughterhouse right in the middle where all the stands can see it. And he's got the wherewithal – he was left thirty million when his poor father died. Even if he spent four hundred thousand, his pocket won't feel it and he'll go down in history. He's got some real desperadoes already, and a woman who fights in a chariot, and Glyco's steward who was caught having fun with his mistress. You'll see quite a quarrel in the crowd between jealous husbands and romantic lovers. But that half-pint Glyco threw his steward to the lions, which is just giving himself away. How is it the servant's fault when he's forced into it? It's that old pisspot who really deserves to be tossed by a bull. But if you can't beat the ass you beat the saddle. But how did Glyco imagine that poisonous daughter of Hermogenes would ever turn out well? The old man could cut the claws off a flying kite, and a snake don't hatch old rope. Glyco – well, Glyco's got his. He's branded for as long as he lives and only the grave will get rid of it. But everyone pays for their sins.

'But I can almost smell the dinner Mammaea is going to give us – two denarii apiece for me and the family. If he really does it, he'll make off with all Norbanus's votes, I tell you he'll win at a canter. After all, what good has Norbanus done us? He put on some half-pint gladiators, so done in already that they'd have dropped if you blew at them. I've seen beast fighters[30] give a better performance. As for the horsemen killed, he got them off a lamp – they ran round like cocks in a backyard. One was just a cart-horse, the other couldn't stand up, and the reserve was just one corpse instead of another – he was practically hamstrung. One boy did have a bit of spirit – he was in Thracian armour,[31] and even he didn't show any initiative. In fact, they were all flogged afterwards, there were so many shouts of "Give 'em what for!" from the crowd. Pure cowards, that's all.

' "Well, I've put on a show for you," he says. "And I'm clapping you," says I. "Reckon it up – I'm giving more than I got. So we're quits." '

46. 'Hey, Agamemnon! I suppose you're saying "What is that bore going on and on about?" It's because a good talker

like you don't talk. You're a cut above us, and so you laugh at
what us poor people say. We all know you're off your head
with all that reading. But never mind! Will I get you some day
to come down to my place in the country and have a look at
our little cottage? We'll find something to eat – a chicken, some
eggs. It'll be nice, even though the weather this year has ruined
everything. Anyway, we'll find enough to fill our bellies.

'And by now my little lad is growing up to be a student of
yours. He can divide by four already. If he stays well, you'll
have him ready to do anything for you. In his spare time, he
won't take his head out of his exercise book. He's clever and
there's good stuff in him, even if he is crazy about birds. Only
yesterday I killed his three goldfinches and told him a weasel
ate them. But he's found some other silly hobbies, and he's hav-
ing a fine time painting. Still, he's already well ahead with his
Greek, and he's starting to take to his Latin, though his tutor is
too pleased with himself and unreliable. He's well-educated but
doesn't want to work. There is another one too, not so trained
but he is conscientious – he teaches the boy more than he
knows himself. In fact, he even makes a habit of coming around
on holidays, and whatever you give him, he's happy.

'Anyway, I've just bought the boy some law books, as I want
him to pick up some legal training for home use. There's a liv-
ing in that sort of thing. He's done enough dabbling in poetry
and such like. If he objects, I've decided he'll learn a trade –
barber, auctioneer, or at least a barrister – something he can't
lose till he dies. Well, yesterday I gave it to him straight: "Believe
me, my lad, any studying you do will be for your own good.
You see Phileros the lawyer – if he hadn't studied, he'd be starv-
ing today. It's not so long since he was humping round stuff to
sell on his back. Now he can even look Norbanus in the face.
An education is an investment, and a proper profession never
goes dead on you."'

47. This was the sort of chatter flying round when Trimal-
chio came in, dabbed his forehead and washed his hands in
perfume. There was a very short pause, then he said:

'Excuse me, dear people, my inside has not been answering
the call for several days now. The doctors are puzzled. But

some pomegranate rind and resin in vinegar has done me good. But I hope now it will be back on its good behaviour. Otherwise my stomach rumbles like a bull. So if any of you wants to go out, there's no need for him to be embarrassed. None of us was born solid. I think there's nothing so tormenting as holding yourself in. This is the one thing even God Almighty can't object to. Yes, laugh, Fortunata, but you generally keep me up all night with this sort of thing.

'Anyway, I don't object to people doing what suits them even in the middle of dinner – and the doctors forbid you to hold yourself in. Even if it's a longer business, everything is there just outside – water, bowls, and all the other little comforts. Believe me, if the wind goes to your brain it starts flooding your whole body too. I've known a lot of people die from this because they wouldn't be honest with themselves.'

We thanked him for being so generous and considerate and promptly proceeded to bury our amusement in our glasses. Up to this point we'd not realized we were only half-way up the hill, as you might say.

The orchestra played, the tables were cleared, and then three white pigs were brought into the dining-room, all decked out in muzzles and bells. The first, the master of ceremonies announced, was two years old, the second three, and the third six. I was under the impression that some acrobats were on their way in and the pigs were going to do some tricks, the way they do in street shows. But Trimalchio dispelled this impression by asking:

'Which of these would you like for the next course? Any clodhopper can do you a barnyard cock or a stew and trifles like that, but my cooks are used to boiling whole calves.'

He immediately sent for the chef and without waiting for us to choose he told him to kill the oldest pig.

He then said to the man in a loud voice:

'Which division are you from?'

When he replied he was from number forty, Trimalchio asked:

'Were you bought or were you born here?'

'Neither,' said the chef, 'I was left to you in Pansa's will.'

'Well, then,' said Trimalchio, 'see you serve it up carefully – otherwise I'll have you thrown into the messengers' division.'

So the chef, duly reminded of his master's magnificence, went back to his kitchen, the next course leading the way.

48. Trimalchio looked round at us with a gentle smile: 'If you don't like the wine, I'll have it changed. It is up to you to do it justice. I don't buy it, thank heaven. In fact, whatever wine really tickles your palate this evening, it comes from an estate of mine which as yet I haven't seen. It's said to join my estates at Tarracina and Tarentum.[32] What I'd like to do now is add Sicily to my little bit of land, so that when I want to go to Africa, I could sail there without leaving my own property.

'But tell me, Agamemnon, what was your debate about today? Even though I don't go in for the law, still I've picked up enough education for home consumption. And don't you think I turn my nose up at studying, because I have two libraries, one Greek, one Latin. So tell us, just as a favour, what was the topic of your debate?'

Agamemnon was just beginning, 'A poor man and a rich man were enemies . . .' when Trimalchio said: 'What's a poor man?' 'Oh, witty!' said Agamemnon, and then told us about some fictitious case or other. Like lightning Trimalchio said: 'If this happened, it's not a fictitious case – if it didn't happen, then it's nothing at all.'

We greeted this witticism and several more like it with the greatest enthusiasm.

'Tell me, my dear Agamemnon,' continued Trimalchio, 'do you remember the twelve labours of Hercules and the story of Ulysses – how the Cyclops[33] tore out his eye with his thumb. I used to read about them in Homer, when I was a boy. In fact, I actually saw with my own eyes the Sybil at Cumae[34] dangling in a bottle, and when the children asked her in Greek: "What do you want, Sybil?" she used to answer: "I want to die." '

49. He was still droning on when a server carrying the massive pig was put on the table. We started to express our amazement at this speed and swear that not even an ordinary rooster could be cooked so quickly, the more so as the pig seemed far larger

than it had appeared before. Trimalchio looked closer and closer at it, and then shouted:

'What's this? Isn't this pig gutted? I'm damn certain it isn't. Call the chef in here, go on, call him!'

The downcast chef stood by the table and said he'd forgotten it.

'What, you forgot!' shouted Trimalchio. 'You'd think he'd only left out the pepper and cumin. Strip him!'

In a second the chef was stripped and standing miserably between two guards. But everyone began pleading for him:

'It does tend to happen,' they said, 'do let him off, please. If he does it any more, none of us will stand up for him again.'

Personally, given my tough and ruthless temperament, I couldn't contain myself. I leaned over and whispered in Agamemnon's ear:

'This has surely got to be the worst slave in the world. Could anyone forget to clean a pig? I damn well wouldn't let him off if he forgot to clean a fish.'

But not Trimalchio. His face relaxed into a smile.

'Well,' he said, 'since you have such a bad memory, gut it in front of us.'

The chef recovered his shirt, took up a knife and with a nervous hand cut open the pig's belly left and right. Suddenly, as the slits widened with the pressure, out poured sausages and blood-puddings.

50. The staff applauded this trick and gave a concerted cheer – 'Hurray for Gaius!' The chef of course was rewarded with a drink and a silver crown, and was also given a drinking cup on a tray of Corinthian bronze. Seeing Agamemnon staring hard at this cup, Trimalchio remarked:

'I'm the only person in the world with genuine Corinthian.'

I was expecting him with his usual conceit to claim that all his plate came from Corinth. But he was not as bad as that.

'Perhaps you're wondering,' he went on, 'how I'm the only one with genuine Corinthian dishes. The simple reason is that the manufacturer I buy from is named Corinth – but what can be Corinthian, if you don't have a Corinth to get it from?

'You mustn't take me for a fool: I know very well where Corinthian metalwork first came from. When Troy was captured that crafty snake Hannibal piled all the bronze, silver and gold statues into one heap and set them on fire, and they were all melted to a bronze alloy. The metalworkers took this solid mass and made plates, dishes, and statuettes out of it. That is how Corinthian plate[35] was born, not really one thing or another, but everything in one. You won't mind my saying so, but I prefer glass – that's got no taste at all. If only it didn't break, I'd prefer it to gold, but it's cheap stuff the way it is.

51. 'Mind you, there was a craftsman once who made a glass bowl that didn't break. So he got an audience with the Emperor,[36] taking his present with him . . . Then he made Caesar hand it back to him and dropped it on the floor. The Emperor couldn't have been more shaken. The man picked the bowl off the ground – it had been dinted like a bronze dish – took a hammer from his pocket and easily got the bowl as good as new. After this performance he thought he'd be in high heaven, especially when the Emperor said to him:

' "Is there anyone else who knows this process for making glass?"

'But now see what happens. When the man said no, the Emperor had his head cut off, the reason being that if it was made public, gold would have been as cheap as muck.

52. 'Now I'm very keen on silver. I have some three-gallon bumpers more or less . . . how Cassandra killed her sons, and the boys are lying there dead – very lifelike. I have a bowl my patron left to me with Daedalus shutting Niobe in the Trojan Horse.[37] What's more, I have the fights of Hermeros and Petraites[38] on some cups – all good and heavy. No, I wouldn't sell my know-how at any price.'

While he was talking, a young slave dropped a cup. Trimalchio looked in his direction.

'Get out and hang yourself,' he said, 'you're utterly useless.' Immediately the boy's lips trembled and he begged Trimalchio's pardon.

'What are you asking me for?' snapped his master, 'as though

I was the trouble! I'm just asking you not to let yourself be such a useless fool.'

In the end however, as a favour to us, he let him off and the boy ran round the table to celebrate . . . and shouted, 'Out with the water – in with the wine!'

We all showed our appreciation of his amusing wit – especially Agamemnon, who knew how to angle for further invitations. But our admiration went to Trimalchio's head. He drank with even greater cheerfulness and was very nearly drunk by now.

'Doesn't anyone want my dear Fortunata to dance?' he said. 'Honestly, no one dances the *Cordax*[39] better.'

Then he stuck his hands up over his forehead and gave us a personal imitation of the actor Syrus, while all the staff sang in chorus:

'Madeia, Perimadeia.'[40]

In fact, he would have taken the floor, if Fortunata had not whispered in his ear. She must have told him, I suppose, that such low fooling did not suit his dignity. But you never saw anyone so changeable – one minute he would be frightened of Fortunata and the next minute he would be back in character again.

53. What really interrupted his coarse insistence on dancing was his accountant, who sounded as though he was reading out a copy of the Gazette:

'26 July: Births on the estate at Cumae: male 30, female 40. Wheat threshed and stored: 500,000 pecks. Oxen broken in: 500.

'On the same date: the slave Mithridates crucified[41] for insulting the guardian spirit of our dear Gaius.

'On the same date: Deposits to the strong-room (no further investment possible): 10,000,000 sesterces.

'On the same date: a fire broke out on the estate at Pompeii beginning at the house of Nasta the bailiff.'

'What!' said Trimalchio. 'When was an estate bought for me at Pompeii?'

'Last year,' said the accountant, 'so it hasn't yet come on the books.'

Trimalchio flared up:

'If any land is bought for me and I don't hear of it within six months, I refuse to have it entered on the books.'

The official edicts were read out and the wills of certain game-keepers. In specific codicils they said they were leaving Trimalchio nothing. Then the names of some bailiffs; the divorce of a freed-woman, the wife of a watchman, on the grounds of adultery with a bath-attendant; the demotion of a hall-porter to a job at Baiae;[42] the prosecution of a steward; and the result of an action between some bedroom attendants.

Finally the acrobats arrived. One was a silly idiot who stood there holding a ladder and made his boy climb up the rungs, give us a song and dance at the top, then jump through blazing hoops, and hold up a large wine-jar with his teeth.

Only Trimalchio was impressed by all this: art wasn't appre-ciated, he considered, but if there were two things in the world he really liked to watch, they were acrobats and horn-players. All the other shows were not worth a damn.

'As a matter of fact,' he said, 'once I even bought some comic-actors, but I preferred them putting on Atellan farces,[43] and I told my conductor to keep his songs Latin.'

54. Just as he was saying this, the boy tumbled down[44] on Trimalchio's couch. Everyone screamed, the guests as well as the servants – not because they were worried over such an awful person (they would happily have watched his neck being broken) but because it would have been a poor ending to the party if they had to offer their condolences for a comparative stranger. Trimalchio himself groaned heavily and leaned over his arm as though it were hurt. Doctors raced to the scene, but practically the first one there was Fortunata, hair flying and cup in hand, telling the world what a poor unfortunate thing she was. As for the boy who had fallen, he was already crawl-ing round our feet, begging for mercy. I had a very uneasy feeling that his pleadings might be the prelude to some funny surprise ending, as I still remembered the chef who had forgotten to gut his pig. So I began looking round the dining-room for

some machine to appear out of the wall, especially after a servant was beaten for using white instead of purple wool to bandage his master's bruised arm.

Nor were my suspicions far out, because instead of punishment, there came an official announcement from Trimalchio that the boy was free, so that no one could say that such a great figure had been injured by a slave.

55. We all applauded his action and started a desultory conversation about how uncertain life was.

'Well,' says Trimalchio, 'an occasion like this mustn't pass without a suitable record.' He immediately called for his notebook, and without much mental exertion he came out with:

> 'What comes next you never know,
> Lady Luck runs the show,
>   So pass the Falernian, lad.'

This epigram brought the conversation round to poetry and for quite a time the first place among poets was given to Mopsus of Thrace[45] until Trimalchio said:

'Tell me, professor, how would you compare Cicero and Publilius?[46] I think Cicero was the better orator, but Publilius the better man. Now could there be anything finer than this:

> 'Down luxury's maw, Mars' walls now wilt.
> Your palate pens peacocks in plumage of gilt:
> These Babylon birds are plumped under lock
> With the guinea hen and the capon cock.
> That long-legged paragon, winged castanet,
> Summer's lingering lease and winter's regret –
> Even the stork, poor wandering guest,
> Is put in your pot and makes that his nest.
> Why are Indian pearls so dear in your sight?
> So your sluttish wife, draped in the diver's delight,
> May open her legs on her lover's divan?
> What use are green emeralds, glass ruin of man,
> Or carbuncles from Carthage with fire in their flint?
> Unless to let goodness gleam out in their glint.

Is it right for a bride to be clad in a cloud
Or wearing a wisp show off bare to the crowd?

56. 'Well now, whose profession do we think is most diffi-
cult after literature? I think doctors and bankers. A doctor has
to know what people have in their insides and what causes a
fever – even though I do hate them terribly the way they put me
on a diet of duck. A banker has to spot the brass under the
silver. Well, among dumb animals the hardest worked are cattle
and sheep. It's thanks to cattle we have bread to eat, and it's
thanks to sheep and their wool that we're well dressed. It's a
low trick the way we eat mutton and wear woollens. Bees, now,
I think are heavenly creatures – they spew honey, though people
suppose they get it from heaven. But at the same time they
sting, because where there's sweet you'll find bitter there too.'

He was still putting the philosophers out of work when tickets
were brought round in a cup and the boy whose job it was read
out the presents.[47] '*Rich man's prison*[48] – a silver jug. *Pillow*[49] – a
piece of neck came up. *Old man's wit and a sour stick*[50] – dry salt
biscuits came up and an apple on a stick. *Lick and spit*[51] got a
whip and a knife. *Flies and a fly-trap*[52] was raisins and Attic
honey. *Dinner-clothes and city-suit*[53] got a slice of meat and a
notebook. *Head and foot*[54] produced a hare and a slipper. *Lights
and letters*[55] got a lamprey and some peas.' We laughed for ages.
There were hundreds of things like this but they've slipped my
mind now.

57. Ascyltus, with his usual lack of restraint, found every-
thing extremely funny, lifting up his hands and laughing till the
tears came. Eventually one of Trimalchio's freedman friends
flared up at him.

'You with the sheep's eyes,' he said, 'what's so funny? Isn't
our host elegant enough for you? You're better off, I suppose,
and used to a bigger dinner. Holy guardian here preserve me! If
I was sitting by him, I'd stop his bleating! A fine pippin he is to
be laughing at other people! Some fly-by-night from god knows
where – not worth his own piss. In fact, if I pissed round him,
he wouldn't know where to turn.

'By god, it takes a lot to make me boil, but if you're too soft, worms like this only come to the top. Look at him laughing! What's he got to laugh at? Did his father pay cash for him? You're a Roman knight, are you? Well, my father was a king.

' "*Why are you only a freedman?*" did you say? Because I put myself into slavery. I wanted to be a Roman citizen, not a subject with taxes to pay.[56] And today, I hope no one can laugh at the way I live. I'm a man among men, and I walk with my head up. I don't owe anybody a penny – there's never been a court-order out for me. No one's said *"Pay up"* to me in the street.'

'I've bought a bit of land and some tiny pieces of plate. I've twenty bellies to feed, as well as a dog. I bought my old woman's freedom so nobody could wipe his dirty hands on *her* hair. Four thousand I paid for myself. I was elected to the Augustan College and it cost me nothing. I hope when I die I won't have to blush in my coffin.

'But you now, you're such a busybody you don't look behind you. You see a louse on somebody else, but not the fleas on your own back. You're the only one who finds us funny. Look at the professor now – he's an older man than you and we get along with him. But you're still wet from your mother's milk and not up to your ABC yet. Just a crackpot – you're like a piece of wash-leather in soak, softer but no better! You're grander than us – well, have two dinners and two suppers! I'd rather have my good name than any amount of money. When all's said and done, who's ever asked me for money twice? For forty years I slaved but nobody ever knew if I was a slave or a free man. I came to this colony when I was a lad with long hair – the town hall hadn't been built then. But I worked hard to please my master – there was a real gentleman, with more in his little finger-nail than there is in your whole body. And I had people in the house who tried to trip me up one way or another, but still – thanks be to his guardian spirit! – I kept my head above water. These are the prizes in life: being born free is as easy as all get-out. Now what are you gawping at, like a goat in a vetch-field?'

58. At this remark, Giton, who was waiting on me, could not suppress his laughter and let out a filthy guffaw, which did

not pass unnoticed by Ascyltus' opponent. He turned his abuse
on the boy.

'So!' he said. 'You're amused too, are you, you curly-headed
onion? A merry Saturnalia[57] to you! Is it December, I'd like to
know? When did *you* pay your liberation tax?[58] ... Look, he
doesn't know what to do, the gallow's bird, the crow's meat.

'God's curse on you, and your master too, for not keeping
you under control! As sure as I get my bellyful, it's only because
of Trimalchio that I don't take it out of you here and now. He's
a freedman like myself. We're doing all right, but those good-
for-nothings, well – . It's easy to see, like master, like man. I can
hardly hold myself back, and I'm not naturally hot-headed –
but once I start, I don't give a penny for my own mother.

'All right! I'll see you when we get outside, you rat, you
excrescence. I'll knock your master into a cocked hat before
I'm an inch taller or shorter. And I won't let you off either, by
heaven, even if you scream down God Almighty. Your cheap
curls and your no-good master won't be much use to you then –
I'll see to that. I'll get my teeth into you all right. Either I'm
much mistaken about myself or you won't be laughing at us
behind your golden beard. Athena's curse on you and the man
who first made you such a forward brat.

'I didn't learn no geometry or criticism and such silly rub-
bish, but I can read the letters on a notice board and I can do
my percentages in metal, weights, and money. In fact, if you
like, we'll have a bet. Come on, here's my cash. Now you'll see
how your father wasted his money, even though you do know
how to make a speech.

'Try this:

> 'Something we all have.
> Long I come, broad I come. What am I?

'I'll give you it: something we all have that runs and doesn't
move from its place: something we all have that grows and gets
smaller.[59]

'You're running round in circles, you've had enough, like
the mouse in the pisspot. So either keep quiet or keep out of

the way of your betters – they don't even know you're alive – unless you think I care about your box-wood rings that you swiped from your girl-friend! Lord make me lucky! Let's go into town and borrow some money. You'll soon see they trust this iron one.

'Pah! a drownded fox makes a nice sight, I must say. As I hope to make my pile and die so famous that people swear by my dead body, I'll hound you to death. And he's a nice thing too, the one who taught you all these tricks – a muttonhead, not a master. We learned different. Our teacher used to say: "Are your things in order? Go straight home. No looking around. And be polite to your elders." Nowadays it's all an absolute muck-heap. They turn out nobody worth a penny. I'm like you see me and I thank god for the way I was learnt.'

59. Ascyltus began to answer this abuse, but Trimalchio, highly amused by his friend's fluency, said:

'No slanging matches! Let's all have a nice time. And you, Hermeros, leave the young fellow alone. His blood's a bit hot – you should know better. In things like this, the one who gives in always comes off best. Besides, when you were just a chicken, it was cock-a-doodle too, and you had no more brains yourself. So let's start enjoying ourselves again, that'll be better, and let's watch the recitations from Homer.'

In came the troupe immediately and banged their shields with their spears. Trimalchio sat up on his cushion and while the reciters spouted their Greek lines at one another in their usual impudent way, he read aloud in Latin in a sing-song voice. After a while, he got silence and asked:

'Do you know which scene they were acting? Diomede and Ganymede were the two brothers. Their sister was Helen. Agamemnon carried her off and offered a hind to Diana in her place. So now Homer is describing how the Trojans and Tarentines fought each other. Agamemnon, of course, won and married off his daughter Iphigenia to Achilles.[60] This drove Ajax insane, and in a moment or two he'll explain how it ended.'

As Trimalchio said this, the reciters gave a loud shout, the servants made a lane, and a calf was brought in on a two-hundred pound plate: it was boiled whole and wearing a helmet. Following it came Ajax, slashing at the calf[61] with a drawn sword like a madman. After rhythmically cutting and slicing, he collected the pieces on the point and shared them among the surprised guests.

60. But we were not given long to admire these elegant turns, for all of a sudden, the coffered ceiling began rumbling[62] and the whole dining-room shook. I leapt to my feet in panic, as I was afraid some acrobat was coming down through the roof. The other guests also looked up to see what strange visitation this announced. Would you believe it – the panels opened and suddenly an enormous hoop was let down, with gold crowns and alabaster jars of toilet cream hanging from it. While we were being told to accept these as presents, I looked at the table . . . Already there was a tray of cakes in position, the centre of which was occupied by a Priapus made of pastry, holding the usual things in his very adequate lap – all kinds of apples and grapes.

Greedily enough, we stretched out our hands to this display, and in a flash a fresh series of jokes restored the general gaiety. Every single cake and every single apple needed only the slightest touch for a cloud of saffron to start pouring out and the irritating vapour to come right in our faces.

Naturally we thought the fish must have some religious significance to be smothered in such an odour of sanctity, so we raised ourselves to a sitting position and cried:

'God save Augustus, the Father of his People!'

All the same, even after this show of respect, some of the guests were snatching the apples – especially me, because I didn't think I was pushing a generous enough share into Giton's pocket.

While all this was going on, three boys in brief white tunics came in. Two of them set down on the table the household deities,[63] which had amulets round their necks; the other, carrying round a bowl of wine, kept shouting: 'God save all here!' . . .

Our host said that one of the gods was called Cobbler, the second Luck, and the third Lucre. There was also a golden image of Trimalchio himself, and as all the others were pressing their lips to it we felt too embarrassed not to do the same.

61. After we had all wished each other health and happiness, Trimalchio looked at Niceros and said:

'You used to be better company at a party. You're keeping very quiet nowadays: you don't say a word – I don't know why. Do me a favour to please me. Tell us about that adventure you had.'

Niceros was delighted by his friend's affable request and said:

'May I never make another penny if I'm not jumping for joy to see you in such form. Well, just for fun – though I'm worried about those schoolteachers there in case they laugh at me. That's up to them. I'll tell it all the same. Anyway, what do I care who laughs at me. It's better to be laughed at than laughed down.'

'*When thus he spake*,' he began this story:

'When I was still a slave, we were living down a narrow street – Gavilla owns the house now – and there as heaven would have it, I fell in love with the wife of Terentius the inn-keeper.

'You all used to know Melissa from Tarentum, an absolute peach to look at. But honest to god, it wasn't her body or just sex that made me care for her, it was more because she had such a nice nature. If I asked her for anything, it was never refused. If I had a penny or halfpenny, I gave it to her to look after and she never let me down.

'One day her husband died out at the villa. So I did my best by hook or by crook to get to her. After all, you know, a friend in need is a friend indeed.

62. 'Luckily the master had gone off to Capua to look after some odds and ends. I seized my chance and I talked a guest of ours into walking with me as far as the fifth milestone. He was a soldier as it happened, and as brave as hell. About cock-crow we shag off, and the moon was shining like noontime. We get to where the tombs are and my chap starts making for the grave-stones, while I, singing away, keep going and start counting the stars. Then just as I looked back at my mate, he stripped off and laid all his clothes by the side of the road. My heart was in my mouth, I stood there like a corpse. Anyway, he pissed a

ring round his clothes and suddenly turned into a wolf. Don't think I'm joking, I wouldn't tell a lie about this for a fortune. However, as I began to say, after he turned into a wolf, he started howling and rushed off into the woods.

'At first I didn't know where I was, then I went up to collect his clothes – but they'd turned to stone. If ever a man was dead with fright, it was me. But I pulled out my sword, and I fairly slaughtered the early morning shadows till I arrived at my girl's villa.

'I got into the house and I practically gasped my last, the sweat was pouring down my crotch, my eyes were blank and staring – I could hardly get over it. It came as a surprise to my poor Melissa to find I'd walked over so late.

' "If you'd come a bit earlier," she said, "at least you could've helped us. A wolf got into the grounds and tore into all the livestock – it was like a bloody shambles. But he didn't have the last laugh, even though he got away. Our slave here put a spear right through his neck."

'I couldn't close my eyes again after I heard this. But when it was broad daylight I rushed off home like the innkeeper after the robbery. And when I came to the spot where his clothes had turned to stone, I found nothing but bloodstains. However, when I got home, my soldier friend was lying in bed like a great ox with the doctor seeing to his neck. I realized he was a werewolf and afterwards I couldn't have taken a bite of bread in his company, not if you killed me for it. If some people think differently about this, that's up to them. But me – if I'm telling a lie may all your guardian spirits damn me!'

63. Everyone was struck with amazement.

'I wouldn't disbelieve a word,' said Trimalchio. 'Honestly, the way my hair stood on end – because I know Niceros doesn't go in for jokes. He's really reliable and never exaggerates.

'Now I'll tell you a horrible story myself. A real donkey on the roof! When I was still in long hair (you see, I led a very soft life from my boyhood) the master's pet slave died. He was a pearl, honest to god, a beautiful boy, and one of the best. Well, his poor mother was crying over him and the rest of us were deep in depression, when the witches suddenly started howling – you'd think it was a dog after a hare.

'At that time we had a Cappadocian chap, tall and a very brave old thing, quite the strong man – he could lift an angry ox. This fellow rushed outside with a drawn sword, first wrapping his left hand up very carefully, and he stabbed one of the women right through the middle, just about here – may no harm come to where I'm touching! We heard a groan but – naturally I'm not lying – we didn't see the things themselves. Our big fellow, however, once he was back inside, threw himself on his bed. His whole body was black and blue, as though he'd been whipped. The evil hand, you see, had been put on him.

'We closed the door and went back to what we had to do, but as the mother puts her arms round her son's body, she touches it and finds it's only a handful of straw. It had no heart, no inside, no anything. Of course the witches had already stolen the boy and put a straw baby in its place.

'I put it to you, you can't get away from it – there are such things as women with special powers and midnight hags that can turn everything upside down. But that great tall fellow of ours never got his colour back after what happened. In fact, not many days later, he went crazy and died.'

64. Equally thrilled and convinced, we kissed the table and asked the midnight hags to stay at home till we got back from dinner.

By this time, to tell the truth, there seemed to be more lights burning and the whole dining-room seemed different, when Trimalchio said:

'What about you, Plocamus, haven't you a story to entertain us with. You used to have a fine voice for giving recitations with a nice swing and putting songs over – ah me, the good old days are gone.'

'Well,' said Plocamus, 'my galloping days finished after I got gout. Besides, when I was really young I nearly got consumption through singing. How about my dancing? How about my recitations? How about my barber's shop act? When was there anybody so good apart from Apelles[64] himself?'

Putting his hand to his mouth he let out some sort of obscene whistle which he afterwards insisted was Greek.

Trimalchio, after giving us his own imitation of a fanfare of

trumpets, looked round for his little pet, whom he called Croe-
sus. The boy, however, a bleary-eyed creature with absolutely
filthy teeth, was busy wrapping a green cloth round a disgust-
ingly fat black puppy. He put half a loaf on the couch and was
cramming it down the animal's throat while it kept vomiting it
back. This business reminded Trimalchio to send out for Scy-
lax, 'protector of the house and the household'.

A hound of enormous size was immediately led in on a
chain. A kick from the hall-porter reminded him to lie down
and he stretched himself out in front of the table. Trimalchio
threw him a piece of white bread, remarking:

'Nobody in the house is more devoted to me.'

The boy, however, annoyed by such a lavish tribute to Scy-
lax, put his own little pup on the floor and encouraged her to
hurry up and start a fight. Scylax, naturally following his canine
instincts, filled the dining-room with a most unpleasant bark-
ing and almost torc Croesus' Pearl to pieces. Nor was the
trouble limited to the dog-fight. A lampstand was upset on the
table as well and not only smashed all the glass but spilled hot
oil over some of the guests.

Not wanting to seem disturbed by the damage, Trimalchio
gave the boy a kiss and told him to climb on his back. The lad
climbed on his mount without hesitation, and slapping his
shoulder blades with the flat of his hand, shouted amid roars of
laughter:

'Big mouth, big mouth, how many fingers have I got up?'

So Trimalchio was calmed down for a while and gave
instructions for a huge bowl of drink to be mixed and served to
all the servants, who were sitting by our feet. He added the
condition:

'If anyone won't take it, pour it over his head. Day's the time
for business, now's the time for fun.'

65. This display of kindness was followed by some savouries,
the very recollection of which really and truly makes me sick.
Instead of thrushes, a fat capon was brought round for each of
us, as well as goose-eggs in pastry hoods. Trimalchio surpassed
himself to make us eat them; he described them as boneless
chickens. In the middle of all this, a lictor knocked at the double

doors and a drunken guest entered wearing white, followed by a large crowd of people. I was terrified by this lordly apparition and thought it was the chief magistrate arriving. So I tried to rise and get my bare feet on the floor. Agamemnon laughed at this panic and said:

'Get hold of yourself, you silly fool. This is Habinnas – Augustan College and monumental mason.'

Relieved by this information I resumed my position and watched Habinnas' entry[65] with huge admiration. Being already drunk, he had his hands on his wife's shoulders; loaded with several garlands, oil pouring down his forehead and into his eyes, he settled himself into the praetor's place of honour[66] and immediately demanded some wine and hot water. Trimalchio, delighted by these high spirits, demanded a larger cup for himself and asked how he had enjoyed it all.

'The only thing we missed,' replied Habinnas, 'was yourself – the apple of my eye was here. Still, it was damn good. Scissa was giving a ninth-day dinner[67] in honour of a poor slave of hers she'd freed on his death-bed. And I think she'll have a pretty penny to pay with the five per cent liberation tax, because they reckon he was worth fifty thousand. Still, it was pleasant enough, even if we did have to pour half our drinks over his wretched bones.'

66. 'Well,' said Trimalchio, 'what did you have for dinner?'

'I'll tell you if I can – I've such a good memory that I often forget my own name. For the first course we had a pig crowned with sausages and served with blood-puddings and very nicely done giblets, and of course beetroot and pure wholemeal bread – which I prefer to white myself: it's very strengthening and I don't regret it when I do my business. The next course was cold tart and a concoction of first-class Spanish wine poured over hot honey. I didn't eat anything at all of the actual tart, but I got stuck into the honey. Scattered round were chickpeas, lupines, a choice of nuts and an apple apiece – though I took two. And look, I've got them tied up in a napkin, because if I don't take something in the way of a present to my little slave, I'll have a row on my hands.

'Oh yes, my good lady reminds me. We had a hunk of

bear-meat set before us, which Scintilla was foolish enough to try, and she practically spewed up her guts; but I ate more than a pound of it, as it tasted like real wild-boar. And I say if bears can eat us poor people, it's all the more reason why us poor people should eat bears.

'To finish up with, we had some cheese basted with new wine, snails all round, chitterlings, plates of liver, eggs in pastry hoods, turnips, mustard, and then, wait a minute, little tunny fish! There were pickled cumin seeds too, passed round in a bowl, and some people were that bad-mannered they took three handfuls. You see, we sent the ham away.

67. 'But tell me something, Gaius, now I ask – why isn't Fortunata at the table?'

'You know her,' replied Trimalchio, 'unless she's put the silver away and shared out the leftovers among the slaves, she won't put a drop of water to her mouth.'

'All the same,' retorted Habinnas, 'unless she sits down, I'm shagging off.'

And he was starting to get up, when at a given signal all the servants shouted 'Fortunata' four or more times. So in she came with her skirt tucked up under a yellow sash to show her cerise petticoat underneath, as well as her twisted anklets and gold-embroidered slippers. Wiping her hands on a handkerchief which she carried round her neck, she took her place on the couch where Habinnas' wife was reclining. She kissed her. 'Is it really you?' she said, clapping her hands together.

It soon got to the point where Fortunata took the bracelets from her great fat arms and showed them to the admiring Scintilla. In the end she even undid her anklets and her gold hair net, which she said was pure gold. Trimalchio noticed this and had it all brought to him and commented:

'A woman's chains, you see. This is the way us poor fools get robbed. She must have six and a half pounds on her. Still, I've got a bracelet myself, made up from one-tenth per cent to Mercury[68] – and it weighs not an ounce less than ten pounds.'

Finally, for fear he looked like a liar, he even had some scales brought in and had them passed round to test the weight.

Scintilla was no better. From round her neck she took a little gold locket, which she called her 'lucky box'. From it she extracted two earrings and in her turn gave them to Fortunata to look at.

'A present from my good husband,' she said, 'and no one has a finer set.'

'Hey!' said Habinnas. 'You cleaned me out to buy you a glass bean. Honestly, if I had a daughter, I'd cut her little ears off. If there weren't any women, everything would be dirt cheap. As it is, we've got to drink cold water and piss it out hot.'

Meanwhile, the women giggled tipsily between themselves and kissed each other drunkenly, one crying up her merits as a housewife, the other crying about her husband's demerits and boy-friends. While they had their heads together like this, Habinnas rose stealthily and taking Fortunata's feet, flung them up over the couch.

'Oh, oh!' she shrieked, as her underskirt wandered up over her knees. So she settled herself in Scintilla's lap and hid her burning red face in her handkerchief.

68. Then came an interval, after which Trimalchio called for dessert. Slaves removed all the tables and brought in others. They scattered sawdust tinted with saffron and vermilion, and something I had never seen before – powdered mica. Trimalchio said at once:

'I could make you just settle for this. There's dessert for you! The first tables've deserted.[69] However, if you people have anything nice, bring it on!'

Meanwhile a slave from Alexandria, who was taking round the hot water, started imitating a nightingale, only for Trimalchio to shout: 'Change your tune!'

More entertainment! A slave sitting by Habinnas' feet, prompted, I suppose, by his master, suddenly burst out in a sing-song voice:

'Meantime Aeneas was in mid-ocean with his fleet.'[70]

No more cutting sound ever pierced my eardrums. Apart from his barbarous meandering up and down the scale, he mixed in Atellan verses, so that Virgil actually grated on me for

the first time in my life. When he did finally stop through
exhaustion, Habinnas said:

'He's never had any real training. I just had him taught by
sending him along to peddlers on the street corner. He's no one
to equal him if he wants to imitate mule-drivers or hawkers.
He's terribly clever, really. He's a cobbler, a cook, a confec-
tioner – a man that can turn his hand to anything. But he's got
two faults; if he didn't have them, he'd be one in a million – he's
circumcised and he snores. I don't mind him being cross-eyed –
so is Venus. That's why he's never quiet and his eyes are hardly
ever still. I got him for three hundred denarii.'

69. Scintilla interrupted him: 'Of course, you're not telling
them all the tricks that wretch gets up to. He's a pimp – but I'll
make sure he gets branded for it.'

Trimalchio laughed: 'I know a Cappadocian when I see one.
He's not slow in looking after himself and, by heaven, I admire
him for it. You can't take it with you.

'Now, Scintilla, don't be jealous. Believe me, we know all
about you women too. As sure as I stand here, I used to bang
the mistress so much that even the old boy suspected; so he sent
me off to look after his farms. But I'd better save my breath to
cool my porridge.'

As though he'd been complimented the wretched slave took
out an earthenware lamp from his pocket and for more than
half an hour gave imitations of trumpet-players, while Habin-
nas hummed an accompaniment, pressing down his lower lip
with his hand. Finally coming right into the middle, he did a
flute-player with some broken reeds, then he dressed up in a
greatcoat and whip and did the Life of the Muleteer, till Habin-
nas called him over, kissed him, and gave him a drink:

'Better and better, Massa!' he said. 'I'll give you a pair of
boots.'

There would have been no end to all these trials if an extra
course had not arrived – pastry thrushes stuffed with raisins
and nuts. After them came quinces with thorns stuck in them to
look like sea urchins. All this would have been all right, but
there was a far more horrible dish that made us prefer even
dying of hunger. When it was put on the table, looking to us

like a fat goose surrounded by fish and all sorts of game, Trimalchio said:

'Whatever you see here, friends, is made from one kind of stuff.'

I, of course, being very cautious by nature, spotted immediately what it was and glancing at Agamemnon, I said:

'I'll be surprised if it isn't all made of wax, or any rate mud. I've seen that sort of imitation food produced at the Saturnalia in Rome.'

70. I hadn't quite finished what I was saying when Trimalchio said:

'As sure as I hope to expand – my investments of course, not my waist-line – my chef made it all from pork. There couldn't be a more valuable man to have. Say the word and he'll produce a fish out of a sow's belly, a pigeon out of the lard, a turtle dove out of the ham, and fowl out of the knuckle. So he's been given a nice name I thought of myself – he's called Daedalus.[71] And seeing he's a clever lad, I brought him some carvers of Styrian steel as a present from Rome.'

He immediately had them brought in and gazed at them with admiration. He even allowed us to test the point on our cheeks.

All of a sudden in came two slaves, apparently having had a quarrel at the well; at any rate they still had water jugs on their shoulders. But while Trimalchio was giving his decision about their respective cases, neither of them paid any attention to his verdict: instead they broke each other's jugs with their sticks. Staggered by their drunken insolence, we couldn't take our eyes away from the fight till we noticed oysters and scallops sliding out of the jugs, which a boy collected and carried round on a dish. The ingenious chef was equal to these elegant refinements – he brought in snails on a silver gridiron, singing all the time in a high grating voice.

I blush to say what happened next. Boys with their hair down their backs came round with perfumed cream in a silver bowl and rubbed it on our feet[72] as we lay there, but first they wrapped our legs and ankles in wreaths of flowers. Some of the same stuff was dropped into the decanter and the lamp.

Fortunata was now wanting to dance, and Scintilla was doing more clapping than talking, when Trimalchio said:

'Philargyrus – even though you are such a terrible fan of the Greens[73] – you have my permission to join us. And tell your dear Menophila to sit down as well.'

Need I say more? We were almost thrown out of our places, so completely did the household fill the dining-room. I even noticed that the chef, the one who had produced the goose out of pork, was actually given a place above me, and he was reeking of pickles and sauce. And he wasn't satisfied with just having a place, but he had to start straight off on an imitation of the tragedian Ephesus,[74] and then challenge his master to bet against the Greens winning at the next races.

71. Trimalchio became expansive after this argument.

'My dear people,' he said, 'slaves are human beings too. They drink the same milk as anybody else, even though luck's been agin 'em. Still, if nothing happens to me, they'll have their taste of freedom soon. In fact, I'm setting them all free in my will. I'm giving Philargyrus a farm, what's more, and the woman he lives with. As for Cario, I'm leaving him a block of flats, his five per cent manumission tax, and a bed with all the trimmings. I'm making Fortunata my heir, and I want all my friends to look after her.

'The reason I'm telling everyone all this is so my household will love me now as much as if I was dead.'

Everyone began thanking his lordship for his kindness, when he became very serious and had a copy of his will brought in. Amid the sobs of his household he read out the whole thing from beginning to end.

Then looking at Habinnas, he said:

'What have you to say, my dear old friend? Are you building my monument the way I told you? I particularly want you to keep a place at the foot of my statue and put a picture of my pup there, as well as paintings of wreaths, scent-bottles, and all the contests of Petraites, and thanks to you I'll be able to live on after I'm dead. And another thing! See that it's a hundred feet facing the road and two hundred back into the field. I want all the various sorts of fruit round my ashes and lots and lots of vines. After all, it's a big mistake to have nice houses just for when you're alive and not worry about the one we have to live in for much longer. And that's why I want this written up before anything else:

THIS MONUMENT DOES NOT GO TO THE HEIR

'But I'll make sure in my will that I don't get done down once I'm dead. I'll put one of my freedmen in charge of my tomb to look after it and not let people run up and shit on my monument. I'd like you to put some ships there too, sailing under full canvas, and me sitting on a high platform in my robes of office, wearing five gold rings[75] and pouring out a bagful of money for the people. You know I gave them all a dinner and two denarii apiece. Let's have in a banqueting hall as well, if you think it's a good idea, and show the whole town having a good time. Put up a statue of Fortunata on my right, holding a dove, and have her leading her little dog tied to her belt – and my little lad as well, and big wine-jars tightly sealed up so the wine won't spill. And perhaps you could carve me a broken one and a boy crying over it. A clock in the middle, so that anybody who looks at the time, like it or not, has got to read my name. As for the inscription now, take a good look and see if this seems suitable enough:

'HERE SLEEPS
GAIUS POMPEIUS TRIMALCHIO
MAECENATIANUS[76]
ELECTED TO THE AUGUSTAN COLLEGE IN HIS ABSENCE
HE COULD HAVE BEEN ON EVERY BOARD IN ROME
BUT HE REFUSED
GOD-FEARING BRAVE AND TRUE
A SELF-MADE MAN
HE LEFT AN ESTATE OF 30,000,000
AND HE NEVER HEARD A PHILOSOPHER
. FAREWELL
AND YOU FARE WELL, TRIMALCHIO'

72. As he finished Trimalchio burst into tears. Fortunata was in tears, Habinnas was in tears, in the end the whole household

filled the dining-room with their wailing, like people at a funeral. In fact, I'd even begun crying myself, when Trimalchio said:

'Well, since we know we've got to die, why don't we live a little. I want to see you enjoying yourselves. Let's jump into a bath – you won't be sorry, damn me! It's as hot as a furnace.'

'Hear! Hear!' said Habinnas. 'Turning one day into two – nothing I like better.' He got up in his bare feet and began to follow Trimalchio on his merry way.

I looked at Ascyltus. 'What do you think?' I said. 'Now me, if I see a bath, I'll die on the spot.'

'Let's say yes,' he suggested, 'and while they're going for their bath, we can slip out in the crowd.'

This seemed a good idea, so Giton led us through the portico till we reached the door, where the hound chained there greeted us with such a noise that Ascyltus actually fell into the fish-pond. Not only that, as I was drunk too, when I tried to help the struggling Ascyltus I was dragged into the same watery trap. However, the hall-porter saved us and by his intervention pacified the dog and dragged us trembling to dry land. Giton had already bought off the beast in a most ingenious way. He had scattered whatever he had got from us at dinner in front of the barking hound, and distracted by the food, it had choked down its fury.

Nevertheless, when, shivering and wet, we asked the hall-porter to let us out through the front door, he said: 'You're wrong if you think you can leave through the door you came in. No guest has ever been let out through the same door. They come in one way and go out another.'

73. What could we do after this piece of bad luck, shut up in this modern labyrinth[77] and now beginning to regret that bath? We asked him to please show us the way to the bath-hall, and, throwing off our clothes, which Giton began drying at the door, we went in. There stood Trimalchio, and not even there could we get away from his filthy ostentation. He told us there was nothing better than a private bath, and that there had once been a bakery on that very spot. Then he sat down as though tired, and being tempted by the acoustics of the bath, with his drunken mouth gaping at the ceiling, he began murdering some

songs by Menecrates[78] – or so we were told by those who understood his words.

The rest of the guests ran round the edge hand in hand, roaring away with a tremendous noise. Some were trying to pick up rings from the floor with their hands tied behind their backs, or were kneeling and trying to bend their necks backwards and touch the tips of their big toes. We left them to their games and sat down in the hot tub, which was being heated to Trimalchio's liking.

Well, after shaking off our drunken stupor, we were taken to another dining-room where Fortunata had laid out an elegant spread ... In fact, I noticed some bronze fishermen on the lamps as well as tables of solid silver, with gold inlaid pottery spread around and wine pouring from a leather wine-flask before our very eyes.

'Today, my friends,' said Trimalchio, 'my little slave had his first shave: he's a careful fellow – no offence meant! – who watches the pennies. So let's whet our throttles and not stop eating till daylight.'

74. Just as he was speaking, a cock crowed. Upset by this, Trimalchio ordered some wine to be poured out under the table and even had the lamps sprinkled with it undiluted. He actually changed his ring to his right hand.[79]

'That trumpeter,' he said, 'didn't give the signal without good reason. There should be a fire next or else somebody will be dying in the neighbourhood – God spare us! So whoever gets me that bringer of bad news, there's a tip for him.'

Before the words were out of his mouth, a cock was brought in and Trimalchio ordered it to be put in the pan and cooked. It was cut up by that very skilful chef and it was thrown into the pot. While Daedalus drew the scalding liquid, Fortunata ground pepper in a box-wood grinder.

After this dish Trimalchio looked at the servants and said:

'Why haven't you had dinner yet? Off you go and let some others come on duty.'

Up came another squad and as the first set called out: 'Good night, Gaius!' the new arrivals shouted: 'Good evening, Gaius!'

This led to the first incident that damped the general high

spirits. Not a bad-looking boy entered with the newcomers and Trimalchio jumped at him and began kissing him at some length. Fortunata, asserting her just and legal rights, began hurling insults at Trimalchio, calling him a low scum and a disgrace, who couldn't control his beastly desires. 'You dirty dog!' she finally added.

Trimalchio took offence at this abuse and flung his glass into Fortunata's face. She screamed as though she'd lost an eye and put her trembling hands across her face. Scintilla was terrified too and hugged the quaking woman to her breast. An obliging slave pressed a little jug of cold water to her cheek, while Fortunata rested her head on it and began weeping. Trimalchio on the other hand said:

'Well, well, forgotten her flute-girl days, has she? She doesn't remember, but she was bought and sold, and I took her away from it all and made her as good as the next. Yet she puffs herself up like a frog and doesn't even spit for luck. Like wood, not woman. But those as are born over a shop don't dream of a house. May I never have a day's good luck again, if I don't teach that Cassandra[80] in clogs some manners!

'There was I, not worth twopence, and I could have had ten million. And you know I'm not lying about it. Agatho, who runs the perfume shop, he took me on one side just recently and said: "You don't want to let your family die out, you know!" But me, trying to do the right thing and not wanting to look changeable, I cut my own throat.

'All right! I'll make you want to dig me up with your bare nails. Just so you'll know on the spot what you've done for yourself – Habinnas! I don't want you to put her statue on my tomb, so at least when I'm dead I won't have any more squabbles. And another thing! Just to show I can get my own back – when I'm dead I don't want her to kiss me.'

75. After this thunderbolt, Habinnas began asking him to calm down: 'There's none of us does no wrong,' he said, 'we're human beings, not gods!' Scintilla said the same, calling him Gaius, and she began asking him, in the name of his guardian spirit, to give in.

Trimalchio held back his tears no longer. 'I ask you, Habinnas,'

he said, 'as you hope to enjoy your bit of savings – if I did any-
thing wrong, spit in my face. I kissed this very careful little
fellow, not for his pretty looks, but because he's careful with
money – he says his ten times table, he reads a book at sight,
he's got himself some Thracian kit out of his daily allowance,
and he's bought himself an easy chair and two cups out of his
own pocket. Doesn't he deserve to be the apple of my eye? But
Fortunata won't have it.

'Is that the way you feel, high heels? I'll give you a piece of
advice: don't let your good luck turn your head, you kite, and
don't make me show my teeth, my little darling – otherwise
you'll feel my temper. You know me: once I've decided on
something, it's fixed with a twelve-inch nail.

'But to come back to earth – I want you to enjoy yourselves,
my dear people. After all, I was once like you are, but being the
right sort I got where I am. It's the old headpiece that makes a
man, the rest is all rubbish. "But right – sell right!" – that's me!
Different people will give you a different line. I'm just on top of
the world, I'm that lucky.

'But you, you snoring thing, are you still moaning? I'll give
you something to moan about in a minute.

'However, as I'd started to say, it was my shrewd way with
money that made me my fortune. I came from Asia as big as
this candlestick. In fact, every day I used to measure myself
against it, and to get some whiskers round my beak quicker, I
used to oil my lips from the lamp. Still, for fourteen years I was
the old boy's fancy. And there's nothing wrong if the boss wants
it. But I did all right by the old girl too. You know what I
mean – I don't say anything because I'm not the boasting sort.

76. 'Well, as heaven will have it, I became boss in the house,
and the old boy, look, was mine, heart and soul. That's about
it – he made me co-heir with the Emperor[81] and I got a senator's
fortune.[82] But nobody gets enough, never. I wanted to go into
business. Not to make a long story of it, I built five ships, I
loaded them with wine – it was absolute gold at the time – and
I sent them to Rome. You'd have thought I ordered it – every
single ship was wrecked. That's fact, not fable! In one single day
Neptune swallowed up thirty million. Do you think I gave up?

This loss, I swear, just whetted my appetite – it was as if nothing had happened. I built more boats, bigger and better and luckier, so nobody could say I wasn't a man of courage. You know, the greater the ship, the greater the confidence. I loaded them again – with wine, bacon, beans, perfumes and slaves. At this point Fortunata did the decent thing, because she sold off all her gold trinkets, all her clothes, and put ten thousand in gold pieces in my hand. This was the yeast my fortune needed to rise. What heaven wants soon happens. In one voyage I carved out a round ten million. I immediately bought back all my old master's estates. I build a house, I invest in slaves and haulage. Whatever I touched grew like a honeycomb. Once I had more than the whole country, then down tools! I retired from business and began advancing loans to freedmen.

'Actually I was tired of trading on my own account, but it was an astrologer who convinced me. He happened to come to our colony, a sort of Greek, Serapa by name, and he could have told heaven itself what to do. He even told me things I'd forgotten. He went through everything for me from A to Z. He knew me inside out – the only thing he didn't tell me was what I ate for dinner the day before. You'd have thought he'd never left my side.

77. 'Wasn't there that thing, Habinnas? – I think you were there: "You got your lady wife out of those *certain circumstances*. You are not lucky in your friends. Nobody thanks you enough for your trouble. You have large estates. You are nursing a viper in your bosom."

'And he said – though I shouldn't tell you – I have thirty years, four months, and two days to live. What's more, I shall soon receive a legacy. My horoscope tells me this. If I'm allowed to join my estates to Apulia,[83] I'll have lived enough.

'Meantime, under the protection of Mercury, I built this house. As you know, it was still a shack, now it's a shrine. It has four dining-rooms, twenty bedrooms, two marble colonnades, a row of box-rooms up above, a bedroom where I sleep myself, a nest for this viper, and a really good lodge for the porter. In fact, when Scaurus[84] came here, he didn't want to stay anywhere else, even though he's got his father's guest house down by the sea. And there are a lot of other things I'll show you in a second.

'Believe me: have a penny, and you're worth a penny. You got something, you'll be thought something. Like your old friend – first a frog, now a king.

'Meantime, Stichus, bring out the shroud and the things I want to be buried in. Bring some cosmetic cream, too, and a sample from that jar of wine I want my bones washed in.'

78. Stichus did not delay over it, but brought both his white shroud and his purple-edged toga into the dining-room ... Trimalchio told us to examine them and see if they were made of good wool. Then he said with a smile:

'Now you, Stichus, see no mice or moths get at those – otherwise I'll burn you alive. I want to be buried in style, so the whole town will pray for my rest.'

He opened a bottle of nard on the spot, rubbed some on all of us and said:

'I hope this'll be as nice when I'm dead as when I'm alive.'

He now ordered wine to be poured into a big decanter and he said:

'I want you to think you've been invited to my wake.'

The thing was becoming absolutely sickening, when Trimalchio, showing the effects of his disgusting drunkenness, had a fresh entertainment brought into the dining-room, some cornet players. Propped up on a lot of cushions, he stretched out along the edge of the couch and said: 'Pretend I'm dead and say something nice.'[85]

The cornet players struck up a dead march. One man in particular, the slave of his undertaker (who was one of the most respectable persons present), blew so loudly that he roused the neighbourhood. As a result, the fire brigade in charge of the nearby area, thinking Trimalchio's house was on fire, suddenly broke down the front door and began kicking up their usual sort of din with their water and axes.

Seizing this perfect chance, we gave Agamemnon the slip and escaped as rapidly as if there really were a fire ...

79. There was no torch available to show us the way, and as it was halfway through the night, the silence gave us little hope of meeting anyone with a light. Add to this too much wine and our ignorance of the place, which would have been a problem

even in daylight. So after we had dragged our bleeding feet over
all the sharp stones and jutting pieces of broken crockery for
nearly a full hour, we were rescued by Giton's ingenuity. Afraid
of losing his way even in daytime, the lad had shrewdly marked
all the pillars and posts with chalk, and the bright marks,
gleaming through even the thickest darkness, showed us the
way. Yet we had to sweat just as much once we arrived at the
inn. The old woman, after soaking herself so long with her
guests, wouldn't have felt it if you'd put a fire under her, and we
should probably have had to spend the night on the doorstep if
the landlord, returning from the coaches, had not turned up.
He naturally didn't make a noise very long but just broke the
inn-door down and finally let us in through the same way.

> Ye gods and goddesses! O what a night!
> How soft the bed! We clung so warm and tight,
> Our lips exchanged our souls in mingled breath.
> Farewell, all worldly cares! O welcome, death!

I congratulated myself too soon. For once the wine had
made me relax my drunken hands; Ascyltus, utterly unscrupu-
lous, took the boy away from me in the night and transferred
him to his bed. And rolled up coolly with someone else's boy-
friend (was Giton conscious of the assault or was he pretending?)
he fell asleep wrapped in an embrace he had no right to, lost to
all sense of justice.

When I awoke and ran my hands over the empty joyless
bed . . . if you can trust what a lover says, I wondered whether
to run my sword through both of them and continue their sleep
into death. Following a safer policy, I roused Giton with my
fists, but looking at Ascyltus with a savage expression I said:

'You have wrecked all mutual confidence and friendship
with your criminal ways, so pack up right away and find some-
where else to practise your filthy habits.'

He made no opposition but once we had shared the loot
equally, he said:

'Right, now let's split the boy too.'

ENCOLPIUS IS JILTED
AND ROBBED

80. I thought this was a parting joke. But he drew his sword with a murderous hand, saying:

'You are not going to enjoy this prize you are sitting on alone. I must have my share even if I cut it off with this sword to avenge myself.'

I did the same and wrapping my cloak round my arm, dropped into a fighting crouch. In the middle of this heart-breaking lunacy the poor boy held on to our knees in tears and begged us not to let the inn see another pair of Theban brothers[1] or to sully the sanctity of our beautiful friendship with each other's blood.

'If there must be bloodshed at any price,' he cried, 'look, I offer you my throat, get your hands on it, press your points home. I'm the one to die, because I broke up a sworn friendship.'

We put up our steel after this plea. Ascyltus was the first to speak:

'I'll put an end to this quarrel. Let the boy himself go with the one he wants, so that he at least may have the liberty of choosing his lover.'

Imagining our long intimacy had come to mean as much as ties of blood, I had no fears. On the contrary, I jumped head-long at the offer and gave the decision to the judge. There was no hesitation, not the slightest appearance of it. The last syllable was scarcely out of my mouth when he got up and chose Ascyltus as his lover. Thunderstruck by this verdict, just as I was, I fell on the bed. I would have laid violent hands on myself like an executioner, if I hadn't begrudged my rival that victory.

Ascyltus left proudly with his prize and abandoned his com-
rade-in-arms, his dearest friend a little while ago, his companion
even in misfortune; he abandoned him in all his misery in a
place full of strangers.

Friendship's a word and friends know its value –
The counters slide merrily all through the game –
Your friends broadly smiling, while fortune was by you:
Their backs even broader when trouble came.

*

[The mime has begun
And the father is there,
And here is the son
And the millionaire.
Then closes the page,
When played is their part,
On the laughter upstage
And the masks of their art –
Then their true faces appear.][2]

81. I soon dried my tears but being afraid that, in addition to
all my other troubles, Menelaus the assistant lecturer might find
me alone in my lodgings, I collected my bags and sadly rented a
quiet place along the seafront. I holed up there for three days,
constantly aware of my loneliness and humiliation; I would beat
my breast, already sore with sobbing, and again and again I'd
cry out loud through all the groans that racked me:
  'Why couldn't that earthquake have swallowed me up? Or
the sea, such a menace even to innocent people? Did I escape
the law, did I outwit the arena, did I kill my host, only to end
up, despite my claims to be a daring criminal, just lying here, a
beggar and an exile, abandoned in a lodging-house in a Greek
town? And who brought this loneliness upon me? An adoles-
cent wallowing in every possible filth, who even on his own
admission had been rightly run out of town, free – for sex, free-
born – for sex, whose youth you'd buy with a ticket, who had
been hired as a girl even by someone who thought he was a
male. As for the other one! Putting on women's clothes the day

he became a man, talked into effeminacy by his mother, doing
only woman's work in the slave pen, and after he couldn't meet
his debts and had to change his sexual ground, he abandoned
the claims of an old friendship and – in the name of decency! –
sold out everything like a whore on the strength of a one-night
stand. Now the loving pair lie clutching each other whole
nights on end and perhaps when they are worn out by their
love-play, they laugh at my loneliness. But they won't get away
with it. As sure as I'm a man and not a slave, I'll right my
wrongs with their guilty blood.'

82. With these words I fastened my sword to my side and,
not to let bodily weakness endanger my mission, I restored my
strength with a heavy meal. Then I rushed out into the street
and went round all the arcades like a madman. But while I was
thinking of nothing but blood and destruction, my face like
thunder and full of rage (I was dropping my hand continually
to my dedicated hilt), a soldier noticed me, a con man or a
thug.

'Hey there, friend,' he said, 'what's your regiment and who's
your company commander?'

Although I lied boldly about my commander and my regi-
ment, he said:

'Well, tell me something. Do the soldiers in your army walk
about in slippers?'

As my face and my very trembling betrayed the lie, he told
me to give up my weapons and keep out of trouble. I'd been
robbed and, worse, my revenge had been nipped in the bud. I
walked back towards my lodgings and gradually, as my bold-
ness decreased, I began to feel grateful for the thug's audacity.

*

Craving the water around, apples above his head,
    Poor Tantalus can neither drink nor eat.[3]
This is the rich man's image: in plenty dogged by dread
    To drink dry-mouthed, to choke and starve on meat.

*

One should not rely a great deal on one's plans as fate has a
way of her own.

*

EUMOLPUS IN THE ART
GALLERY

83. I went into an art gallery, which had a wonderful variety of paintings. For instance, I even saw work by Zeuxis still unaffected by the ravages of time. And I examined, not without a certain thrill, some sketches by Protogenes, so lifelike they were a challenge to nature herself. I practically worshipped that masterpiece of Apelles[1] that they call The Goddess on One Knee. The lines of the paintings were so subtle and clear-cut that you could see them as expressing the subjects' very souls. Here the eagle, way up high, was carrying off the Idaean youth[2] to heaven, there a dazzling white Hylas[3] repulsed the lascivious Naiad. Apollo cursed his murderous hands[4] and decorated his unstrung lyre with a new flower. Surrounded by the faces of these lovers, I burst out as though I were alone:

'So love affects gods, too. Jupiter didn't find anything to love in heaven, but at least when going to sin on earth he injured no one. The nymph that snatched Hylas away would have controlled her passion if she had thought Hercules would come to restrain her. Apollo called back the boy's soul into a flower – all of them enjoyed embraces free from rivalry. But I took to my heart a crueller friend than Lycurgus.'[5]

All of a sudden, however, as I was arguing with the wind, a white-haired old man entered the gallery. His face was lined and seemed to have in it a promise of something impressive. But his clothes were shabby and this made it clear that he belonged to the class of intellectuals so hated generally by the rich. He therefore came and stood by my side . . .

'I am a poet,' he said, 'and a poet of no mean ability, I like to think, at least if poetry prizes are to be trusted when favouritism confers them even on mediocrity. "Why," you ask, "are you so badly dressed then?" For this one reason – concern for the intellect never made anyone rich.

> 'The trader trusts the sea: his goods are sold;
> The soldier from campaigns wears belted gold;
> Cheap flatterers sprawl drunk in purple shirts;
> Seducers courting newly married flirts
> Are rich from playing their seductive parts.
> Only a poet is a tattered thing,
> Cold scarecrow, mute and endlessly sighing
> For the lonely, lost and now deserted arts.

84. 'No doubt about it. If a man sets his face against every temptation and starts off on the straight and narrow, he's immediately hated because of his different ways. No one can approve of conduct different from his own. And secondly, those who are interested in piling up money don't want anything else in life regarded as better than what they have themselves. So lovers of literature are sneered at by whatever means possible to show that they too are inferior to wealth.'

*

'I suspect somehow that poverty is the twin sister of talent.'

*

'I'd like to think that the man who hounds me in my hard life were honest enough to be conciliated. As it is, he's hardened in crime and cleverer than the very pimps.'

*

85. [*Eumolpus*] 'When I was taken out to Asia on the paid staff of a treasury official, I accepted some hospitality in Pergamum.[6] I was very pleased to accept this invitation not only because of the elegance of the quarters but also because my host had a very good-looking son, and I thought up a way to prevent his father becoming suspicious of me. Whenever any mention was made at the table of taking advantage of pretty boys, I flared up so violently and I was so stern about my ears being offended by obscene talk that the mother especially regarded me as a real old-world philosopher. From then on I escorted the young lad

to the gymnasium, I organized his studies, I taught him and gave him good advice. After all, we didn't want any greedy seducer admitted to the house.

*

'One holiday, when the celebrations had given him time to play, we were lounging in the dining-room, since the long day's enjoyment had made us too lazy to go to bed. About midnight, I realized the boy was awake. So in a very nervous whisper I breathed a prayer.

'"Dear Venus," I said, "if I can kiss this boy without his knowing it, I'll give him a pair of doves tomorrow."

'Hearing the price of my pleasure, the boy started snoring, and I therefore went to work on the faker and kissed him several times. Content with this beginning, I rose early next morning and brought him the choice pair of doves he was expecting and fulfilled my vow.

86. 'Next night, given the same opportunity, I altered my prayer.

'"If I can run my hands all over him," I said, "without his feeling anything, I'll give him two really savage fighting cocks for his patience."

'At this offer the boy moved over to me of his own accord. I think he was getting afraid I might fall asleep. Naturally I dispelled his worries and his whole body became a whirlpool in which I lost myself, although I stopped short of the ultimate pleasure. Then when day came, I brought the delighted boy what I'd promised.

'The third night gave me similar licence, and I got up, and close to his ear, as he tossed restlessly, I said:

'"O eternal gods, if I can get the full satisfaction of my desires from him in his sleep, for this happiness tomorrow I shall give the boy the finest Macedonian thoroughbred – but with this proviso, only if he feels nothing."

'The lad had never slept so soundly before. First I filled my hands with his milk-white breasts, then I clung to his lips, and finally I reduced all my longings to one climax.

'In the morning he sat in his room and waited for me to follow my usual practice. Of course, you know how much easier it is to buy doves and cocks than a thoroughbred, and besides, I was nervous in case such an extravagant gift should make my kindness suspect. So after walking round for a few hours, I returned to my host's house and gave the boy nothing more than a kiss. He looked round, as he threw his arms about my neck, and said:

' "Please, sir, where's my thoroughbred?"

*

87. 'This offence had lost me the headway I had made, nevertheless I returned to my old freedom. A few days later when a similar chance left us in the same position, hearing the father snoring, I began asking the boy to become friends with me again, and I said all the other things that a strong physical urge dictates. But clearly annoyed, he only said:

' "Just go to sleep or I'll tell father."

'Nothing is too hard to get if you're prepared to be wicked. Even while he was saying, "I'll wake father," I slipped into the bed and without much of a fight from him I took my pleasure by force. Actually he was not displeased that I'd been so naughty, and after complaining for a long time that he'd been tricked and that he'd been laughed at and talked about among his schoolfriends because he had boasted to them of my wealth, he said finally:

' "But you'll see I'm not like you. Do it again, if you wish."

'Well, I was back in the boy's favour with all his hard feelings gone, and after taking advantage of his kindness, I fell asleep. The boy, however, being fully mature and of an age very much able to take it, was not content with the repeat performance. He woke me up from my sleep saying:

' "Don't you want anything?"

'Of course it wasn't a tiresome job yet, so somehow, ground between the panting and sweating, he got what he wanted and I fell back asleep, exhausted with passion. Less than an hour later he began poking me with his hand and saying,

' "Why aren't we getting on with it?"

'Being woken up so often, I really flared up. I gave him his own back:

' "Just you go to sleep or I'll tell your father." '

*

88. Cheered by this conversation, I began to ask my mentor . . .
about the age of the pictures and the subject of some of the
obscure ones, at the same time pressing him for reasons for the
present decadence, when the loveliest of the arts were dying
out, not least painting, which had vanished without the slight-
est trace. His reply was:

'Financial greed has caused this change. In former days
when sheer merit was still sufficient, the liberal arts flourished
and there was great competition to bring to light anything of
benefit to posterity. Democritus, for instance, distilled all forms
of vegetable life and spent his days in scientific experiments to
discover the properties of minerals and plants. Eudoxus grew
old on the top of one of the highest mountains to further his
knowledge of astronomy, and Chrysippus[7] purged his brain
three times with hellebore to allow himself to continue his
investigations.

'To turn to the plastic arts, Lysippus was so preoccupied
with the lines of one statue that he died of poverty, and Myron,[8]
who almost captured the souls of men and animals in his
bronzes, left no heir. But we, besotted with drink and whoring,
daren't study even arts with a tradition. Attacking the past
instead, we acquire and pass on only vices. What has happened
to dialectic? Astronomy? Or the road most cultivated to wis-
dom? Who has ever gone into a temple and prayed to become
eloquent – or to approach the fountainhead of philosophy?
People do not even ask for a sound mind or body, but before
they touch the threshold one man immediately promises an
offering if he can arrange the funeral of a rich relation, another
if he can dig up some treasure, another if he can come into a
safe thirty million. Even the senate, the standard of rectitude
and goodness, habitually promises the Capitol a thousand
pounds of gold, and to remove anyone's doubts about financial
greed, tries to influence even Jove with money.

'So don't be surprised that painting is on the decline, when a
lump of gold seems more beautiful to everybody, gods and
men, than anything those crazy little Greeks, Apelles and Phi-
dias,[9] ever made.

89. 'But I notice you can't pull yourself away from that

painting of the Fall of Troy.[10] Well, I'll try and interpret its sub-
ject in verse:

> 'The tenth harvest, tenth year of the Troy-siege,
> The Phrygians forlorn, doubt-fraught and frightened,
> Calchas the soothsayer downcast,
> A dark daunting upon him.
> The Delian doled out his destinies
> And tall trees toppled on Ida,[11]
> Their boles borne from the mountain;
> Trunks trimmed, massed for its making,
> For hewing the horse, shaping the fell shape.
>
> A cave is uncovered, a cavern to capture the foe-camp.   10
> Into it, taut from the ten-year taking,
> Their valour is hidden, deep in the gods' vail;
> Doughty Danaans dwell in the depths of it.
>   The thousand-fold fleet we felt was in full flight,
>   Your fields, O my fatherland, freed from the fighting.
> Words so declared on horse side,
> Sinon,[12] steady in death's sight, said it,
> And our hearts ever steady for our destruction.
>
> Uncaged, careless of combat, the crowd came,
> Praising and prayerful. Cheeks washed with weeping,   20
> Joy in the faint heart, tears yet trickling –
> Terror retracts them.
>   Priest of the sea god,
> Loud Laocoön,[13] locks lank, hails the assemblage,
> His flung spear wounding the wide womb:
> Fate slows his sinews; blade-point rebounding
> Makes us trust; more truth in the treachery.
> Yet again Laocoön, hardening his halt hands,
> Aims at the sheer side his double axe-stroke.
> Hear cry of captives, lo, at their murmuring   30
> The oak-bulk breathes of foreigners' faintness –
> The captured captains move to Troy's capture,
> With fresh frauds reviving the fighting.

Other prodigies press us and portents.
Where tall Tenedos[14] breaks back the billows,
Swollen the straits surge up with sea-surf,
And the waters, broken, wince back, breaking the sea-calm.
As in the nightwatch oars sound from far-off,
Of fleets faring through sea foam, sea face
40   Groaning of grazes from fir-keels coursing.
Back stare we.
Waves speed snakes, sinuously doubling, rockwards;
As tall ships, their breasts scatter spindrift;
Tails tolling thunder, head fringes, foam-freed,
Shine as their eyes shine. Thundery skin-sheen
Shines on the water, as waves hiss and tremble.
Men stand mindless. Laocoön's loved ones,
In sacred ribbons and Phrygian tiring, his twin sons,
Are suddenly twined in the twinkling snake-coils.

50   They lock little fingers into the snake-jaws,
Each for the other, neither from self-love –
Brother for brother, their love is requited,
Death a deliverance from mutual mourning.
Added then unto their doom is the old one,
Hopeless as helper.
The serpents, sated from slaying,
Beset him, bear to the earth his body,
He lies mid the altars, priest now a victim,
Making the ground groan.
60   What is sacred is soiled, Troy, doomed to destruction,
Destroys first its godhead.

Full moon aloft had lifted its white glow,
Leading the lesser lights with radiant torchbrand:
The sons of Priam were sleeping and wine-soaked –
"Undo the bolts, ye Danaans, bring out your brave ones!"
Chieftains acquitting themselves in combat,
As in Thessalian hills a horse out of halter
Shakes its neck and its mane, for the onrush.
Swords now unsheathed, brandishing bucklers,

They fly to the fray, dealing death to the drunken,   70
Sent in their sleep to the death-sleep;
Here brands are brought from the altars
To turn against Troy town the worship of Trojans.'

90. Some of the people walking about in the colonnades interrupted Eumolpus' recitation with a shower of stones. Being familiar with this sort of appreciation of his genius, he covered his head and fled from the sanctuary. I was nervous myself in case they should call me a poet too. So I followed his fleeing figure and arrived at the seafront. As soon as we were out of range and could stop, I said:

'Listen, what's wrong with you? You've been with me for less than two hours and you've spoken more often like a poet than a human being. I'm not surprised people chase you with stones. I'm going to fill my pockets with rocks and whenever you start taking wings, I'll let some blood from your head.'

His face changed and he said:

'My lad, today is not the first time I've tested the air like that. In fact I've never gone into a theatre to give a recitation without getting this sort of unexpected reception from the spectators. But I don't want to quarrel with you as well, so I'll keep off the stuff for the whole day.'

'Right,' I said, 'if you swear off this madness for today, we'll dine together.'

*

I gave the landlord of my little place the task of preparing a simple meal.

*

91. I saw Giton leaning against the wall with towels and scrapers, and looking depressed and confused. You could tell he didn't like his menial position. To confirm my observation . . . He turned towards me, his face softening with pleasure:

'Don't be hard on me, my dear. Where there are no weapons around, I speak freely. Take me away from this bloody criminal and punish me as savagely as you like for what I've been regretting. I feel so bad about everything, it will be a sufficient consolation to die because you wanted me to.'

I told him to stop complaining in case someone should guess
our plans, and abandoning Eumolpus, who was reciting a poem
in the main bath, I dragged Giton through a dark and sordid
exit and flew hastily to my lodgings. Then, with the doors
barred, I rushed to take him in my arms and press my cheeks to
his tearful face. For a long time neither of us recovered his
voice. The boy's lovely breast heaved with a succession of sighs.

'Oh, this shouldn't happen,' I said, 'for me to love you,
though I was deserted, and for there to be no scar on my heart
from that great wound. What have you to say after giving
yourself to another lover? Did I deserve this treatment?'

When he realized he was still loved, he raised his eye-
brows . . .

'I left the decision about our love to no other judge but you.
But I won't complain of anything any more, I won't remember
anything any more, if you prove your regrets by behaving hon-
ourably.'

As I poured all this out with sobs and tears, he wiped my
face with a cloak and said:

'Encolpius, please, I appeal to your memory to be honest.
Did I desert you or did you betray me? I admit this and I'm not
ashamed of it – when I saw two armed men, I went to the
stronger.'

I kissed that wise little breast and threw my arms round his
neck, and to let him fully realize that I was reconciled and I was
renewing our friendship as sincerely as ever, I hugged him to
my heart.

92. It was well into the night and the woman had taken care
of our orders for dinner, when Eumolpus hammered on the
door.

'How many of you are there?' I asked, and meanwhile began
peeping carefully through a chink in the door to see if Ascyltus
had come with him. Then seeing my guest by himself, I let him
in immediately. As he threw himself on the bed and saw Giton
in full view fixing the table, he nodded his head, saying:

'There's a pretty Ganymede. It should be a nice day.'

Such a studied opening did not make me happy and I was

afraid I had joined up with someone just like Ascyltus. Eumolpus pressed on, and when the boy gave him a drink, he said:

'I prefer you to the whole bathful of them,' and after greedily emptying the glass, he said he had never had such a disagreeable time and he explained:

'You know, I was almost beaten up even while I was taking my bath, just because I tried to recite a poem to the people sitting round my tub. After I'd been thrown out of the bath, I began going round every nook and cranny and calling out "Encolpius" in a loud voice. And somewhere else a naked young man, who had lost his clothes, was demanding someone called Giton with equally indignant shouts. And while the boys just ridiculed me for a lunatic with the most impudent imitations, a huge crowd surrounded him with applause and the most awestruck admiration. You see, he had such enormous sexual organs that you'd think the man was just an attachment to his penis. What a man for the job! I think he starts yesterday and finishes tomorrow. So he found help in no time. Someone or other, a Roman knight and notorious for his tastes, the loungers said, covered him with his own clothes as he went wandering round and took him off home – to enjoy such a piece of luck on his own, I suppose. Whereas I wouldn't have got even my own clothes back from the sneaky attendant there if I hadn't produced someone who knew me. A polished wick is much more profitable than a polished wit.'

While Eumolpus was telling us this, my expression kept changing all the time, now through amusement at my rival's misfortunes, now through annoyance at his successes. But all the same, I said nothing and passed the food, pretending the story had no personal interest for me.

*

RECONCILIATION
WITH GITON

93. 'What's legitimate[1] we hold cheap; our wayward hearts
love our offences.

> 'Pheasants snared in Colchis, in Africa game-birds,
> These are the rarities that have to be chased;
> White goose and duckling,
> Gaudy in their gay plumes,
> Are left to the populace, not to our taste.

> Parrot-wrasse from far shores, haul from Syrtes,
> Bought at the price of some great shipwreck,
> These are for the table –
> Mullet's indigestible –
> Don't ask the cost: you can pay by cheque.

> Wives are out of fashion. Better get a girl-friend –
> A little more expensive but really very nice.
> Rose leaves are out of date,
> Cinnamon's the thing now.
> Anything hard to get is well worth the price.'

'Is this how you keep your promise,' I said, 'not to produce
any verse today? As a favour, at least let *us* off – we never threw
stones at you. Because if anyone drinking in the same house
we're in smells the suggestion of a poet, he'll rouse the whole
neighbourhood and finish us all off for the same reason. Have
some thought for us and remember the art gallery or the public
baths.'

Giton, being a very gentle boy, remonstrated with me for this way of speaking, and said it wasn't right for me to abuse someone older than myself, while forgetting my obligations and letting my insults spoil the meal I had provided in all kindness. And there was a lot of other moderate and courteous things he said, which came very well from his pretty lips.

*

94. [*Eumolpus to Giton*] 'What a lucky mother,' said he, 'to have such a child! Bravo! Your good looks and your good sense make a rare mixture. Don't think you've wasted all that breath: you've found someone who loves you. I'll fill poems with your praises. I'll follow you as your teacher and guardian, even when you don't ask me to. And Encolpius is not losing, he's in love with someone else.'

That soldier who took away my sword was a piece of luck for Eumolpus too. Otherwise I would have cooled the spleen I'd felt against Ascyltus in Eumolpus' blood. Giton was not unaware of this. He went out of the room on the pretext of getting some water and by his prudent withdrawal damped my anger. Then a few moments later, as my fury rekindled, I said:

'Eumolpus, I prefer you even speaking in verse to the sort of thoughts you are having. Now I'm a hot-tempered man and you are a lecherous one. You can see how these temperaments don't go together. So you have to regard me as a madman and give in to my insanity – now get out quick!'

Confused by this outburst, Eumolpus did not ask the reason for my anger, but going straight out over the threshold, suddenly slammed the door of the room, and, as I was expecting nothing of the sort, shut me in; he swiftly removed the key and ran off to look for Giton.

Shut up inside like that, I decided to finish everything by hanging myself. I had already put the bed frame against the wall, tied a belt to it, and was inserting my neck in the noose when the door was unlocked and Eumolpus came in with Giton and in a race against death brought me back to life. In his grief Giton, unlike Eumolpus, went mad with rage; he raised a great outcry and pushing me with both hands precipitated me on top of the bed.

'You're wrong, Encolpius,' he said, 'if you think by any possible chance you can die before me. I tried first: I looked for a sword in Ascyltus' rooms. If I had not found you, I was going to throw myself to my death. To make you realize death isn't far away if you look for it, see in your turn what you wanted me to see.'

With this he snatched a razor from Eumolpus' hired servant and slashing his throat once and then twice, collapsed at our feet.

Thunderstruck, I let out a cry and following his collapsing body to the floor, I looked for a way to die with the same instrument. But Giton showed not the slightest suspicion of a wound nor could I feel any pain myself. It was a practice razor and blunted for the purpose: to give apprentices the courage a barber needs, it had a sheath fitted round it. This was the reason why the servant had not panicked at his snatching the razor and why Eumolpus had not intervened in this fake death scene.

95. While this love drama was being played out, the landlord came in with the rest of our little dinner and at the sight of the disgraceful sprawling heap on the floor, he shouted:

'Hey, are you people drunk or runaway slaves? Or both? Who turned that bed up? What's the meaning of all this criminal behaviour? But of course – you were going to do a moonlight flit to avoid paying your room rent. But you're not getting away with it. Because I'll have you know the place doesn't belong to some widow but to Marcus Mannicius.'

Eumolpus yelled back: 'Are you threatening us?' and at the same time he hit the man hard in the face with the flat of his hand. Reckless from so much drinking with the guests, the fellow hurled an earthenware pot at Eumolpus' head, split his forehead in midshout, and flung himself out of the room. Eumolpus was not standing for this insult; he snatched up a wooden candlestick, followed him as he made off and avenged his pride with a tremendous shower of blows. The whole household came rallying round, as well as a crowd of drunken guests. I, however, took this opportunity for my revenge by shutting Eumolpus out. Having put paid to the bastard, I was of course without a rival and I went on to put the room and the evening to their full use.

Meanwhile the kitchen staff and the people who lived in the building were beating up Eumolpus now that he couldn't get inside – one was aiming for his eyes with a spit covered with sizzling tripes, while another went through his battle-drill with a butcher's hook. One old woman in particular, a bleary old hag, dressed in the filthiest clothes and wearing odd wooden clogs, came dragging along an enormous dog on a chain and set him on Eumolpus. But he defended himself from all these threats with his candlestick.

96. We were watching everything through a hole left in the door when the handle had been pulled off a little while ago, and I was cheering every blow that reached Eumolpus. Giton, however, with his usual compassion pressed me to open the door and rescue him. As my resentment was still with me, I didn't restrain myself but smashed him on the head with a sharp bended knuckle for his pains. He sat down on the bed in tears while I applied each eye alternately to the hole and feasted my eyes on the sight of Eumolpus in trouble – this was rich food indeed! I was recommending him to a good lawyer when the manager of the lodging house, Bargates by name, who had been disturbed at his dinner, was carried into the centre of the brawl by two porters – he had bad feet, it seems. After coming out with a long and furious diatribe in a foreign accent about drunken sots and runaway slaves, he then looked at Eumolpus and said:

'It was you, was it, you wonderful poet? Now why don't these no-good slaves get off quick and stop fighting? . . .'

'The woman I'm living with is acting high and mighty with me. So be a friend and write some nasty verses about her so she'll know her place.'

*

97. While Eumolpus was talking privately to Bargates, a town crier entered the hotel accompanied by a policeman and quite a number of other people. Waving a torch that gave out more smoke than light, he made the following announcement:

'LOST, A SHORT WHILE AGO IN THE BATHS, A BOY AGED ABOUT SIXTEEN. HE IS CURLY-HAIRED, SOFT-SKINNED, GOOD-LOOKING, AND GOES BY

THE NAME OF GITON. THERE IS A REWARD OF ONE THOUSAND SESTERCES FOR ANYONE WHO WILL BRING HIM BACK OR GIVE ANY INFOR-MATION OF HIS WHEREABOUTS.'

Not far from the announcer stood Ascyltus, wearing a multi-coloured shirt and displaying the description and the reward on a silver plate.

I ordered Giton to get immediately under the bed and tie his hands and feet to the webbing that held the mattress on the frame – the way Ulysses had once clung to the ram[2] – and so stay out of the hands of the searchers.

Giton was not slow to obey and in a moment he inserted his hands in the fastenings and beat Ulysses at his own tricks. To avoid leaving any room for suspicion, I filled the bed with clothes and made up the traces of a man about my size.

Meanwhile Ascyltus, after going round all the occupied rooms, came to mine and became more hopeful because he found the doors more carefully bolted. The policeman, how-ever, inserting an axe where the doors joined, loosened the bolts from their hold.

I fell at Ascyltus' knees and, appealing to the memory of our friendship and our companionship in misfortune, I begged him at least to let me see my little friend. In fact, to lend some sin-cerity to my hypocritical appeals, I said:

'I know you've come to kill me, Ascyltus. Why else have you brought an axe? Well, vent your rage on me. Look, I'm show-ing you my neck, spill the blood you really came for under the pretence of a search.'

Ascyltus rejected the injustice of the charge and assured me he was only looking for the runaway who belonged to him and didn't want to kill a helpless man, least of all a man he regarded as a very dear friend even after that fateful quarrel.

98. The policeman on the other hand did not take things so easily. Snatching a rod from the innkeeper he pushed it under the bed and even tried all the cracks in the wall. Giton pulled himself away from the poking, and holding his breath in a great panic, pressed his mouth to the very bedbugs . . .

But as the broken door could keep no one out of the room, Eumolpus burst in excitedly:

'I've got the thousand sesterces,' he said. 'I'm going after the advertiser now – he's only just leaving. I'm fully justified in betraying you; I'll explain that Giton is in your possession.'

He was determined about this even as I clasped his knees and begged him not to kill two dying men.

'You would be quite right to be flaming mad,' I added, 'if you could bring forward your prisoner. The boy just got away among the crowd and I haven't a suspicion where he's going to. For pity's sake, Eumolpus, bring the lad back – even hand him over to Ascyltus.'

While I was persuading him till he almost believed this, Giton, through holding his breath to bursting point, sneezed three times in rapid succession, so hard that the bed shook. At the noise Eumolpus said: 'God bless you, Giton!'

When the mattress was pulled back too, he saw our Ulysses, and even a hungry Cyclops would have had pity on him. Turning to me, he said:

'What's this, you thief? You didn't have the courage to tell me the truth even when you were caught. Why, if the god in charge of human destinies hadn't forced a sign from the lad as he hung there, I'd have been wandering round the bar-rooms like a fool.'

*

Giton, far more conciliatory than I, first of all bound up the cut on his forehead with cobwebs soaked in oil; then he replaced his tattered clothes with his own little cloak, and embracing the now mollified poet and pressing kisses on him like poultices, said to him:

'My dear, dear father, we are all completely in your hands. If you love your little Giton, now is the time to save him. I wish some terrible fire would burn me up, just me, or some freezing sea would cover me. I'm the object of all these crimes, I'm the cause. If I were to die, it would reconcile the people at each other's throats.'

*

99. [*Eumolpus*] 'Always and everywhere I have lived as though each day were my last and would never return.'

*

With tears flowing from my eyes, I begged him to become my friend again too: the madness of jealousy was not in a lover's control. Nevertheless I would take great care never to say or do anything again that could offend him. Only let him, as befitted a poet and scholar, smooth away without a scar all the rancour festering in his heart.

'The snows cling longer in rough and uncultivated regions, but where the ground has come under the plough, the light frost vanishes from its bright expanse even while you are speaking. It's the same way with anger in human breasts: it chokes an untutored heart, but slips away from a cultivated mind.'

'What you say is true,' said Eumolpus, 'and to prove it, look, I'll even kiss you and put an end to our quarrel. Well now, I hope everything will be all right. Get your things together and follow me, or if you prefer, you lead the way.'

He was still talking when the door was pushed and creaked open, and a rough-bearded sailor stood in the doorway.

'You're late, Eumolpus,' he said. 'You'd think you didn't know we have to hurry.'

We all got up without delay, and Eumolpus ordered his servant, who had been asleep for some time, to start moving with his baggage. Giton and I got together what we had for the journey; I sent up a prayer to the stars and passed aboard.

*

100. 'It's annoying that our new acquaintance likes the boy. But aren't the best things in life free to all? The sun shines on everyone. The moon, accompanied by countless stars, leads even the beasts to pasture. What can you think of lovelier than water? But it flows for the whole world. Is love alone then to be something furtive rather than something to be gloried in? Exactly, that's just it – I don't want any of the good things of life unless people are envious of them. One man, and old at that, will be no trouble: even if he wished to try something, he'll give himself away through panting.'

I put forward these considerations with something less than

confidence and managed to overcome my inward disagreement. Then, with my head buried in my tunic, I began pretending to sleep.

But suddenly as though fortune were determined to take all the heart out of me, a voice on deck could be heard complaining:

'So he made a fool of me, did he?'

It was a male voice that sounded to my ears like an old friend and sent me into palpitations. Then a woman, apparently cut to the quick and equally indignant, blazed out with even greater vehemence:

'If only some god would put Giton into my hands, what a welcome I'd have for the wanderer!'

Both of us were so shaken by these unexpected sounds that the blood drained from our faces. Myself in particular, as though caught up in some distressing nightmare, found my voice only after a long interval and with trembling hands I pulled at Eumolpus' cloak, just as he was falling off to sleep.

'For heaven's sake, sir, can you tell us whose ship this is and who are aboard?'

He was annoyed at being awakened.

'Was this the reason why you wanted us to occupy the most secluded place on the ship, so that you could stop us sleeping? Anyway, suppose I told you that Lichas of Tarentum was the owner of this boat and that he was taking Tryphaena to Tarentum into exile, what does it matter?'

ABOARD SHIP WITH LICHAS
AND TRYPHAENA

101. Thunderstruck[1] by this, I broke out trembling and, baring my throat, I said:

'Fate has utterly defeated me at last.'

Giton indeed fainted across my chest and went on lying there. When the sweat broke out and revived us, I gripped Eumolpus by the knees.

'Show some pity for us,' I said, 'we're as good as dead. In the name of our common education, lend us a helping hand. Our last hour has come and unless you prevent it, it can only be a blessing.'

Overwhelmed by this wrongful accusation, Eumolpus swore by all the gods and goddesses that he neither knew what had happened nor had he planned any deliberate treachery – with the most straightforward of intentions and in all good faith he had brought his friends to the boat he'd long before planned to take.

'Anyway,' he said, 'what is the trap here? Who is the Hannibal[2] sailing with us? It's just Lichas of Tarentum, a very respectable man, who is not only the owner of this boat which he's in command of, but also of a number of farms and a trading company. He's carrying a commercial cargo to market. This is your Cyclops and pirate-captain, and we owe our passage to him. And as well as this man, there's Tryphaena, the loveliest woman in the world, who travels from place to place in the service of pleasure.'

'These are the people we're running away from,' said Giton and went on to explain briefly to the frightened Eumolpus the reasons for their hatred and the seriousness of the danger.

Confused and not knowing what to do, Eumolpus suggested we each put forward our ideas:

'You have to imagine we've got into the Cyclops' cave. Some way of escape has to be found, short of involving ourselves in a shipwreck and extricating ourselves from every possible risk.'

'No,' said Giton, 'better get the pilot to take the ship back into some port – not for nothing, obviously – and tell him your brother is not a good sailor and is in the final stages. You can cover up the deception by looking worried and shedding some tears, so the pilot will be touched and do what you want.'

Eumolpus argued that this wasn't possible. 'You see,' he said, 'large ships make their way into well-curved harbours, and it is not likely that my brother could have fallen ill so quickly. And another thing, perhaps Lichas will want to look at the sufferer out of a feeling of duty. You can see how very useful that would be to us, deliberately summoning the captain to the very ones running away from him. But suppose the ship could be diverted from its long voyage and suppose Lichas did not go round the sick-beds no matter what, how could we leave the ship without being seen by everyone? With heads covered or bare? Covered? Then everyone would want to give a hand to the invalids. Bare? Then that would be simply advertising ourselves.'

102. I interposed: 'Why don't we rely on really bold measures, slip down a rope, get into the ship's boat, cut the painter and leave the rest to fortune? Not that I'm calling on Eumolpus to share this risk. I'm happy if luck's on our side as we go down.'

'Not a bad plan,' said Eumolpus, 'if it would work. But everyone will notice you leave, especially the pilot, who stays on watch all night and also observes the movement of the stars. Now you might trick him somehow, even with his eyes open, if you were taking your leave by another part of the ship. As it is, you have to slide down by the stern, by the very steering gear where the painter hangs down. Besides, I'm surprised, Encolpius, that it hasn't occurred to you that one sailor stays in the boat on continuous day and night watch and you couldn't get rid of him without killing him or throwing him overboard by

brute force. For this you must ask yourselves how brave you
are. As for my coming with you, I shirk no danger that offers
any hope of safety. I presume that not even you would want to
risk your lives for nothing as though they were trifles. See
whether you like this idea: I'll drop you into two leather bags,
tie them up with straps and put you among my clothes, leaving
the tops a little way open of course, so you can get air and
food. Then I'll raise the alarm that my two slaves have thrown
themselves in the sea during the night through fear of worse
punishment. Then on arrival in port, I'll carry you off like lug-
gage without any suspicion.'

'Oh, really,' I said, 'you'd tie us up as though we were solid
right through and our bellies didn't give us any trouble, or as
though we didn't even sneeze or snore? Or just because this
type of trick did work nicely once?[3] But suppose we could
stand being tied up for one day. What happens if either a calm
or bad weather holds us up longer? What would we do? Clothes
tied up too long get ruined by creases and papers tied together
lose their shape. We're young and not used to hard work; will
we stand up to being tied and covered like statues?

'Some safe way still has to be found. You look at my idea.
Eumolpus as a literary man surely has some ink. So let's use
this as a dye and change our colour – hair right down to finger-
nails. Disguised as Ethiopian slaves, we can wait on you quite
happily without any chance of being tortured and at the same
time we can trick our enemies by our change of colour.'

Giton added: 'Why not circumcise us too, so we look like
Jews, and bore holes in our ears to imitate Arabs, and whiten
our faces so Gauls would take us as fellow-countrymen. As
though this colouring by itself could change our shapes. A lot
of details have to be consistent to keep up the deception! Sup-
pose a face could stay stained for some time. Suppose no drops
of water produce spots on our skins and our clothes don't cling
to the ink. Well then, can we also puff out our lips into that
hideous swollen look? Can we change our hair with a curling-
iron? Can we cut our foreheads with scars? Can we open our
legs till they're bandy? Can we touch the ground with our
ankles? Can we produce foreign-looking beards? Artificial dye

stains your body, it doesn't change it. Listen to my coward's way out – let's tie our heads in our clothes and throw ourselves to the bottom.'

103. 'Gods and men forbid,' Eumolpus exclaimed, 'that you should end your lives in so ugly a fashion. Better do what I tell you. My hired man, as you know from the razor, is a barber. Let him shave the hair off both of you right away, not just your heads but your eyebrows too. I'll follow up by marking your foreheads with an artistic inscription, so you'll appear to have been punished with branding. The letters will simultaneously lull the suspicions of the people looking for you and hide your faces under cover of the punishment marks.'

No time was lost working the trick. We went stealthily to the side of the ship and presented our heads and eyebrows to the barber to be shaved. Eumolpus covered both our foreheads with the huge letters and with a liberal hand extended the notorious inscription for runaway slaves over the whole of our faces.

As it happened, one of the passengers, who was leaning against the side of the ship and emptying his sick stomach, noticed in the moonlight the barber bent over his unseasonable office. Swearing at the bad omen which was reminiscent of a last offering in a shipwreck, he flung himself back to his berth. Pretending to ignore the seasick man and his curse, we returned to our melancholy procedures and, wrapped in silence, spent the remaining hours of the night sleeping fitfully.

*

104. [*Lichas*] 'I dreamt Priapus said to me: "Since you are looking for him, I want you to know that Encolpius has been brought aboard your boat through my agency."'

Tryphaena shuddered and said:

'You would think we'd slept in the one bed. I dreamt that the statue of Neptune that I'd noticed in the great temple at Baiae said: – "You will find Giton on Lichas' ship."'

'You should realize from this,' said Eumolpus, 'how godlike a man Epicurus[4] was. He condemned this sort of nonsense in a very humorous way.' . . .

But Lichas, to play safe with Tryphaena's dream, said: 'Who's going to stop us searching the boat? That way we'll avoid any appearance of condemning the workings of the divine mind.'. . . The man who had noticed our furtive and worried behaviour in the dark (Hesus was his name) suddenly shouted:

'Then those are the ones who were having a shave in the dark – and that's a terrible thing to do, by god! I'm told no mortal soul should cut his nails or hair on a ship unless the wind and the sea are at odds.'

105. Lichas, shocked by this report, started blazing:

'Is it true that someone cut his hair on the ship, and in the dead of night at that? Bring the culprits out here immediately, so I'll know whose heads should roll to purify the ship.'

'I gave the orders,' said Eumolpus. 'And as I was going to be on the same ship I didn't intend any bad omen for myself, but since they had long shaggy hair, in case I appeared to be making a prison out of the ship, I gave orders for the condemned men to be cleaned up. Another reason was to allow the marks of the letters to be entirely visible to the eyes of readers and not hidden by their covering of hair. Among other things they spent my money on a whore the two of them kept, and I dragged them from her last night soaked in wine and scent. In fact they still smell of what was left of my inheritance.' . . .

So to appease the guardian spirit of the ship, it was decided to give each of us forty lashes. So there was no delay. The furious sailors laid into us with ropes and tried to placate the ship's guardian with our worthless blood. I personally absorbed three lashes with Spartan disdain.[5] But Giton after one blow cried out so loudly that Tryphaena's ears could hear nothing but that well-known voice. And it was not merely the mistress who was thrown into confusion; her maids too, pulled by the familiar tones, rushed to the victim. Giton with his marvellous body had already made the sailors drop their whips and his silent appeal had even begun working on their savage hearts before the maids cried out in chorus:

'It's Giton, Giton! Keep your cruel hands off him. It's Giton, lady. Help him!'

Tryphaena lent an already believing ear to their cries and

flew quickly to the boy's side. Lichas, who knew me best, as though he too had vocal testimony, ran to me and without considering my hands or face, but immediately stretching out an investigating hand to my private parts, he said:

'How are you, Encolpius?'

Will anyone now be surprised that Ulysses' nurse after twenty years[6] found a scar sufficient identification when this shrewd man so cleverly went straight to the one thing that identified the runaway, despite the total confusion of the lines we use for physical identification?

Tryphaena began to cry, taking the punishment for real – for she believed that the marks really had been branded on our foreheads – and in a rather subdued manner she began to ask what prison had got hold of us in our travels, and whose hands had been cruel enough to carry out this punishment, making it clear, however, that some of the maltreatment had been richly deserved by us for running away and for hating a situation where we were so well off . . .

106. Highly irritated, Lichas leapt forward:

'You simple-minded woman! As though burns from the iron had absorbed the letters. I wish they *had* branded themselves with the inscription. We would have had this consolation at the very least. As it is we have been the victims of a pure farce and made ridiculous by a mere outline.'

Tryphaena was prepared to be merciful, seeing she had not lost her pleasures forever, but Lichas, still remembering his wife's seduction and the affronts he had received in the colonnade of Hercules,[7] exclaimed with a violently contorted face:

'You've realized, I suppose, Tryphaena, that heaven takes some interest in human affairs. It brought the culprits unawares to our ship and warned us of what they'd done in a pair of corroborating dreams. So think, what possibility is there of pardoning men that the god himself has handed over for punishment? As for me, I'm not a cruel man, but I'm afraid I'd suffer whatever penalty I remitted.'

Swayed by so superstitious an argument, Tryphaena said she would not interfere with the punishment; on the contrary, she

was even in favour of such richly deserved reprisals. She had
suffered no less serious an injury than Lichas – her reputation
as a decent woman had been impugned at a public meeting.

*

107. [*Eumolpus*] 'They chose me for this task, I suppose,
because I'm well known and they asked me to reconcile them
to their own one-time dearest friends. Unless perhaps you think
the young men fell into this trap accidentally, even though the
first thing every traveller asks is into whose care he is commit-
ting himself. So let your hearts be softened now reparations
have been made and allow these free citizens to go where they
are bound without interference. Slave owners who are brutal
and unrelenting actually hinder the satisfaction of their sadistic
impulses if conscience is ever likely to bring runaways back.
And we don't kill enemies who are handed over to us. What
more are you after? What more do you want? Lying before
your eyes, begging for mercy, are two young men, respectable,
honest and what is more important than either of these things,
once bound in friendship to you. For god's sake, if they had run
off with your money or had betrayed your trust, yet you might
still be well satisfied by these punishment marks you see. Look,
you can trace the brand of slavery on their foreheads and their
respectable faces have voluntarily undergone a penalty that
puts them outside society.'

Lichas interrupted this plea for mercy and said:

'Don't confuse the issue, but deal with each item. And first
of all, if they came of their own accord, why did they cut all the
hair from their heads? Anyone who disguises his face is plan-
ning deception, not satisfaction. And another thing, if they
were trying to ingratiate themselves through an intermediary,
why did you do everything you could to keep your protégés out
of sight? It is obvious from this that the culprits fell into the
trap through sheer chance and you looked for a way to baffle
our revenge. As for the odium you are bringing on our heads by
shouting about their respectability and honesty, watch you
don't damage your case through over-confidence. What should
the injured parties do when the guilty come running to be pun-
ished? They were our friends, of course! Then they deserve all

the greater punishment. A man who attacks strangers is called a criminal, a man who attacks friends, a monster.'

Eumolpus refuted this unjust attack.

'I see,' he said, 'that the greatest objection to these poor young men is the fact that they cut off their hair during the night. According to this argument, they apparently came on the ship by accident, not deliberately. Now I'd like you to hear an account as frank as the matter was simple. Before they embarked, they wanted to rid their heads of a troublesome and superfluous burden, but the unexpectedly favourable wind caused them to delay carrying out their intention. However they didn't think it mattered when they began doing what they had wanted to do, because they didn't know about sailors' superstitions and the code of the sea.'

To this Lichas said:

'What use was it in their helpless position to shave their heads? Unless perhaps bald men tend to be more pitiful objects? In any case what use is it looking for the truth from an interpreter?

'What have you to say, you criminal? Did a salamander burn your eyebrows off?[8] What god did you dedicate your hair to? Speak up, you poisonous creature!'

108. I simply gaped, terrified by the thought of being punished, and I could find nothing to say, the case was so open and shut. I was such a confused and ugly object – for besides the disgrace of my shorn head, my eyebrows were as bare as my forehead – that didn't seem right for me to say or do anything. But once a dripping sponge had been wiped over my tearful face, and the wetted ink, streaming over it, reduced all my features to a dark cloud, anger turned to hatred . . .

Eumolpus however said he would not allow anyone to outrage respectable people contrary to all moral and legal principles, and he not only verbally but bodily interposed himself between us and their threatening temper.

His travelling servant was there to help him in his intervention as well as one or two very feeble passengers – giving moral support in the dispute rather than any physical aid. And I was not asking anything for myself, but holding my fists before

Tryphaena's eyes I said loudly in firm clear tones that I would resort to what force I had, if that criminal woman, the only one who deserved a thrashing on the whole ship, did not leave Giton alone. At my boldness Lichas blazed up into further anger: he was indignant with me for forgetting my own situation to shout so loudly for someone else. Tryphaena, blazing at the insult, was in just as much of a rage and she forced the whole ship's company to take sides. On our side Eumolpus' man armed himself and distributed his razors amongst us. On their side Tryphaena's entourage put up their bare fists and even the maids, yelling away, did not abandon the front line. There was only the navigator, who threatened to give up steering the ship if this madness brought on by the lust of the dregs of society did not stop. But the crazy struggle continued raging none the less, they fighting for revenge, we for our lives.

A good many went down on both sides without any fatalities. Even more retreated from the battlefield bleeding from their wounds. And yet no one's anger abated. Then Giton, like the hero he was, held his menacing razor over his genitals and threatened to cut off the cause of all our misery. Tryphaena averted this extreme action by an unambiguous pardon. Several times I myself put the barber's razor to my throat with no more intention of killing myself than Giton had of carrying out his threat. But he played his tragic role more boldly because he knew he had the razor he'd already cut his throat with.

Both lines stood there in position. So when it was obvious that it was going to be no ordinary battle, the navigator managed with difficulty to persuade Tryphaena to accept the role of ambassador and make a truce. The requisite promises were solemnly offered and accepted. Tryphaena then extended an olive branch plucked from the ship's figurehead and boldly began the negotiations.

> 'What madness,' she cries, 'makes peace become war?
> What guilt is on our hands? No hero from Troy
> Elopes on this ship, no Paris with the betrothed
> Of Menelaus tricked. No maddened Medea[9]
> Makes of her brother's blood a weapon.

Rejected love is the driving force.
Ah me! Who takes to arms and calls for death
Amid these waves?
    Is one death not enough?
Surpass not the sea – send no fresh floods
To swell the savage waves.'

109. As the woman poured all this out in shrill distressed tones, the lines hesitated a moment and our hands dropped peaceably – the fight was over. Eumolpus took command and made full use of this change of heart. Prefacing it with a violent attack on Lichas, he wrote out and signed a treaty, the formula of which was:

'You, Tryphaena, sincerely undertake not to complain of any past injury done to you by Giton or to bring up, avenge, or by any other method attempt to pursue any action committed before today. You undertake not to impose any service on the boy against his will, whether it be an embrace, kiss, or sexual intercourse, unless for each service you pay one hundred denarii in cash.

'Secondly: you, Lichas, sincerely undertake not to persecute Encolpius with insulting words or looks or make any inquiries as to where he sleeps at night. Otherwise you are to pay two hundred denarii in cash for each separate offence.'

Once the treaty was concluded on these terms, we put away our weapons and, to avoid any lingering resentment after the ceremony, we agreed to put the past behind us with an exchange of kisses. Amid the general encouragement our hatred simmered down and a picnic was brought out on the battlefield, which restored everyone's high spirits. The whole ship rang with the songs and as a sudden calm had interrupted the voyage, we had one man trying to harpoon the fish as they jumped out of the water and another trying to drag the struggling catch aboard with baited fishhooks. And surprise, sea-birds had even perched along the yard and a clever bird-catcher got at them with reeds woven together. They stuck to the limed twigs and were brought down into his hands. The air took hold of the floating plumes and the light spray whirled the feathers over the sea.

Lichas was beginning to be friendly to me again. Tryphaena was splashing Giton with the dregs of her drink, when Eumolpus, being well into his cups, got the idea of throwing out some quips about bald heads and brandmarks, until, exhausting his weak witticisms, he went back to his poetry and began reciting a little elegy on hair:

'Your hair has fallen out – your only good feature;
A cruel storm has stripped the foliage of spring.
Each temple misses its natural shade
And a bare expanse grins under worn stubble.
Oh, the gods, the gods cheat us!
Our Youth's first glories are Youth's first forfeits.

*

Poor boy,
One moment your hair
Was shining gold
And you were more beautiful
Than Phoebus or his sister.
Now you are shinier
Than a bronze
Or the round cap
Of a mushroom after rain.
You run nervously
From the laughter of ladies.
Death's sooner than you think,
You must believe –
See now, Death has begun at the top.'

110. He was ready to give us more of the same, I think, or worse, but Tryphaena's maid takes Giton down to the lower half of the ship and dresses the boy's head in one of her mistress's curly wigs. In fact, she even produces eyebrows from a box and, by cunningly following the outlines of the missing features, entirely restored his appearance.

Tryphaena recognized the real Giton and, moved to tears, gave the boy this time a really sincere kiss.

For myself, although I was delighted to see the boy restored to his pristine glory, I began covering my face more than ever. I realized how bizarre my deformity was – not even Lichas thought me worth talking to. But the same girl got me out of my depression by taking me to one side and fixing me up with an equally handsome head of hair. In fact, my face was brighter and more attractive, because mine was a yellow wig.

*

However, Eumolpus, our champion in time of trouble and the author of the present harmony, to prevent the general merriment lapsing into silence without a few stories, began a succession of gibes about feminine fickleness – how easily they fell in love, how quickly they forgot even their children. There was no woman so pure that she could not be driven crazy by some stranger's physical attractions. He wasn't thinking of old tragedies or famous historical names but of something that happened within his own living memory, and he would tell us about it if we wanted to hear it. So when everyone's eyes and ears were turned to him, he began the following story.

111. 'There was once a lady of Ephesus[10] so famous for her fidelity to her husband that she even attracted women from neighbouring countries to come just to see her. So when she buried her husband, she was not satisfied with following him to his grave with the usual uncombed hair or beating her breast in front of the crowd, but she even accompanied the dead man into the tomb, and when the corpse was placed in the underground vault, she began watching over it from then on, weeping day and night. Neither her parents nor her relations could induce her to stop torturing herself and seeking death by starvation. Finally the magistrates were repulsed and left her, and this extraordinary example to womankind, mourned by everyone, was now spending her fifth day without food. A devoted servant sat with the ailing woman, added her tears to the lady's grief, and refilled the lamp in the tomb whenever it began to go out. Naturally there was only one subject of conversation in the whole town: every class of people admitted there had never been such a shining example of true fidelity and love.

'In the meantime the governor of the province ordered the crucifixion of some thieves to be carried out near the humble abode where the wife was crying over the corpse of the lately deceased. Next night the soldier who was guarding the crosses to prevent anyone removing one of the bodies for burial noticed a light shining clearly among the tombs and, hearing the sounds of someone mourning, he was eager to know – a general human failing – who it was and what was going on. Naturally he went down into the vault and, seeing a beautiful woman, at first stood rooted to the spot as though terrified by some strange sight or a vision from hell. When he observed the dead man's body and noted the woman's tears and scratched face, surmising rightly that here was a woman who could not bear her intense longing for the dead man, he brought her his bit of supper and began pleading with the weeping woman not to prolong her hopeless grief and break her heart with useless lamentation. The same end, the same resting-place awaited everyone, he told her – along with all the other things that restore grief-stricken minds to sanity. But in spite of the stranger's consoling words, the woman only tore at her breast more violently and draped her mangled hair over the body of the dead man. The soldier still refused to withdraw; instead, using the same arguments, he tried to press food on her servant until the girl, seduced by the smell of the wine, first gave in herself, stretched out her hand to his tempting charity, and then, refreshed by the food and drink, began to lay siege to her mistress's resolution.

' "What good is it," she said to her, "for you to drop dead of starvation, or bury yourself alive or breathe your last innocent breath before fate demands it?

Believe you that ashes or the buried ghosts can know?[11]

Won't you come back to life? Won't you give up your womanly error and enjoy the comforts of life as long as you can? That very corpse lying there should be your encouragement to live."

'No one is ever reluctant to listen when pressed to eat or stay alive. Parched from taking nothing day after day, the woman allowed her resolution to be sapped and filled herself with food no less avidly than the girl who had given in first.

112. 'But you know what temptations follow on a full stom-

ach. The inducements the soldier had used to persuade the lady
into a desire to live became part also of an attempt on her vir-
tue. For all her chastity the man appealed to her: he was neither
unpleasing nor ill-spoken, she thought. Moreover, her maid
spoke on his behalf and quoted the line:

Would you fight even a pleasing passion?[12]

'Need I say more? The woman couldn't refuse even this grat-
ification of the flesh and the triumphant soldier talked her into
both. They then slept together, not just the night they first per-
formed the ceremony but the next night too, and then a third.
The doors of the vault were of course closed, so if a friend or
a stranger came to the tomb, he thought that the blameless
widow had expired over her husband's body.

'Actually the soldier, delighted with the lady's beauty and
the whole secret liaison, had bought whatever luxuries he could
afford and carried them to the tomb on the very first night. As
a result, the parents of one of the crucified men, seeing the
watch had been relaxed, took down the hanging body in the
dark and gave it the final rites. The soldier, tricked while he lay
enjoying himself and seeing next day one of the crosses without
a corpse, in terror of punishment, explained to the woman
what had happened. He would not wait for the judge's verdict,
he said – his own sword would carry out sentence for his dere-
liction of duty. Only let her provide a place for him in death
and let the tomb be the last resting place for both her lover and
her husband. The woman's pity was equal to her fidelity:

' "Heaven forbid," she said, "that I should see simultane-
ously two funerals, for the two men I hold dearest. I'd rather
hang the dead than kill the living."

'Suiting the deed to the word, she told him to take the body
of her husband from the coffin and fix it to the empty cross.
The soldier followed the sensible woman's plan, and next day
people wondered how on earth the dead man had managed to
get up on the cross.'

113. The sailors greeted the story with roars of laughter;
Tryphaena blushed rather and laid her cheek affectionately on

Giton's neck. Lichas however was not amused. Shaking his
head angrily, he said:

'If his commander-in-chief had been an honourable man,
he should have put the husband's body back in the tomb and
nailed the woman to the cross.'

No doubt he had remembered Hedyle and the robbery on his
ship before the lecherous elopement. But the terms of the treaty
did not permit him to recall this and the prevailing high spirits
left no room for bad temper. Tryphaena however was settled on
Giton's lap, covering his chest with kisses and occasionally titi-
vating his depilated appearance. Being depressed and annoyed
with the recent treaty, I took nothing to eat or drink, but looked
at both of them with oblique and hostile glances. All the kisses
and all the endearments that the lecherous woman thought up
wounded me deeply. Yet I still wasn't sure whether I was more
angry with the boy for stealing my mistress or with my mistress
for seducing the boy. Both acts were offensive to my eyes and
more saddening than my past captivity. Added to this was the
fact that Tryphaena would not talk to me like an old friend and
once pleasing lover, and Giton did not regard me as worth even
the usual toasts – at least he didn't address me in the general
conversation, which was the least he could do. He was nervous,
I imagine, of opening some fresh scar in the initial stages of the
reconciliation. Tears of vexation choked me, and my groans,
which I smothered into sighs, almost made me faint.

*

[*Lichas*] tried to get invited to the party, putting on no lordly
airs but acting like a friend asking a favour.

*

[*Tryphaena's maid to Encolpius*] 'If you had[13] any decent blood
in your veins, you wouldn't regard him as anything more than
a whore. If you were a man, you wouldn't go to such a per-
verted creature.'

*

Nothing embarrassed me more than the possibility of Eumol-
pus' realizing what had gone on, and, with his usual fluency,
taking revenge in verse.

*

Eumolpus swore in the most solemn terms.

*

114. While we were talking about this and similar things, the sea grew rough; clouds gathered from all directions and turned the day into darkness. The sailors scampered nervously to their duties and took down the sails before the storm. But there was no consistent wind driving the waves and the helmsmen did not know which way to head the ship. Sometimes the south-east wind blew towards Sicily, then time and again the north-east wind, dominating the Italian shoreline, would take over and turn the helpless ship this way and that. And what was far more dangerous than all the gales, the sudden pitch-black darkness had quenched the light so completely that the navigator could not even see the length of the prow. When the strength of the storm was at its height, Lichas, trembling, stretched out his hands to me pleadingly and said:

'You're the one, Encolpius. Save us from this danger. Just restore to the ship that sacred robe and the goddess's rattle.[14] In heaven's name, have some pity for us, as surely you used to.'

And then in mid-shout the wind flung him into the sea. He was caught up in a raging whirlpool and the blast whirled him round and sucked him under. Loyal servants however caught hold of Tryphaena, who was almost lifeless, put her in a boat with most of the luggage and snatched her from certain death . . . Clasping Giton to me with a cry, I wept and said:

'We deserved this of heaven – death alone would unite us. But our cruel luck does not allow it. Look, the waves are already overturning the ship. Look, the angry sea is trying to break our affectionate embraces. If you ever really loved Encolpius, kiss him while you can and snatch this last pleasure from the jaws of death.'

As I said this, Giton took off his clothes and, covered in my tunic, brought up his head for a kiss. And in case the envious waves should drag us apart even when clinging together like this, he tied his belt round both of us and said:

'If nothing else, we will float longer if we are tied together in death, or if out of pity the sea is likely to throw us up on the same shore, either some passing stranger will throw stones over us out of common humanity or, as a last favour that even the angry waves cannot refuse, the heedless sand will cover us.'

For the last time I felt bonds about me and as though laid out on a bier I waited for death – no longer an enemy. Meanwhile the storm executed the commands of fate and carried away all that was left of the ship. No mast, no helm, no rope or oar was left, but like a rough and shapeless log it went with the waves.

*

Fishermen came hurrying out in little boats to do some looting. When they saw there were people to defend their property, their greed was replaced by the wish to help.

*

THE JOURNEY TO CROTON[1]

115. We heard a strange murmur and moaning from the captain's cabin, as though an animal were trying to escape. We followed the sound and found Eumolpus sitting there and turning out verses on a great sheet. Surprised that he had leisure in the face of death to write poems, we dragged him out protesting and told him not to worry. But he was blazing with anger for being interrupted, and said:

'Allow me to get this line right. The poem is almost finished.'

I grabbed the lunatic and told Giton to come and drag the bellowing poet to land.

*

Finally the job was done and we sorrowfully entered the fisherman's cottage. Satisfying ourselves somehow with spoilt food from the wreck we passed a very miserable night. Next day, when we were discussing where in the world we could safely go, I suddenly saw a body turning in a gentle eddy and drifting to the shore.

I stopped sadly and began gazing at this example of the sea's treachery with moist eyes.

'Perhaps somewhere,' I said aloud, 'a carefree wife waits for him, perhaps a son, not knowing about the storm. Or perhaps it was his father he left, at least someone he kissed when he set out. So much for mortal schemes and mortal desires. Look at him – how the man floats!'

I was still mourning for what I supposed was a stranger, when the tide turned his undamaged face to the shore and I recognized almost underneath my feet what had been a little while ago the terrible and implacable Lichas. I could hold back my tears no longer. In fact, I beat my breast again and again and said: 'Where are your bad tempers and your ungovernable rages now? You have been at the mercy of fishes and other horrible creatures. A little while ago you boasted of your power and your position, but you haven't even a plank left from the wreck of your great ship. Go now, mortals, and fill your hearts with great schemes. Go and carefully invest your ill-gotten gains for a thousand years. Yesterday he must have looked at the accounts of his investments, he must have fixed the day he would reach his home town. O heavens, how far away he lies from his destination! Yet it is not only the seas that serve mortals like this. Weapons play a man false in wartime; the collapse of his family shrine buries a man giving thanks to heaven; a man falls from his carriage and hastily gasps his last. Food chokes the glutton, abstinence the abstemious. If you think it over properly, there is shipwreck everywhere. Mind you, a man drowned at sea does not get buried – as though it matters what destroys a perishable corpse – fire, water, or time! Whatever you do, all these things come to the same thing. But of course, wild beasts will mangle the carcass. As though it were better that fire should have it – and yet we consider this the severest possible punishment when we are angry with our servants. So what is the point of this craze to make sure that no part of us is left behind after burial?'

*

And the pyre, built by his enemies' hands, reduced Lichas to ashes.

While Eumolpus was composing an epigram on the dead man, he gazed into the distance in search of inspiration.

*

116. We gladly performed this duty and then we took the road we had decided on and in a short time we were sweating our way up a mountain, from which we saw in the near distance a town situated on a lofty height. Being lost, we did not know what town it was until we learnt from some farm overseer that it was Croton, a very ancient city, once the foremost in Italy. We then inquired most carefully what sort of people lived in this noble area and what type of business they particularly

favoured, since their wealth had been diminished by a long ser-
ies of wars.

'My dear sirs,' he said, 'if you are businessmen, change your
plans and look for some other source of livelihood. If, however,
you are a more sophisticated type and you can take incessant
lying, you are following the right road to riches. You see, in this
city no literary pretensions are honoured, eloquence has no
standing, sobriety and decent behaviour are not praised and
rewarded – no, whatever people you see, you must consider as
divided into two classes. Either they have fortunes worth hunt-
ing or they are fortune-hunters.[2] In this city no one raises chil-
dren because anyone who has heirs of his own is not invited
out to dinner or allowed into the games; he is deprived of all
amenities and lives in ignominious obscurity. But those who
have never married and have no close ties attain the highest
honours – only these have real courage, or even blameless char-
acters. You are on your way to a town that is like a plague-
ridden countryside, where there is nothing but corpses being
pecked and crows pecking them.'

117. Eumolpus, the wiser head, turned his thoughts to this
novel situation and confessed that this method of enrichment
appealed to him. I imagined that the old man was joking, just
like a poet, until he said:

'I wish we had more elaborate stage-properties, more civil-
ized costumes, and a more splendid set-up to give plausibility
to the imposture. I wouldn't postpone grabbing it, by god! I'd
lead you straight to a fortune. Even so, I promise . . .'

*

. . . whatever he should ask for, provided that our old compan-
ion in crime, the robe I'd stolen,[3] would do and also whatever
Lycurgus' burgled villa had yielded. The mother of the gods
with her usual good faith would send us money for immediate
use.

*

'Why delay the start of the show then?' said Eumolpus. 'Make
me your master, if you like the business.'

No one dared condemn a scheme that would cost nothing.
And so, to safeguard the imposture in which we were all

involved, we swore an oath dictated by Eumolpus, that we would be burned, flogged, beaten, killed with cold steel or whatever else Eumolpus ordered. Like real gladiators we very solemnly handed ourselves over, body and soul, to our master. After swearing the oath we saluted our master in our role as slaves, and we were all instructed that Eumolpus had buried his son, a young man of great oratorical abilities and high promise, and the unhappy old man had therefore left his native city so that he should not have daily cause for tears at the sight of his son's followers and friends or his tomb. Shipwreck was next added to this grief, in which he had lost more than twenty million sesterces. But he was not worried by the loss, except that being deprived of his servants he did not see about him what was proper to his rank. Besides, he had thirty million invested in Africa in farms and loans; in fact, he had such a large number of slaves spread among his estates in Numidia that they could even capture Carthage.

Following this pattern, we told Eumolpus to cough a lot, get first constipation, then diarrhoea, and curse all his food openly. He was to talk about gold and silver, unreliable farms and his invariably unproductive lands. Moreover he was to sit down every day at his accounts and renew the terms of his will every month. And, to complete the farce, whenever he tried to call one of us he was to call out the wrong name, to make it clear that their master remembered even the ones who were no longer with him.

After making these arrangements, we prayed to heaven that it would all turn out well and happily, and set off down the road. Giton however, could not manage the unaccustomed pack and Corax the hired man, a constant grumbler in his job, kept putting his bag down, hurling insults at us for hurrying, and vowing that he'd throw away the bags and run off with his load.

'What *is* this, you people?' he said. 'Do you think I'm a beast of burden or a ship for carrying stones? I contracted for a man's job, not a dray-horse's. I'm a free man as much as you are, even if my father did leave me poor.'

Not content with cursing, every so often he lifted his leg right up and filled the road with obscene sounds and smells.

Giton laughed at his bad behaviour and followed each of his farts with an equally loud imitation.

*

118. 'Poetry, my young friends,' said Eumolpus, 'has cheated many people. As soon as each of them has made his lines scan and woven some idea into a delicate web of words, he thinks he's gone straight up Helicon. Tired by their legal practice they often fly to the calm waters of poetry, as though it were a lucky port in a storm, believing it must be easier to construct an epic poem than a speech that glows with scintillating epigrams. But noble inspiration hates empty verbiage and a mind cannot conceive or bear fruit unless it is soaked in a mighty flood of great works. One must avoid all vulgarity of language and one must select expressions not in common use; the effect should be "I hate the vulgar crowd and fend them off".[4] Besides this, one must be careful that witty lines are not made to stand out from the body of the narrative, but add their colour and brilliance to the texture of the poem. Witness Homer and the lyric poets, Roman Virgil, and Horace's careful felicity. Other poets either have not seen the way to approach poetry, or if they have seen it have been frightened to take it. Above all, whoever attempts the great theme of the Civil War[5] without being full of the great writers will fail under the task. For it is not historical fact that has to be handled in the poem – historians do this far better. No, the unfettered inspiration must be sent soaring from the catapult of wit through dark messages and divine interventions and stories, so that it gives the impression of prophetic ravings rather than the accuracy of a solemn speech before witnesses.

'As an example, if you like, here's this bold attempt, even though it has not yet received the final touches:

I

119.　　　'All-conquering Rome was mistress of the globe,
　　　　　By land and sea an empire to the poles,
　　　　　　　　but still unsatisfied.
　　　　　Sea-lanes battered by heavy hulks;

A hidden bay, a gold-producing region –
    this was the ENEMY.
The Fates are bent on war,
The search for wealth continues.
Ordinary pleasures,
10   plebeian enjoyments
      are tedious,
Soldiers connoisseurs of Corinthian bronze.
Gems from deep mines
    flash challenges to purple.
From Numidia marble –
    From China new silks –
The Arabian countryside
    stripped bare for profits.
Further disasters, more stabs at a stricken Peace (hear ye!):
20 Wild beasts are stalked in the woods of Taurus,
Ammon in darkest Africa
    flushed for the monster
"which is slain
    because his tooth sells dear".[6]
Starvation in strange forms
    weighs down the ships;
The prowling tiger hauled in a bronze cage
To gorge on human blood for the cheering PLEBS.
Shame chokes my spleen and voice.
30 How to reveal those doomed lives?
The genitals removed,
Organs mutilated under the knife
And broken into the services of lust.
    The solemn march of time is checked,
    The speeding years retarded,
    Nature seeking herself finds nothing.
    Each man has his catamite
    (The soft enervated gait,
    The floating hair,
40   The fashions in clothes,
    Tokens of absent virility.)

Eye-catching tables of citron-wood from Africa (look ye!)
Mirror the splash of purple and lackeys;
Imitate in mottled surfaces disvalued gold.
About the useless wood, the pride of fools,
The mob moves tipsily.

Footloose, the soldier hefts his tackle,
        an esurient mercenary.

The Belly, miracle of ingenuity,
Brings the parrot-wrasse,   50
Submerged in Sicilian water,
Alive to the table;
Pulls oysters from the Lucrine Lake,
To make a sale to the palate,
The high price most of the flavour.

The Phasian Lake emptied of birds,[7]
Along that silent shore
Only the wind breathes upon the deserted leaves.
The same madness in politics:
A bribed electorate changing sides for silver.   60
On sale: one people and one senate

                        CHEAP!

Votes are for selling.
Even old men forget
        the strenuous requirements of freedom.
A change of government for small change,
Auctoritas corrupt and humiliated.
        Cato is defeated,[8]
                rejected by the electorate;
The victorious candidate is embarrassed,   70
Ashamed to snatch
        the *fasces* from Cato.
Not the defeat of a candidate,
The death-blow of a great people –

Rome a lost city,
      merchant and merchandise,
      plunderer and plundered.
A vile vortex, a gaping whirlpool,
The people drowning.
80   With *Usura*[9] comes there greed,
      With usura hath no man a house,
      With usura hath no man a hand free,
      A canker born in the hidden marrow,
      A madness raging in the limbs of the body politic
      And wandering with its sorrows
      Like a pack of hounds.
      And out of this Revolution,
      Revolution from poverty.

War tempts the poor.
90   Dissipated fortunes are recouped by murder,
Boldness with nothing has nothing to lose.
Drowned in this filth, sodden with this sleep,
What practitioner's skill can rouse Rome surely?
Furor militaris
None but the soldier's, *furor militaris*,
      desire pricked by the sword.[10]

II

120.   'Fortune produced three captains.
Enyo,[11] murderous goddess of War,
Crushed each on different battlefields.
100 Parthia kept Crassus,
In the Libyan Sea lay Pompey (surnamed Magnus)
And Julius –
      his blood incarnadined ungrateful Rome.
The earth,
Intolerant of so many tombs together
Divided their ashes.

Such are fame's privileges.
  The scene:[12]
  Deep in a hollow cleft
  Between Neapolis and Puteoli,   110
  A cleft awash with water from Cocytus,
  Hot with eternal exhalations,
  Damp with a deadly dew.
  No autumn green here,
  No green fields of pleasant turf,
  No echoing thickets
     Or sweet discords of spring song.
  But CHAOS,
     foul black pumice rock,
  In triumphant isolation,   120
  And a ring of depressed cypresses above.
Father Dis,[13] appearing from below,
Head powdered with white ash
And flames from funeral pyres,
Sardonically to Fortune, winged goddess:
  "O mistress of all divine and human things,
  Hater of all security of power,
  Lover of the new, forsaker of triumphs,
  Art thou not crushed
  By the weight of Rome?   130
  Canst thou raise higher that doomed mass?
  The new generation frets at its strength,
  Burdened by accumulated wealth.
  See, everywhere rich pickings of victory,
  Prosperity raging to its ruin.
  They build in gold and raise their mansions to the stars.
  The seas are dammed by dykes of stone
  And other seas spring up within their fields –
  A rebellion against the order of all things.
  The tunnelled earth yawns under insane buildings;   140
  Caverns groan in hollowed mountains;
  As long as frivolous employments are found for stone,
  My ghosts confess their hopes of heaven.

On then, Fortune –
Change thy looks of peace for the face of war.
Rouse Rome and give my kingdom its dead.
I have felt no blood on my face,
My Tisiphone has not bathed her parched limbs,
Since Sulla's sword[14] drank deep

150   And the bristling earth produced its bloody crops."

121.   'He tries to take her right hand,
But the ground breaks into a yawning chasm.

Fickle-hearted Fortune so replies:
"Father, lord of inmost Cocytus,[15]
If I may with impunity reveal
     what must come to pass,
Thy wishes are granted.
The mad rage inside me no less than thine,
A more wayward fire eats my heart.

160   All I have heaped upon the Roman citadels
I now detest,
     resenting my generosity.
The same power that built
     will destroy their mighty works.
I have in mind
     to immolate their warriors,
Choke their decadence with blood.
Now rings through timorous ears the clash of arms:
I see Philippi strewn with double slaughter,

170   Thessalian pyres, Spanish and Libyan dead;
I see Nile's barriers groaning,
The bays of Actium,[16]
     warriors terrified of Apollo's
       martial port.
Go then, open the thirsty territories of thy kingdom
To beckon in new ghosts.
The ferryman Charon[17] will be too weak
To ferry the shades in his boat –
     there will be need of a fleet.

Glut thyself on the great disaster, pale Tisiphone,   180
Bite into the open wounds.
The torn world is led to the Stygian shades."

122.   'As she finished a cloud shook
        And with abrupt flashes of fire
        Broke apart for a gleaming thunderbolt,
        Closing behind the jetting flame.
        The father of the shades retreated,
        Pater umbrarum
        Closed the gaping breast of the earth
        in panic,   190
        Paling before fraternal bolts.[18]

III

'At once mankind's disaster, the dooms to come,
Are revealed by heavenly omens.
Hyperion, ugly with bloody face,
        hid his orb in darkness,
As though he saw civil war already.
Elsewhere Cynthia[19] dimmed her full face,
Withdrew her light from the scene of the crime.
Mountain ridges thundered into fragments,
    As peaks collapsed,   200
And rivers wandered no longer free,
        dying slowly between familiar banks.
Heaven a pandemonium of military excursions;
A tremulous trumpet from the stars
        took Mars by the ears.
Etna,[20] eaten by strange fires,
    flung its eruptions into the skies.
Amid the tombs and unburned bones
    the faces of the dead appear
With terrible menacing shrieks.   210
A comet trailing new stars, bearing fire;

A new Jove,
A new sky descending in bloody rain.
Portents soon clarified by God.

Caesar brooks no delay,
Pricked by lust for revenge
He abandons the Gallic,[21]
        begins the Civil
        War.

IV

220   'In airy Alps
Where the rocks once pounded by a Greek divinity[22]
Slope softly to let men enter,
Est locus,
    a holy place with altars there to Hercules.
Winter blocks it with tight-packed snow
And lifts it to the stars with a blanching peak.
The heavens might have fallen from its top.
It does not melt in midsummer rays, spring breezes,
Its packed surface stays stiff with ice and winter frost,
230   It could carry the globe on its threatening shoulders.
When Caesar tramped these ridges with his exulting
        soldiers and chose his site,
He looked out
    over the wide Italian plains from the summit,
Pointed both hands to the stars:
    "Jupiter Omnipotent,
    Saturnian land[23] once glad of my armies,
    And loaded down with my triumphs,
    I call you to witness:
240   Mars summons me to war,
        an unwilling warrior.
    I bring unwilling hands to the execution,
    Forced by my grievances,
    Driven from my city

THE JOURNEY TO CROTON

    while I reddened the Rhine with blood
And blocked the Gauls from the Alps
(Their second attempt on the Capitol).
Exile the surer for my victory!
In German blood my guilt is rooted,
    in a hundred triumphs.   250
Yet who are they my glory terrifies?
Who are they who would end my wars?
Cheap operators bought and sold,
    hirelings,
My Rome their step-mother.
But not with impunity, nor without revenge, I think,
Shall a coward tie my hands.

Run mad, my victorious ones!
Go, comrades, plead my case with a sword!
The same charge laid at our doors,   260
The same disaster over us all.
I owe you thanks –
    I did not win alone.
So, since there are penalties
    for the acquisition of trophies,
And victory celebrations see us in convicts' dress,
    Fortune be the judge –
Let the die be cast.
Begin the war and try your mettle.
Yet my case is already won –   270
With so many brave around me
    I do not know the meaning of defeat."
'At the trumpet of his voice
A raven, *Delphicus ales*,[24]
Was a glad omen in the sky,
Cleaving the air.
From the left of the dread grove
Strange voices sounded
    and flames rose.
The brightness of the Sun grew brighter than its wont   280
And set a burning halo of gold about its face.

123.   'Caesar deployed his standards of war,
         Heartened by omens,
         First to attempt these new audacities.
         The icy surface and frost-hard ground
         Made no resistance,
                    lay quiet, crunching gently.
         But the squadrons shattered the bound clouds,
         The horses panicking unfettered the ice,
290   the snow melted.
         Rivers of sudden origin ran from the mountain heights,
         Yet these too (as at a command)
         Halted and the flow was still,
                    (chained downpour).
         One moment a mire, then a hardened floor.
         Treacherous before, it now mocked at their steps,
                    deceived each foot.
         Men, horses equally, arms and armour
         Lay piled in sorry confusion.
300   Now the clouds, hit by the cutting wind,
         Let fall their loads,
         Winds torn by whirlwinds,
         Skies rent by swollen hailstones.
         The very clouds were tatters
                    and fell about their armour.
         The frozen ice heaved like ocean waves.
         The earth was covered by the storm of snow,
         The stars were covered
         And the rivers stuck to their banks
310   covered too.
         Only Caesar above it –
         Leaning on his great spear,
         With sure strides breaking across the cracking fields,
         Like Hercules, Amphitryonides,[25] striding, head-high,
         From the Caucasian peak,
         Or like a frowning Jupiter,
         Rushing from the towering tops of Olympus,
         Hurling his bolts at the doomed race of Giants.[26]

V

While Caesar angrily trod underfoot
    the haughty pinnacles,   320
Winged Rumour, wings fluttering in terror,
Took flight to the high ridges of the Palatine,[27]
And with this thunder of rumours smote
Every statue in the city:
  "The fleets are on the sea,
   The whole Alps a blaze of squadrons
   Spattered with German blood."
Armies, blood, slaughter, fire, whole wars
Flit before their eyes.
Their hearts battered by this din   330
Were torn in two and much afraid.
Flight by land, said one –
The sea is better, said another:
The sea is now safer than our country.
Not wanting were those who favoured fight,
Accepting the command of Fate.
The people trailed from the desolate city,
To wherever their stunned minds moved,
    saddest of scenes.
Rome's heart is in the rout,   340
Beaten already the Quirites[28]
Leave their sad homes when they hear the rumour.
One clutches his children in trembling hands,
One hides his family gods beneath his coat,
Leaving the sad hallway
    cursing to death the distant enemy.
Some clasp wives to their sad breasts
And young men who never felt a load
Clasp aged fathers,
Carrying only what they fear for most.   350
Others unwarily take all they have,
Carrying booty to battle.
In a storm at sea,

When great Auster[29] starts to roughen the deep
And sends the driven waves toppling,
When rigging and rudder fail,
One man battens down,
Another looks for safe harbour, tranquil shore,
And another hoists sail to fly the storm,
360   Trusting his all to Fortune.

An end to these minor catastrophes:
Pompeius Magnus with both consuls,
Pompey, terror of the Pontus,
Explorer of savage Hydaspes,
The rock that wrecked the pirates,[30]
For all his three triumphs that made Jupiter tremble,
For all the veneration of Pontus
After he sheered through its maelstrom,
And the submission of the waves of the Bosphorus,
370   Took to flight,
                    Shame on 't!
His title to power forgotten,
So fickle Fortuna might see the back
              Of even Pompeius Magnus.

VI

124.   'Such a great infection spread even to the skies,
The timorousness of heaven set the seal on flight.
And through the world a gentle host of gods,
Abominating earth's madness, abandoned earth,
Avoiding the armies of the doomed.
380   First Pax, first of them all,
Bruising her white arms, hid her defeated head
In a helmet, left earth in haste
For the implacable kingdom of Dis.
Submissive Honour her companion,
And Justitia, hair ragged,
Concordia sobbing in her torn dress.

The flight not all in one direction:
Where the realm of Erebus[31] yawned,
Emerged in broad array the troop of Dis:
Bristling Erinys, Bellona, menacing,   390
Megaera[32] with her armoury of torches,
Doom, Treachery and the pale image of Death.

In their midst went Furor, Madness,
Like a horse trailing broken reins,
Her bloody head held up to the world
Her face, pitted with a thousand wounds,
Hid in a bloodstained helmet:
The battered shield of Mars,
        heavy with innumerable arrows,
Gripped in her left hand,   400
In her right the threat of a burning torch
Carrying fires to earth.

VII

The earth feels the weight of the gods,
Stars shifted, losing equilibrium,
The whole kingdom of heaven divided.
Dione first heads the armies of her Caesar,
Pallas moving to her side and Romulus (Mavortius)
        beating his great spear.
Phoebus and Phoebus' sister,
And Mercury, on Cyllene born,[33] took Pompey away,   410
And Hercules Tirynthius[34] like him in all his deeds.
        The trumpets sounded.
Discordia with her torn hair
Raised to the gods above her Stygian head.
Clotted blood in her mouth,
Tears in her battered eyes,
Her teeth mailed with a scurf of rust,
Her tongue dripping with foulness,
Her face in a ring of snakes;

420   With bosom convulsed beneath her tattered dress,
         She waved in a shaking hand a bloody torch.
         Left Tartarus, the darknesses of Cocytus,
         Striding up to the high ridges
         Of the lordly Appennines,
         Vantage-point for all lands, all seas,
         And the forces flooding the world.
         From her mad breast these cries erupted:
         "To arms, ye nations – now your hearts are on fire.
         To arms and throw your torches
430   into the hearts of cities.
         Whoever hides will be defeated.
         Let no woman lag behind, or child,
                  Or age-torn man.
         Earth trembles, the ripped houses revolt.
         Cling to your Law, Marcellus.[35]
         Shake up the masses, Curio.
         Lentulus, quench not that brave and martial ardour.
         And you, son of heaven,[36]
         Why do you delay with your armies?
440   Why are you not battering at gates,
         Tearing away town walls, hauling off treasure?
         Can you not guard the Roman fortress, Pompey?
         Look then to the walls of Epidamnus,[37]
         And dye Thessalian bays[38] with human blood."
         And all Discordia commanded
                  so came to pass on earth.'

When Eumolpus had poured all this out in a great flow of words, we finally entered Croton. Here we recuperated at a little inn and next day, looking for a house on a larger scale, we fell in with a crowd of legacy-hunters, who asked us what sort of people we were and where we came from. Following our concerted plan we told the gullible inquirers where we were from and who we were.

Immediately they did their best to outdo each other in putting their financial resources at Eumolpus' service . . . All of the legacy-hunters vied with each other to get into Eumolpus' good graces with presents.

*

THE SEDUCTIONS OF CIRCE

125. While all this was taking place in Croton over a considerable period of time ... Eumolpus, full of happiness, was so forgetful of his previous fortune, that he often boasted that no one in the place could stand up against his influence, and his own people, through the good offices of his friends, would get off scot-free for any crime they committed.

Personally, although I fattened myself up every day with more and more of these over-abundant luxuries and thought Fortune had taken her eyes off me, yet quite often I was worried not from any real cause, but from thinking of my usual luck: 'What if some shrewd legacy-hunter sends a spy to Africa and exposes our whole deception? What if the hired man gets tired of our present happy position, turns over evidence to our friends, and uncovers the whole scheme by his spiteful treachery? We'll obviously have to run away once more and just when we were rid of it, we'll be reduced to poverty again for a fresh period of beggary. Heavens above, how terrible it is to live outside the law – one is always expecting what one rightly deserves.'[1]

*

126. [*Circe's maid, Chrysis, is talking to Polyaenus, i.e. Encolpius*] 'Because you're aware of your sexual charms, you put on an arrogant air and sell your favours instead of giving them free. Otherwise, what's the point of your combed wavy hair, the heavy make-up, the soft sulkiness in your eyes, the self-conscious walk, the carefully measured steps? What's the object unless you're prostituting your good looks for money? You look at me – I'm no fortune-teller, and I don't go in for astrology, but

I tell people's characters from their faces, and when I've seen how someone walks, I know what he's thinking. If you're selling what I've come for, there's a customer waiting. Or if you're giving it free – which is nicer – put me under an obligation for your kindness. You say you're just a poor slave, but you're only exciting her desire to boiling point. Some women get heated up over the absolute dregs and can't feel any passion unless they see slaves or bare-legged messengers. The arena sets some of them on heat, or a mule-driver covered with dust, or actors displayed on the stage. My mistress is one of this type. She jumps across the first fourteen seats from the orchestra and looks for something to love among the lowest of the low.'

I said in a voice full of sweetness: 'Tell me, are you the one who is in love with me?'

The maid laughed heartily at such an unlikely notion.

'I wouldn't make you so pleased with yourself. I have never yet gone to bed with a slave, and heaven forbid I should ever see a lover of mine crucified. That's for ladies who kiss the whip-marks. Even though I'm a servant, I've never sat anywhere except in the lap of knights.'

I couldn't help some surprise at such contrasting sexual desires. I thought it very strange that the maid should cultivate the superior outlook of a lady and the lady the low taste of a maid.

Then as the joking continued, I asked her to bring her mistress to the copse of plane trees. The girl agreed to the suggestion. She tucked up her tunic and turned into the laurel grove bordering the walk. Without any long delay she brought out of the shadows a woman who was lovelier than any work of art, and led her to my side.

No words could do justice to her charms – whatever I said would not be enough. Her curls flowed naturally over the whole breadth of her shoulders and waved back at the hairline from her exquisitely narrow brow. Her eyebrows ran down to the contour of her cheeks and almost met over the bridge of her nose. Her eyes were brighter than stars shining outside the glow of the moon. Her nostrils curved in a little, and her little mouth was as Praxiteles imagined Diana's.[2] Now her chin, now her neck, now her hands, now the pearly lustre of her feet

clasped by a thin gold chain – each in turn would have put Par-
ian marble[3] to shame. Then for the first time I despised my old
passion for Doris.[4]

*

What has happened, Jove, what has happened
To make you throw down your arms,
To become an old story in heaven,
To disdain these terrestrial charms?

Now here was a worthy occasion
To beetle your brows and put on
Two horns or cover your white hair
With the feathers and form of a swan.[5]

Here, here is a real Danaë –
She would kindle your lust even higher.
One touch, one mere touch of her body
And your limbs would be melting in fire.

*

127. She was delighted and smiled so sweetly I thought the full
moon had shown her face out of a cloud. Then modulating her
voice to her gestures, she said:
  'If you don't find a smart lady distasteful, one who had a
man for the first time only this year, let me introduce to you a
new girl-friend,[6] young man. Of course, you have a boy-friend
too – I wasn't ashamed of making inquiries, you see – but
what's to stop you adopting a girl-friend as well? I shall come
on the same footing. You have only to agree to put up with my
kisses as well, whenever you like.'
  'On the contrary,' I replied, 'I must beg you, you beautiful
creature, not to disdain to number a poor stranger among your
adorers. You will find him religiously devoted if you permit
him to worship you. And don't imagine I am entering this tem-
ple without an offering. I give up my boy-friend for you.'
  'What?' she said. 'Are you giving up for me the boy you
cannot live without, the lips you cling to, the one you love the
way I want to love you?'
  As she said this, there was such charm in her voice, such a

sweet sound caressed the enraptured air that it was as though the song of the Sirens sang through the breezes. And then in my amazement – the whole sky seemed somehow brighter – it occurred to me to ask the goddess her name.

'So my maid hasn't told you,' she said, 'that I'm called Circe? Not that I am the child of the Sun – my mother never stopped at will the course of the revolving heavens. Yet if the fates unite us, I shall have something to thank heaven for. A god, in fact, is already working his mysterious purposes to some end. It is not by chance that Circe is in love with Polyaenus[7] – a great flame is always kindled between these names. Take me in your arms, if you wish: there is no reason to fear any prying eyes. Your beloved boy is a long way from here.'

Saying this, Circe drew me, entwined in arms softer than swansdown, on to the grassy ground.

> Flowers such as the Earth Mother spread on Ida's top
> When Jove and his wifely love united[8]
> (His breast one raging fire).
> Roses, violets, soft rushes glinting there
> And the white lilies smiling
>   from the green meadows.
> Such a place cried for love on its soft grass
> The day brightened like a blessing
> On our secret amours.

Side by side there in the grass we kissed a thousand times in our love-play, groping towards more strenuous pleasures.

*

128. [*Circe to Polyaenus*] 'What is it?' she said. 'Does my mouth offend you in some way? Does my breath smell through not eating? Is it the unwashed sweat from my armpits? If it's not any of these, am I to suppose you're somehow frightened of Giton?'

Flushed with obvious embarrassment, I even lost whatever virility I had. My whole body was limp, and I said:

'Please, my queen, don't add insults to my misery. I've been bewitched.'

*

[*Circe*] 'Tell me, Chrysis – but the truth, mind! Am I somehow unpleasant? Am I untidy? Am I somehow obscuring my beauty because of some natural defect? Don't deceive your mistress. I've done something wrong.'

Then as Chrysis remained silent, she snatched a mirror from her and after trying every expression that lovers usually put on to amuse each other, she shook out her dress, rumpled from contact with the ground, and rushed into the shrine of Venus. On my part, like a guilty thing, trembling as though I'd seen a horrible vision, I began asking myself mentally whether I had been robbed of the chance of true pleasure.

> Any soporific midnight an instance,
> When the unfocused eyes are dream-deluded:
> The spaded earth exposing gold,
> Guilty hands fingering criminal gains,
> Snatching at jewels,
> Sweat too bathing the face,
> And a deep fear in the mind
> That mere awareness of gold on the person
> May dislodge it
>   even from the breast pocket.
> The images of joy recede from the mocked brain;
> Reality returns
> To a heart longing for lost pleasures
> Lingering in vanished illusions.

*

[*Giton to Encolpius*] 'So thank you for loving me in such an honourable Platonic way.[9] Alcibiades himself couldn't have been safer when he slept in his teacher's bed.'

*

129. [*Encolpius to Giton*] 'Honestly, dear lad, I can't realize I'm a man, I don't feel it. The part of my body that once made me an Achilles[10] is dead and buried.'

*

The boy was frightened of being discovered alone with me and giving rise to gossip, so he rushed off and took refuge in the inner part of the house.

*

Chrysis however entered my room and delivered to me a letter[11] from her mistress, which read as follows:

Dear Polyaenus,

If I were a sensual woman, I would complain I had been tricked. As it is, I am positively grateful for your weakness. I've played too long in the mere shadows of pleasure. However I'm writing to ask how you are and whether you got home on your own feet. Doctors say a man can't walk if he has no strength. I'll tell you something, my young friend – beware of paralysis. I have never seen a sick man in such great danger – you are as good as dead, for heaven's sake. If that same chill got into your knees and hands, you could send for the undertaker. To come to the point: although I was deeply offended, still I don't begrudge a sick man his prescription. If you wish to get better, send Giton away. You will get your strength back, I can tell you, if you sleep without your darling boy for three days. As far as I am concerned, I'm not afraid of meeting someone who will like me less. The mirror doesn't lie, nor does my reputation.

Get well soon – if you can.

Circe

When Chrysis saw I had read the whole insulting screed, she said:

'These things tend to happen, particularly in this part of the country, where women even drag down the moon ... This problem will be taken care of too. Just write a soothing reply to my mistress and restore her good spirits with a frank and natural answer. If the truth must be told, from the moment she was so insulted, she has not been her usual self.'

130. I gladly took the maid's advice and wrote some such letter as this:

Dear Circe,

I admit I have done many bad things. After all, I am a man and still young. But I have never till today committed a really deadly sin. You have the culprit's confession. Whatever you order, I deserve it. I have been guilty of treachery, I've killed a man, and

I've robbed a temple – find a punishment for these crimes. If you wish to kill me, I'll come and bring my sword. If you are content with just whipping, I'll run naked to my beloved. Remember this one thing, not I but my instruments were at fault. The soldier was ready, but had no weapons. Who caused this trouble I don't know. Perhaps my thoughts ran ahead of my lagging body; perhaps in my keen desire to enjoy every last thing, I used up the pleasure in dallying. I have not discovered what I did. Still, you tell me to beware of paralysis – as though it could become any worse, now it has deprived me of the ability to possess you of all women. However this is what my excuses come to: I will give you satisfaction, if you allow me to atone for my fault.

Your slave,
Polyaenus

*

I sent Chrysis off with this sort of promise and carefully attended to my treacherous body. Omitting a bath, I used a very moderate amount of oil to rub myself down, then dining on more solid dishes than usual, onions and the heads of snails without seasoning, I drank a sparing quantity of wine. After this, setting myself up with a very gentle stroll before bed, I went to my room without Giton. So great was my anxiety to placate her that I was afraid my boy-friend might impair my virility.

131. Getting up next day without any mental or physical strain, I went down to the same grove of plane-trees, although I was nervous of such an inauspicious place, and began waiting among the trees for my guide, Chrysis. I walked round for a short while and I had only just sat down where I had been the day before when she turned up, bringing a little old woman[12] with her. When she greeted me, she said:

'How are you, my fine friend? Have you begun to feel in better spirits?' . . .

The old woman brought out of her dress a string of variously coloured threads twisted together and bound it round my neck. Then mixing some dust with spittle, she took it on her middle finger and ignoring my repugnance, marked my forehead with it.

*

After completing this spell, she instructed me to spit three times and drop down my chest, again three times, some pebbles which she had charmed and wrapped in purple. Then she began to test my virility with her hands. Faster than you could speak, the nerves obeyed the command, and the little old woman's hands were filled with a mighty throbbing. Leaping with joy, she said: 'Do you see, my dear Chrysis, do you see how I've started a hare for others to hunt?'

*

The lofty plane-tree spreads its summer shade,
Metamorphosed Daphne[13] near by, crowned with berries.
Cypresses tremulous, clipped pines around
Shuddering at their tops.
            Playing among them
A stream with wandering waters,
Spume-flecked, worrying the stones
            with a querulous spray.
            A place right for love.
Witness the woodland nightingale,
      and Procne turned urban swallow[14] –
Everywhere amid the grass and soft violets,
Their woodland homes a temple of song.

*

She lay relaxed, her marble neck resting on a golden couch, and she beat the tranquil air with a branch of flowering myrtle. When she saw me, she blushed a little, obviously remembering yesterday's affront. Then when everyone had gone, and I had sat down beside her at her invitation, she placed the branch over my eyes, and with this wall between us she became bolder.

'How are you, you paralytic?' she said. 'Have you come intact today?'

'Why ask me?' said I. 'Try me!' and I threw myself bodily into her arms and kissed her till I could kiss no more – no magic spells there.

*

132. Her sheer[15] physical beauty cried out to me and she pulled me down to make love to her. Our lips ground noisily together in kiss after kiss. Our locked hands found every possible way of

making love. Our bodies wrapped in a mutual embrace united even our very souls.

*

Smarting from these open insults, the lady finally rushes to have her revenge. She calls her attendants and has them hoist me up and whip me. And not content with such a drastic punishment she calls round all her wool workers and the lowest types of servant and has them spit at me. I put my hands over my eyes, and without any begging for mercy because I knew what I deserved, whipped and spat on, I was flung through the door. Proselenus is thrown out too, Chrysis is beaten, and the whole household gloomily muttered to each other and wondered who had dashed their mistress's high spirits . . .

*

And so, after weighing things up, I became more cheerful. I concealed the marks of the whips with some doctoring so that my ill-treatment would neither amuse Eumolpus nor sadden Giton. Then I did the only thing I could do to save my face, I feigned weariness; and wrapped up in bed, I directed the whole blaze of my anger on what had been the cause of all my troubles.

> Three times I took the murd'rous axe in hand,
> Three times I wavered like a wilting stalk
> And curtsied from the blade, poor instrument
> In trembling hands – I could not what I would.
> From terror colder than the wintry frost,
> It took asylum far within my crotch,
> A thousand wrinkles deep.
> How could I lift its head to punishment?
> Cozened by its whoreson mortal fright
> I fled for aid to words that deeper bite.[16]

And so leaning on my elbow I made quite a speech, abusing it for its disobedience. 'What have you got to say?' I said. 'You insult to mankind, you blot on the face of heaven – it's improper to give you your real name when talking seriously. Did I deserve this from you – that you should drag me down to hell when

I was in heaven? That you should betray me in the prime of life and reduce me to the impotence of the last stages of senility? Go on, give me a serious argument.' As I poured this out angrily:

> Turning away, she kept her eyes down-cast,
> Her visage no more moved by this address
> Than supple willow or drooping poppyhead.[17]

Once this vile abuse was finished, I too began to feel regret – for talking like this – and I blushed inwardly at forgetting my sense of shame and bandying words with a part of the body that more dignified people do not even think about. Then after rubbing my brow for some time, I said to myself: 'Still, where's the harm in relieving my feelings by some natural abuse? Anyway, how is it we curse such parts of the body as the stomach or the throat and even the head, when we have the occasional headache? In fact, didn't Ulysses argue with his heart, and don't some tragic heroes abuse their eyes as though they could hear them? People with gout curse their feet, people with arthritis their hands, people with ophthalmia their eyes, and when people stub their toes, they often blame the pain on their feet.

> Cato[18] frowns and knits his brows,
> The Censor wants to stop us,
> The Censor hates my guileless prose,
> My simple modern opus.
> My cheerful unaffected style
> Is Everyman when in his humour,
> My candid pen narrates his joys,
> Refusing to philosophize.
>
> Find me any man who knows
> Nothing of love and naked pleasure.
> What stern moralist would oppose
> Two bodies warming a bed together?
> Father of Truth, old Epicurus[19]
> Spoke of bodies, not of soul,

And taught, philosophers assure us,
Love is Life's sovereign goal.

*

There is nothing on earth more misleading than silly prejudice
and nothing sillier than hypocritical moralizing.

*

133. After finishing this speech, I called Giton and said:

'Tell me, my dear, but on your honour. That night Ascyltus
stole you away from me, did he stay awake and assault you or
was he content with a lonely and honourable night?'

The lad touched his eyes and solemnly swore that Ascyltus
had offered him no violence.

*

Kneeling on the threshold, I offered up a prayer to the hostile
deity:[20]

'Comrade of Nymphs, comrade of Bacchus,
Deity of the rich forests
    whom fair Dione appointed,
Famed Lesbos, green Thasos obey your wishes
And the Lydians spread over the seven rivers
Bow before you —
They built you a temple in your own Hypaepa —
Come to me, guardian of Bacchus, darling of Dryads,[21]
Hear my timid orisons.
I come before you —
    unstained by guiltless blood.
I was no enemy of religion
    when I robbed the temples.[22]
Need and the attrition of poverty,
    these were the agents —
Not my true self.
The man who sins through poverty
    is a venial offender.
My prayer is:
    Relieve my mind,
    Forgive the venial sin,
And whenever fortune smiles on me,

I shall not let your glory go unhonoured —
A horned goat, O holy one, sire of his herd,
Will come to your altars,
The farrow of a grunting sow, a milky victim,
Will come to your altars.
Wine of the newest vintage will foam in the chalices
And inebriated young men
Will march in triumph
Three times around your shrine.'

*

While I was doing this and keeping a close eye on the dear departed, the old woman entered the temple. She looked a sight with her torn hair and black clothes. She put a hand on me and led me outside the vestibule.

*

134. [*The old woman, Proselenus, to Encolpius*] 'Were they witches who enervated you? Did you tread on some shit in the dark at a crossroad? Or a corpse? You haven't even rescued yourself from the boy. Instead, you're soft, weak, and tired, like a cart-horse on a slope; you just wasted all this effort and sweat. And not content to be a sinner on your own, you've set heaven against me too.'

*

And without any protest from me, she led me through into the priestess's room where she threw me on a bed, and snatching a rod from behind the door, still without a murmur from me, gave me a thrashing. If the rod had not shattered at the first stroke and lessened the force of the blows, she might perhaps have broken my arms and head as well. I howled particularly at the cuts aimed at my groin. With my tears flowing freely I leaned my head on the mattress and covered it with my right hand. She was equally upset and tearful. She sat on the other side of the bed and complained in tremulous tones of living too long, until the priestess came in and found us . . .

'Why have you come to my room like mourners to a funeral?' she said. 'Especially on a holiday, when even miserable people show a smile . . .'

*

[*Proselenus to Oenothea, priestess of Priapus, talking of Encol-pius*] 'Oh, Oenothea,' she said, 'it's this young man you see here. He was born under an evil star. He can't make a sale to boy or girl. You've never seen a man so unlucky – he's got a piece of wet leather, not a prick. In fact, what do you think of someone who could get out of Circe's bed without having had any pleasure?'

Hearing this, Oenothea sat down between us and shook her head for quite a time.

'I'm the only one who can cure that trouble,' she said. 'And don't think I'm doing anything puzzling – I want the young man to sleep the night with me. May I drop dead if I don't make it as stiff as a horn:

'All things on earth obey me. At my wish
The flowering earth grows arid, the sap dry.
At my wish its benisons spill forth.
Rocks and jagged cliffs gush out Nile waters;
For me the ocean flattens its white tops;
The zephyrs lay their blasts hushed before my feet.
The rivers obey me,
Hyrcanian tigers,[23] and dragon sentinels.
Small things to boast of! —
The orbed image of the moon descends
At the pull of my spells.
　　　The Sun-god
Turns round his foaming horses
And fear-driven retraces his orbit.
Such power have words.
The hot breath of bulls is quenched
By the rites of virgins;
Sun-child Circe transformed Ulysses' crew
With magic spells.
Proteus[24] turns into whatever shape he likes.
Expert in magical experience,
I will root Idaean trees in the sea.
Plant rivers on the topmost height.'

135. I shuddered: I was terrified by such a fabulous promise and I began scrutinizing the old woman very warily . . .

'Well,' cried Oenothea, 'now do what I tell you.' . . . And carefully washing her hands she lay on the bed and kissed me a couple of times . . .

Oenothea placed an old table in the middle of the altar and heaped red-hot coals on it. She took down a broken old cup and repaired it with some warmed pitch, then she replaced in the smoky wall a wooden nail which had come out with the cup as she pulled it down. Wearing a square cloak, she placed a great kettle on the hearth and drew out from her larder with a fork a cloth bag containing beans and an ancient piece of pig's cheek, very knocked about and with a thousand bruises on it. When she unfastened the string of the bag, she poured part of the beans on the table and ordered me to shell them carefully. I obeyed her instructions and with meticulous fingers separated the beans from their filthy pods. But with some caustic comments on my slowness, she took them herself, stripped the pods off with her teeth and spat them to the ground like dead flies.

*

I was amazed at the ingenious shifts of poverty and the sort of artistry individual objects displayed:

> No gleam of Indian ivory inlaid in gold,
> No radiance of marble underfoot,
> The earth not mocked by the earth's profusion;
> Just a thicket of husked straw on a willow frame,
> New . . . clay pots,
>   the hasty products of cheap wheels.
> Here a tank of soft limewood,
> Tough platters of wicker work,
> A wine-stained cup.
> The walls around were a stiffness
> Of dry straw and random mud —
> Held by a scattering of rustic nails,
> And hanging there a slim broom of green rushes.
> The provisions of the humble place

Hung from its smoky beam:
Bland sorb-apple,
Dried savory and raisins in bunches,
Twined in sweet-smelling wreaths . . .
In such a hut on Attic ground
Lived Hecale, hostess worthy of worship,
Whom in the years of eloquence
The Muse of inspired Callimachus[25] described
With wond'rous art.

*

136. While she cut off a small piece of the meat too, . . . and as
she put back the cheek, which was as old as she was, into the
cupboard with the fork, the rotten stool, which had given her
short body the necessary height, broke and, because of her
weight, sent the old woman sprawling into the hearth. The
neck of the kettle was broken and put out the fire, just as it was
beginning to blaze up. She burnt her elbow on a glowing piece
of wood and blackened the whole of her face with ashes she
stirred up. I got to my feet in alarm and set the old woman on
her feet, not without some amusement . . . To prevent anything
delaying the sacrifice, she immediately rushed off to some place
in the neighbourhood to relight the fire . . .

I went to the door of the cottage . . . when all of a sudden
three geese – I suppose they generally got their daily rations
from the old woman at midday – made a rush at me and to my
dismay surrounded me with an obscene and infuriated hissing.
One tore my tunic, another undid my shoe-laces and tugged at
them, and the ring-leader in this savage assault went so far as to
peck at my leg with its serrated beak. Without any messing
about, I tore a leg off the tiny table and with this weapon began
hammering at the most ferocious of the birds. And not content
with a half-hearted stroke, I avenged myself by killing the goose:

They fled like the heavenward flight
Of Stymphalian birds
From Hercules' powerful arts;
Like the Harpies,[26] dripping with filth,
When Phineus' deceptive feasts dribbled poison;

The aether tremulous and afraid,
The heavenly kingdoms confused
At the strange wailing . . .

*

The rest had already snapped up the beans, which had rolled away and spread out over the whole floor; and now, deprived, I suppose, of their leader, they had returned to the temple.

Pleased with both my bag and my revenge, I throw the dead goose behind the bed and bathe the wound in my leg, which was not deep, with vinegar. Then, fearing a row, I made up my mind to leave. Collecting my clothes I began to make my way out of the cottage, but I had not crossed the threshold when I noticed Oenothea on her way with a potful of fire. I naturally retreated, threw off my clothes and stood in the doorway as though waiting for her impatiently.

She placed the fire in the hearth – it was in some dry reeds – and after putting a lot of sticks on top, she started to explain her delay. Her friend had not let her go without her getting through the ritual three drinks.

'Here,' she said, 'what have you done while I was away? Well, where are the beans?'

I thought I'd done something to be proud of, so I gave her the whole battle in detail, and to cheer her up I offered her the goose as compensation for the loss. When the crone saw it she raised such a loud shriek that you'd have thought the geese were back in the place again. Naturally confused, in fact thunderstruck, as though my action was some strange crime, I asked her why she had flared up and why she was more sorry for the goose than for me.

137. She beat her hands together:

'You criminal,' she said, 'why go on talking? You've no idea of the great offence you've committed. You've killed Priapus' darling, the pet goose of all the ladies. Don't think it's a mere nothing you've done. If the authorities knew of this, you'd be crucified. You've polluted my house with bloodshed – the first time it's ever happened, and you've given any enemy who likes an opportunity to expel me from my post as priestess.'

*

'Please don't shout,' said I, 'I'll give you an ostrich in place of the goose.'

*

While I stood stupefied at all this, and she sat on the bed and wailed over the fate of the goose, Proselenus arrived with the provisions for the sacrifice. Seeing the dead goose, she asked how it happened and then began to cry copiously herself, and said she was deeply sorry for me – as though I'd killed my father, not a communal goose.

So, bored and tired of it all, I said:

'Tell me, can one pay compensation for sacrilege? . . . even if I insulted you, even if I'd committed a murder. Look, I'm putting down two gold pieces – you can buy gods and geese with this.'

When Oenothea saw them, she said:

'I apologize, young man. I'm worried for your sake. It's a sign of affection, not ill-will. We'll do our best to prevent anyone knowing about it. You just pray heaven forgives you for what you've done.'

> With money you've a yacht with a following breeze;
> With money you've got Lady Luck on her knees;
> You could marry Danaë[27] with cash on the nail
> And make her and her father believe the same tale.
> If you're a poet or speaker, the crowd thinks you're great,
> If you plead at the bar, Cato sounds second-rate.
> You can prove and disprove, be a lawyer of note,[28]
> Whose cases are vital for textbooks to quote.
> Whatever you wish for, if you can disburse,
> Will be there – you've a Jupiter locked in your purse.

*

She put a cup of wine under my hands and after rubbing my outstretched fingers clean with leeks and garlic, she threw some filberts into the wine, murmuring a prayer. She made various deductions from whether they came to the top or settled, but I didn't fail to notice that the empty nuts filled with air naturally stayed on the surface of the liquid, while the heavy, full nuts were carried to the bottom.

*

Cutting open the goose's breast, she extracted a very fat liver and foretold my future from it. And more, to get rid of every trace of the crime, she cut up the whole goose, spitted the pieces and prepared an elegant feast for a man who a little while ago, by her own account, was doomed . . .

Cups of strong wine passed quickly round as this went on.

*

138. Oenothea brought out a leather dildo: this she rubbed with oil and ground pepper and crushed nettle seed, and began inserting it gradually up my anus . . .

The vicious old woman then sprinkled my thighs with this liquid.

*

She mixed the juice of cress with some southern-wood, and after soaking my genitals in it, she took a green nettle-stalk and began whipping me steadily everywhere below the navel.

*

Although staggering with drink and desire, the old crones took the same route and followed in my tracks for several streets, shouting 'Stop thief!' But I got away, every one of my toes bleeding through my headlong rush.

*

'Chrysis, who detested your earlier position, intends to follow you in your present situation even at the risk of her life.'[29]

*

'What did Ariadne or Leda have to compare with her loveliness? What could Helen or Venus[30] do against her? Paris[31] himself, judge in the contest of goddesses, if he'd seen her with his roving eyes when making his comparison, he would have given up Helen *and* the goddesses for her. If I were allowed just to take a kiss, or embrace that divine and heavenly breast, perhaps my body would recover its strength and the parts that I'm positive are drugged by some witches' brew would revive. It's not her insults that make me reluctant. I overlook the whipping. I was thrown out, but I regard that as a joke. Only let me back into her good graces . . .'

*

139. I tossed and turned in bed, groping continually, after some image of my beloved . . .

*

> Others have been hounded by gods
> And implacable fate, not I alone.
> Hercules hounded from Argos,
> And propping heaven on his shoulders.
> Impious Laomedon
> And those two angry immortals:
> He paid the price of his offences.
> Pelias felt the weight of Juno.
> Then there was Telephus —
> He took up arms in his ignorance.
> Even Ulysses went in fear of Neptune's power.
> Now I too take my stand among these —
> Over land and white Nereus' sea, I am hounded
> By the mighty rage of Priapus of Hellespont.[32]

*

I started by asking my dear Giton whether anyone had been asking for me.

'No one today,' he said, 'but yesterday quite an elegant lady came to the door and after a long conversation, when she wore me out with irrelevant chatter, she finally said you ought to be punished and you would suffer as a slave should if you took offence and persisted in your ill-feelings.'

*

I had not yet finished when Chrysis arrived and clasped me in a most unrestrained embrace, saying:

'I've got you in my arms just as I'd hoped. You are my only desire, my only pleasure in life. You will never put out the fire I feel unless you quench it in my blood.'

*

One of the new servants hurried up and swore that our master was furious with me because I'd been absent from my duties for over two days. I'd be well advised to prepare some suitable excuse, as it was highly unlikely his rage would calm down without someone getting the whip.

*

EUMOLPUS AND THE
EXTORTIONISTS

140. There was one highly respectable matron, Philomela by name, who had extorted a great many legacies while she had the advantages of her youth. By now she was an old woman and her bloom had gone, so she forced her son and daughter on childless old men and by means of these deputies managed to continue her profession. Naturally she came to Eumolpus and started by handing over her children to his wisdom and upright nature; to him alone could she entrust herself and her prayers. He was the only one on earth who could manage every day to instil sound principles into young people. In fact, she was leaving her children in Eumolpus' house so that they could listen to his talk ... which was the only legacy that could be given to young people.

She was as good as her word. She left the very pretty daughter with her youthful brother in his room and pretended she was going off to the temple to say the appropriate prayers.

Eumolpus, who was such a sexual miser that he even regarded me as a boy, did not hesitate a moment to invite the girl to the rituals of the buttocks. But he had told everyone that he had gout and a weakness in the loins, and if he did not keep this pretence intact, he would be in danger of ruining the whole show. So to ensure that his deception was not discredited, he begged the girl to sit on top of the upright nature to which she had been entrusted, and ordered Corax to get under the bed he was lying in and, with his hands placed on the floor, to move his master with his own thighs. He carried out the order phlegmatically and the expertise of the girl responded with similar movements. When things were looking forward to the climax, Eumolpus called loudly to Corax to press on with the job. Placed in this way between his servant and his lady friend the old man looked as though he was playing on a swing. Eumolpus repeated this performance a few times amid howls of laughter, including his own.

And so I for my part, not to get out of the habit through lack of practice, approached the brother, as he admired his sister's tricks through the key-hole, and tried to see if he would accept my advances. The well-trained little fellow did not withdraw from my caresses, but divine hostility dogged me there too.

*

'There are mightier gods who have restored me to full health. Mercury,[1] who leads souls away and leads them back, by his kindnesses has returned me what was cut off by the hand of vengeance. So you may take it that I am more favoured than Protesilaus[2] or anyone like him in history.'

With this I lifted my tunic and showed all I had to Eumolpus. At first he was horrified, then to convince himself fully, he held in both hands the gifts of the gods.

*

'Socrates, the wisest of all in the opinion of the gods and men, used to boast that he had never looked inside a tavern and never trusted his eyesight at any assembly with a large crowd. There is nothing more profitable than a continuous dialogue with wisdom' . . .

'All of that is true,' I said, 'and no one should come to grief quicker than those who are after what belongs to others. How would a confidence man or a pickpocket survive, if he didn't drop little boxes or chinking purses into the crowd to hook his victims? Just as dumb animals are snared with food, so men can't be caught unless they are nibbling hopefully at something.'

*

141. 'The ship with your money and servants has not arrived from Africa as you promised. The legacy-hunters are already drained dry and are cutting down on their generosity. So if I'm not mistaken, fortune is beginning to have her regrets again.'

*

'All those who have legacies in my will, except for my freedmen, will receive what I have left them only on this condition – that they cut up my corpse and eat it in front of the people.'

*

'We know that among certain races the custom of the dead being eaten by their relations is still observed. So much so that sick people are often reproached for causing their flesh to deteriorate. I therefore call on my friends not to shrink from my demands, but eat my body in the same spirit as they damned my soul . . .'

The enormous reputation of his money blinded the eyes and hearts of the poor fools.

Gorgias[3] was ready to carry out the terms . . .

*

'I have no worries about your stomach's balking. It will obey your command if you promise it a lot of luxuries as compensation for one hour's disgust. Just close your eyes and pretend you are eating a million sesterces, not human offal. Then for another thing, we'll find some seasonings to change the taste. After all, no meat is pleasant by itself; it's artfully adulterated in some way and made acceptable to the reluctant stomach. And if you want the idea to be justified by examples too, there are the Saguntines, who ate human flesh when they were besieged by Hannibal – and they weren't expecting a legacy. The Petelians did the same in the last stages of a famine and all they were after with this feast was to avoid dying of starvation. When Numantia[4] was captured by Scipio, there were some mothers found carrying around at their breasts the half-eaten bodies of their own children.'[5]

THE FRAGMENTS AND
THE POEMS

I

Servius (late 4th c. A.D.) on Virgil, *Aeneid* 3.57: *auri sacra fames*] *sacra* means accursed. The expression derives from a custom of the Gauls. Whenever the inhabitants of Massilia suffer from a plague, one of their poor people offers himself to be fed at the public expense for a whole year on special religious foods. Afterwards he is dressed in sprigs of sacred foliage and certain ritually prescribed clothing and led round the whole city with curses, so that the ills of the whole city will fall upon him. He is then cast out. This is in Petronius.

II

Servius on Virgil, *Aeneid* 12.159 (on the feminine gender of nouns ending in *-tor*): If, however, the nouns are not derived from a verb, they are of common gender. Both the masculine and feminine end similarly in *-tor*, e.g. a male and a female *senator,* a male and female *balneator* (bath attendant), although Petronius employs a form *balneatrix* in his writings.

III

Pseudacro (*c.* A.D. 400) on Horace, *Epodes* 5.48: *Canidia rodens pollicem*] he has described the bearing and movements of Canidia in a fury. Petronius, to describe someone in a rage, says 'with her thumb bitten to danger point'.

IV

Sidonius Apollinaris (*c*. A.D. 450), *Carmen* 23:

145.   What shall I say to you, glories of Latin eloquence,
          Cicero of Arpinum, Livy of Padua, and Mantuan Virgil . . .
155.   And you, Arbiter, worshipper of the sacred stump
          Amid the gardens of Massilia,
          A match for Priapus of the Hellespont.

V

Priscian (early 6th c. A.D.), *Principles of Grammar* 8.16 (*GL* 2.381) and 11.29 (*ibid.* 567) (among examples of past participles of deponent verbs with passive meaning): Petronius 'soul embraced (*amplexam*) to our breast'.

Vb

Boethius (A.D. 480–524) in his comments on Porphyry's *Introduction to Aristotle's Categories* (translated by Victorinus), *Dialogue* 2.32: 'I will do that very willingly,' I said, 'but since the morning sun, as Petronius has it, has smiled upon the roofs, let us get up and if there is anything in that matter, it will be discussed later with more careful consideration.'

VI

Fulgentius (A.D. 532–567) *Mythologies* 1 p. 12 ff. (*Helm*): You do not know . . . how much ladies shrink from satire. Although even lawyers give way under a woman's flood of words and schoolteachers do not even mumble, although rhetoricians are silent and public announcers hush their noise, there is one thing alone that imposes some moderation on their madness, though it be Petronius' character Albucia who is in heat.

VII

Fulgentius *ibid*. 3.8 p. 73 (on the extreme heat of myrrh extract): So Petronius Arbiter too tells us he drank a draught of myrrh to arouse his sexual desires. [This is in Book XIV, where Quartilla is in the company of Ascyltus and Encolpius and, to allow the latter to drink a second toast, gave him Ascyltus' portion to drink. Then Quartilla says 'Has Encolpius drunk all the satyrion there was?']

VIII

Fulgentius in his *Treatise on the Contents of Virgil's Works* p. 98 ff.: Now we earlier explained the fable of the three-headed Cerberus by way of a quarrel and litigation in court; compare Petronius' hostile description of Euscios – 'he was a Cerberus in court'.

IX

Fulgentius in his *Explanation of Archaic Words* 42 p. 122: A mess of various meats is called a course or dish (*ferculum*), compare Petronius – 'after the course was brought to the table'.

X

Fulgentius *ibid*. 46 p. 123: *valgia* (wry twists) are contortions of the lips due to vomiting; compare Petronius 'with his lips wryly twisted'.

XI

Fulgentius *ibid.* 52 p. 124: *alucinare* (to have hallucinations) is
the term for dreaming nonsensical dreams. It derives from *alu-
citae*, which we call mosquitoes. So Petronius says, 'for the
mosquitoes (*alucitae*) were bothering my companion'.

XII

Fulgentius *ibid.* 60 p. 126: *manubies* (booty) means the orna-
ments that kings wear; compare Petronius, 'the *manubies* of so
many kings found in the possession of a runaway slave'.

XIII

Fulgentius *ibid.* 60 p. 126: *Aumatium* (little eye) is the term for
a public privy of the sort found in theatres or in the circus;
compare Petronius, 'I flung myself into a privy'.

XIV

Isidorus Hispalensis (A.D. 602–36) in the *Origines* v. 26.7:
dolus (guile) is mental cunning, so termed because it beguiles
(*deludat*): it does one thing and feigns another. Petronius thinks
otherwise for he says: 'What is guile, gentlemen of the jury?
Surely when something has been done which guys the law. You
have your guile, now let me tell you about an evil (*malum*).'

XV

From the *Glossary of St Dionysius (Petrus Daniel)*: *petaurus*
(= *petaurum*, a spring-board or see-saw) is a kind of game;

compare Petronius, 'and at the demand of the spring-board now higher (now lower)'.

XVI

Ibid.: Petronius, 'there was general agreement that they did not usually go through the Neapolitan tunnel without bending'.

[XVII *Bücheler*]

[Another Glossary (used by Pierre Pithou): *suppes suppumpis*, that is 'with feet bent backwards'. *Tullia, media vel regia* (Tullia, middle or royal).]

[XVIII *Bücheler*]

[Nicoló Perotti, *Cornucopiae* p. 200, 26 (Aldine edition, 1513) Cosmus was an excellent manufacturer of perfumes and Cosmian perfumes are named after him. The same author has 'and though he be smothered in a whole jugful from Cosmus' (Juvenal 8.86). Petronius, 'bring us, he said, an alabaster box of Cosmian'.]

XIX

Terentianus Maurus (late 2nd c. A.D.), *On the Metres of Horace* (*GL* 6.399):

> We see the poet Horace
> Nowhere used such verses
> In regular succession,
> But the Arbiter so eloquent
> Packs them in his writings.
> You can recognize them

In lines we like to chant, as:
'Girls of Memphis origin,
Trained for godly services'
'Tinged with darkness' colouring,
Boy with hands loquacious'.

Marius Victorinus (d. *c.* A.D. 360) 3.17 (*GL* 6.138): We know that certain lyrical poets inserted some verses of this metre and form in their poems, as we find also in the Arbiter. An example of his is:

'Girls of Memphis origin,
Trained for godly services'

and again,

'Tinged with darkness' colouring,
Choruses Egyptian.'

XX

Terentianus Maurus *op. cit.* (*GL* 6.409, 2849–2858, 2861–2865):

The division which we speak of
Gives the metre old Anacreon
Used in his sweet singing.
We find Petronius used it,
When he says that lyric poet
Sang songs befitting Muses
(And many others used it).
But that verse of our Petronius —
iuverunt segetes meum laborem:
(The harvest helped my labour)
I'll show you its caesura —
iuverunt starts as hexameter:

What's left, *segetes meum laborem*
Is like *triplici vides ut ortu*
'Seest thou with triple rising
The Moon her fire revolving,
And Phoebus with swift axle
Traverse the rapid globe.'

Marius Victorinus 4.1 (*GL* 6.153): ... The metre will be Anacreontic, inasmuch as Anacreon used it most frequently, but many poets used it in our literature, among them the Arbiter has this in his writings:

'Seest thou with triple rising
The Moon her fire revolving,
And Phoebus with swift axle
Traverse the rapid globe.'

XXI

Diomedes Thrax (late 4th c. A.D.) in his *Grammar* (*GL* 1.518): From this comes also that caesura, an example of which Petronius offers in:

'An old woman stewed in wine,
With trembling lips.'

XXII

Servius (late 4th c. A.D.) in his *Exposition of the Grammar of Donatus* (*GL* 4.432, 22): Again, he uses '*Quirites*' (citizens) only in the plural. But we read in Horace '*hunc Quiritem*' (this citizen) as though the nominative were 'this *Quiris*'. Again Horace also writes '*quis te Quiritem?*' ('Who – you a citizen?') where the nominative would be *hic Quirites,* a form used by Petronius.

Pompeius (5th c. A.D.) in his *Commentary on the Grammar of Donatus* (GL 5.167, 9): No one says '*hic* (this) *Quirites*' (citizen) but '*hi* (these) *Quirites*' (citizens), although we will find the former. Read in Petronius and you will find this done with the nominative singular, and so Petronius says '*hic Quirites*'.

XXIII

Anonymous, *On Nouns of Uncertain Gender* (GL 5.578, 23): *Fretum* (sea-strait) is neuter and its plural is *freta*, cf. Petronius '*freta Nereidum*' (straits of the sea-nymphs).

XXIV

St Jerome (*c.* A.D. 348–420) in his *Letter to Demetriades* 130.19: curled and waved boys, their skins smelling like foreign mice, the virgin should avoid like some plague and poison of chastity. The Arbiter's line refers to them:

['he who always smells nice has not a nice smell']

XXV

Fulgentius, *Mythologies* 2.6 p. 45 f. (*Helm*): although Nicagorus tells us that (*Prometheus*) first gave rise to the image and describes the exposure of his liver to the vulture as an allegory of spite. Hence too Petronius' lines:

> The vulture that picks through the torn liver,
> Tears out the breast, each inmost part,
> Is not the creature witty poets aver,
> But Lust and Spite, the cankers of the heart.

XXVI

AL 690:

So the crow flies against Nature's way
By laying eggs when the corn is high;

So the bear gives birth, then licks its cub
Into shape; fish spawn, uncoupled in love;

So Apollo's tortoise, free of parental chains,
Cares for its eggs with warm nostrils in the sand;

So the sexless bee, roused from its web of wax,
Swarms and refills its empty ranks.

Nature's not happy with a limited range,
But delights in all variety and change.

XXVII

AL 466:

Fear invented the gods.
Lightning flashing from a high heaven,
Walls riven by the flame,
Athos kindled beneath the blow,
Phoebus descending beneath the traversed earth
For his new risings,
The decay of the moon and its glory recovered,
Stars scattered over all the world,
And the year divided into changing months.
The vice took hold – vain superstition
Bade farmers offer first fruits to Ceres,
Bind Bacchus with full palms,
Let Pales rejoice at the shepherds' hands.
A hazard to every sailor,

Neptune from the depths claims the waters,
Pallas the streets and inns.
Every guilty wish, every venial instinct
Invents its own gods in greedy competition.

XXVIII

AL 476:
People would rather swallow a lighted candle
Than keep a secret that smacks in the least of scandal.
The quietest whisper in the royal hall
Is out in a flash buttonholing passers-by against a wall;
And it's not enough that it's broadcast to the nation —
Everyone gets it with improvement and elaboration.
So the servant, not being sufficiently stealthy
To play the gossip and stay alive and healthy,
Dug a hole and split the news into that
About the ears His Majesty was hiding under the royal hat.
The hole took the story to its bosom and in less time than it takes
    to utter,
The reeds started to mutter
And begin
To let out the whole story that Midas was trying to keep in.

XXIX

AL 650:
Our eyes deceive, the vagrant senses lie,
When reason's overborne. You tower hard by
Rises four-square, but from the distant ground
Looks circular, its angles worn and round.
Full stomach shrinks from honey, often the nose
From cinnamon. Conflicts in taste arose,
Because the senses in predestined suit
Wrangle in their continual dispute.

XXX

AL 651:

Dreams,
The fleeting shadow-play that mocks the mind,
Issue from no temples,
No heavenly power sends them —
Each man creates his own.
When prostrate limbs grow heavy
And the play of the mind is unchecked,
The mind enacts in darkness
The dramas of daylight.

The shatterer of cities in war,
Who fires unlucky towns,
Sees flying spears, broken ranks, the death of kings,
Plains awash with spilt blood.
The barrister pleads again in nightmare,
Sees the twelve tables, the court, the guarded bench.
The miser salts away his money
To find his gold dug up.
The hunter flushes the woodland with his hounds.
The sailor dreams he is doomed,
Drags out of the sea the upturned poop,
Or clings to it.
The mistress scribbles a note to her lover;
The guilty lover sends a gift . . .
And the hound in his slumbers bays at the hare's tracks.
[The pangs of unhappiness last
Into the watches of the night.]

XXXI

AL 464:

Each to his taste: what this one scorns
Another likes; roses one plucks, another thorns.

XXXII

AL 465:

> Autumn had shattered the shadows' glowing line,
> The cool-reined sun looked down on colder skies,
> The plane-tree's leaves were falling and the vine
> Had stripped to count its grapes: before our eyes
> The old year's promises were now redeemed.

XXXIII

AL 467:

> I would not steep my hair in the same old oil,
> Nor woo my stomach with too familiar wine.
> Bulls love to change the valley where they graze;
> And wild beasts fill their maw with changing prey.

XXXIV

AL 468:

> I should love my wife like my income:
> But I must confess to my shame
> That I wouldn't love my income
> If I thought it would stay the same.

XXXV

AL 469:

> Youth, leave your home for alien shores.
> For you now dawns a mightier day;
> Be strong, and the Danube, that last boundary,
> The icy North and the safe Egyptian realms,
> The nations of the morn and setting sun,
> Will learn of you: he who descends
> On distant sands becomes a greater man.

XXXVI

AL 470:
There's some use in everything, sometime, somehow —
In trouble, what you've thrown away seems so useful now;
When the boat goes down and the strongroom bullion too,
It's the floating oars that save the drowning crew;
When the trumpet sounds, the sword's at the rich man's throat,
And the poor man stands there safe, in his ragged coat.

XXXVII

AL 471:
My little house has its safe roof above;
Wine-laden grapes hang from the fruitful elm.
The boughs are hung with cherries; my orchards grow
Their reddening apples and the olive grove
Is cracking with its lavish freight. And where
The airy garden drinks its channelled streams,
The saffron plant, the creeping mallows thrive,
And poppies promising their carefree sleep.
Then, should I wish to weave my snares for birds,
Or set my traps to catch the quivering deer,
Or pull up timid fish on slender lines,
These are the only tricks my fields have known.
So go and sell the hours of life that flies
For rich men's feasts. The same death waits for me:
May it find me here to judge the time I've spent.

XXXVIII

AL 472:
Is it not enough, engulfed by maddened youths,
With damned and blackened name, we're swept off course?
Look, slaves and home-born rabble run amok
And wanton through our hard-won hoard of wealth.

Cheap slaves have kings' estates, and prison cells
Scorn Vesta and the hut of Romulus.
So virtue lies abject in deepest mud:
The fleet of the unjust flaunts whiter sails.

XXXIX

AL 473:
So the body will immure the belly's wind,
Which, labouring to emerge from those deep depths again,
Searches with blows for a way; and the cold shiver
That masters the constricted bones will never cease
Till the warm sweat bedews the loosened frame.

XL

AL 474:
O shore and sea more sweet to me than life!
What luck to come so soon to lands I love!
O lovely day! In these fields long ago
I used to rouse the Naiads as I swam.
The pool of the spring is here; yonder the kelp
In the bay. A haven safe for secret loves.
I have lived. And Fortune's bite can never wrench
From me those joys time past once gave.

XLI

AL 475:
This said, he tore white hair from 's trembling head,
And rent his cheeks; from 's eyes a rain of tears,
But as the evil flood sweeps through the dales,
When melts the frigid snow, and soft south wind
Brooks not the ice to press the prison'd earth,
So in full spate his face ran tears; his heart
In deepest grief resounds with troubled moans.

XLII

AL 477:
There sea and sky in battle win by turns;
Here smiles the sward, pierced through with dainty streams.
There sailors mourn their sunken barque;
Here shepherds water sheep from gentle banks.
There death confronts and stops the gape of greed;
Here Harvest gladly bows to sickle blades.
There thirst, dry-jawed, burns up amid the foam;
Here lavish kisses shower on faithless men.
Let Ulysses in tatters tire the tide;
The fair Penelope will live on land.

XLIII

AL 478:
If there's no haste to die, to force the fates
To break the tender threads with eager hands,
Then test thus far the anger of the deep.
Look where the ebbing tide flows back and bathes
One's feet, still safe, with gentle waves.
Look where the mussel rolls in seaweed green
And the slipp'ry shell with raucous whorl is trapped.
Look where the tides toss back the rolling sands,
And coloured pebbles end on rippled flats.
Whoever can tread here, here let him play,
Safe on the shore, and think just this is sea.

XLIV

AL 479:
Beauty is not enough; who wishes to be fair
Must not content herself with average care.
Talk, be witty and smile to show your wit —

If Nature's unaided, nothing comes of it.
Art is Beauty's aid, her finest dress:
Beauty, if scornful, dies of nakedness.

XLV

AL 691:

India bore me on shores purple as Tyre,
Where the white dawn rises in an orb of fire;
A creature born here, divine honours among,
I changed a barbaric noise for the Latin tongue;
Delphic Apollo, dismiss your every swan —
My parrot voice a worthier myrmidon.

XLVI

AL 692:

Shipwrecked, a sailor finds another
            stunned by the same blow
And tells his story.
Crops ruined by hail,
            a whole year's labour with them,
The farmer weeps out his troubles
On a breast similarly afflicted.
At funerals the bereaved weep in concert —
Death the leveller.
We too will hammer at the stars
            with antiphonal complaints.
I have heard that prayers
Fly more bravely linked.

XLVII

AL 218:

> You send me golden apples, Marcia dear,
> You send me gifts of shaggy chestnut too;
> For those I'm grateful, but if you came here,
> You'd bring your choicest gift, my love, just you.
> And if you wish, crab-apples you may bring,
> Your honeyed lips would make them sweet to taste.
> Yet if you must deny my welcoming,
> Just kiss the fruit; I'll eat it up in haste.

XLVIII

AL 693:

> If you are Phoebus' sister, I entrust my cause
> To you to plead it in your brother's ears,
> Delia. Address him so: O Delphic one,
> I built for you a temple of Sicilian stone,
> And sang you honest songs on slender reed.
> O God Apollo, show me the coins I need.

XLIX

AL 694:

> All that might hush our piteous earthly cries
> An honest god has set before our eyes.
> These common herbs, the berries in the rough
> Brambles are for our belly pangs enough.
> With rivers near, who but the fool feels drought,
> Or leaves his hearth to face East winds without?
> The sword of law blocks in the ravening bride;
> No girl in lawful sheets needs ever hide.
> Rich Nature gives enough to satisfy:
> Endless the claims of unchecked vanity.

L

AL 695:

>   In a soldier's bonnet there nested a dove
>   To prove the alliance of Mars and of Love.

LI

AL 696:

>   A Jew may adore his god in the sty
>   And pour out his woes in the ears of the sky,
>   But unless he will shorten his scabbard to see
>   That the tip of his penis will always hang free,
>   He'll be driven from home to a city in Greece
>   And spend all his Sabbaths – eating in peace.

LII

AL 697:

>   Brave hands are the one nobility,
>   Sole sign of a heart that is free.

LIII

AL 698:

>   My bed was soft, the early night was bliss.
>   My drowsy eyes surrender – Love broke my rest
>   And shook me by the hair in wild protest.
>   Nails ripped my flesh. 'To waste a night like this!
>   You're mine,' he said. 'You broke a thousand hearts,
>   Can you, hard-hearted, lie alone and rest?'
>   I leap from bed, barefoot and barely dressed;
>   I try each road, but all roads are false starts.

I run, but hate to go or to retreat,
Then stand ashamed to halt, so late abroad.
No song of birds, no watchdog even roared,
No human voice, no bustle in the streets.
Alone of all, I fear my bed and sleep:
At your command, great Love, your watch I keep.

LIV

AL 699:

Long may our hearts, Nealce, guard that night,
When first you came to me as I lay still;
The bed, its guardian spirit, the silent light –
They saw your soft submission to my will.
So come, let us endure, though youth has passed,
And use those years that have so short a stay.
Justice and Law allow old loves to last:
Make our quick love go not so quick away.

LV

AL 700:

Its joys are short and nasty,
And end in quick disgust
So let us not be hasty:
In blind and beastly lust
Love wanes, its glow departing –
So let's be slow in starting;
Let's lie here sharing kisses
On an endless holiday.
There's no sweeter rest than this is
(Without a blush to pay),
An endless new beginning
That never dies away.

LVI

AL 701:

> Reproach and Love, all in one moment,
> For Hercules himself would be a torment.

LVII

AL 786:

> Before my birth the gods, they say,
> Discussed what sex I'd be.
> 'Boy!' said Phoebus; 'Girl!' said Mars;
> Said Juno, 'I disagree.'
> So I was born hermaphrodite,
> But how was I to die?
> The goddess was first with the answer:
> 'The sword!' Said Mars, 'The cross!'
> But Phoebus decided on drowning.
> So I had to die of them all.
> A tree hung over a stream,
> Wearing my sword, I climbed –
> A slip, we were driven together:
> My feet caught in a branch,
> My head dipped into the stream –
> Not woman, not man, yet both:
> River and Sword and Cross.

List of Characters*

Agamemnon: Teacher of rhetoric at Puteoli, with whom Encolpius is arguing at the opening of the work. He takes the three heroes to dinner with Trimalchio. He is named after Agamemnon, leader of the Greek expedition to Troy, and his assistant is appropriately named Menelaus after Agamemnon's brother, the husband of Helen.

Agatho: A cosmetician (74.15). Literally, 'Goodman'.

Albucia: An unknown woman (Fgt. VI). Literally, 'Littlewhite'.

Ascyltus: Encolpius' companion and later enemy. In Greek his name means 'untroubled' or 'unmolested' or perhaps 'indefatigable'.

Bargates: A landlord and friend of Eumolpus. The name is Semitic.

Cario: A slave of Trimalchio. The name signifies a Carian and was a common slave name.

Carpus: Another common slave name. Here it is the name of Trimalchio's carver (36 ff.). It means 'harvest' in Greek.

Cerberus: The three-headed watchdog of Hades. Used metaphorically in Fgt. VIII.

Chrysanthus: A lately dead friend of Seleucus and others in Trimalchio's circle (42.3). Literally 'Goldflower'.

Chrysis: Circe's supercilious maid (128 ff.). Literally, 'Golden Girl'.

Cinnamus: Trimalchio's steward. Literally, 'Cinnamon'.

Circe: The would-be mistress of Encolpius, named after the witch who captivates Odysseus in Homer's *Odyssey*.

Corax: Eumolpus' hired servant. The name, often given to slaves, means literally 'raven'.

Corinth: Trimalchio's manufacturer of Corinthian ware (50.4).

Croesus: Trimalchio's little favourite (64.5). The name of a wealthy king of Lydia.

---

* I have listed the main characters in the *Satyricon* and the accepted Fragments, giving where requisite the literal meaning of the names which, no doubt, Petronius chose deliberately. JPS

Daedalus: Trimalchio's ingenious cook. In mythology Daedalus was the prototype of the great inventor.

Dama: A friend of Trimalchio's (41.10). The name is Greek for 'tamer'.

Diogenes: C. Pompeius, a friend of Trimalchio's (38.10). Literally, 'Heaven-born'. The reader might think of Diogenes the Cynic.

Dionysus: A young slave of Trimalchio's. In mythology, the great god of wine and ecstasy.

Doris: Apparently a former mistress of Encolpius. Literally, 'a Dorian woman'.

Echion: A friend of Trimalchio's, a rag-collector. Literally, a sort of plant.

Encolpius: The hero (or anti-hero) of the work. In other authors, such as Martial, his name is given to homosexual favourites. Literally, the name means 'embraced'.

Endymion: A mysterious boy who appears in the novel, probably due to an interpolator. In mythology, he is a beautiful and eternally sleeping youth beloved by the moon-goddess, Selene.

Eumolpus: A pederastic poet, critic, and fraud, who befriends Encolpius and masterminds the affair at Croton. In Greek the name means 'sweet singer'.

Euscios: A vague character mentioned in Fgt. VIII. Literally in Greek 'Pleasantly Shadowy'.

Fortunata: Trimalchio's wife. Literally in Latin, 'Blessed by Fortune'.

Gaius: i.e. Petronius. Cf Introduction, p. xiv.

Ganymedes: A guest of Trimalchio's. In mythology Ganymede, a Trojan prince, became cup-bearer and lover of Zeus. The English noun 'catamite' is derived from the name.

Giton: Encolpius' beloved. His name is Greek for 'neighbour'.

Gorgias: A Crotonian legacy-hunter, who seems to stop at nothing. His famous namesake was a great orator and Sophist.

Habinnas: Close friend of Trimalchio's, a monumental mason and one of the more important men at Puteoli. The name is Semitic.

Hedyle: Apparently the wife of Lichas, whom Encolpius seems to have seduced (113.3). Literally, 'Little Sweety'.

Hermeros: A guest of Trimalchio's. He seems to be sitting next to Encolpius and takes exception to Ascyltus' sneers. Literally, 'Love of Hermes'. A gladiator of the period with the same name is mentioned in c. 52.

Hesus: A superstitious passenger on board Lichas' ship. The name has connotations of 'clinging'.

Julius Proculus: A guest of Trimalchio (38.16).

Lichas: A ship captain from Tarentum and an old enemy of Encolpius. The name would be connected with 'licking'.

Lycurgus: A mysterious figure from some missing portion of the work; he had been a cruel host to Encolpius, who has apparently murdered him. His villa may have been the source of the trio's gold. The wolfish name also belonged to a cruel mythical King of Thrace.

M. Mannicius: Owner of the block of flats in which Encolpius and Eumolpus are staying.

Massa: A favourite young slave of Habinnas. Literally, 'Lump'.

Menelaus: Agamemnon's second in command at his school.

Menophila: The mate of Philargyrus, one of Trimalchio's slaves. Literally, 'Lover of Strength'.

Niceros: One of the most interesting guests of Trimalchio. The name connotes both victory and passion.

Oenothea: A dissolute priestess of Priapus at Croton. Her name means literally 'wine-goddess'.

Pannychis: An immature slave girl, belonging to Quartilla. Literally, 'the All-night Girl'.

Petraites: 'Rocky' was a gladiator of the period.

Philargyrus: A slave belonging to Trimalchio. Literally, 'Lover of Silver'.

Phileros: A guest of Trimalchio. Literally, 'Fond of Love'.

Philomela: A corrupt matron at Croton, who sells her children for legacies. The name also of the song-loving nightingale.

Plocamus: A guest of Trimalchio. Literally, 'Lock of Hair'.

Polyaenus: Encolpius' pseudonym at Croton. An Homeric epithet of Ulysses, meaning 'much-praised'.

C. Pompeius: See DIOGENES.

Priapus: The god of fertility who hounds Encolpius through the book and whom he constantly and inadvertently offends.

Proculus: See JULIUS PROCULUS.

Proselenus: An old bawd adept at magic. Literally, 'Older than the Moon'.

Psyche: The maid of Quartilla. Literally, 'Soul'.

Quartilla: Priestess of Priapus. The name is a diminutive of the Roman first name for 'Fourth in sequence'.

Scintilla: The wife of Habinnas. Literally, 'Spark'.

Scissa: Literally, 'Cut Up'; a sentimental friend of Habinnas.

Scylax: Trimalchio's dog. The name is Greek for 'puppy'.

Seleucus: A guest of Trimalchio. The name belonged to various powerful Eastern rulers in the fourth and third centuries B.C.

Serapa: Trimalchio's astrologer. The name belonged to an Egyptian deity.

Stichus: A slave of Trimalchio, who is in charge of Trimalchio's funeral arrangements. Literally, 'Line', a common slave name.

Trimalchio (the name means literally 'thrice-blessed' and is basically Semitic): the great vulgarian ex-slave, whose dinner occupies most of the extant fragments of the work.

Tryphaena (the Greek meaning of the name is 'luxury'): a prostitute from South Italy with whom Encolpius and Giton had dealings in some lost part of the work and who figures in c. 100.7 ff.

Notes

The Satyricon

At the School of Rhetoric

1. *I got these wounds fighting for your freedom*: Our text begins with Encolpius in mid-rant about the state of education today. Elite young Romans would be thoroughly trained in the art of oratory, and Agamemnon, to whom Encolpius is directing his diatribe, is a teacher of rhetoric. Displaying one's wounds in order to impress an audience was a common oratorical technique, a well-known example of which is Marius' performance in Sallust, *Jugurtha* 85.29.

2. *pompous subjects . . . thunder of platitudes*: Encolpius' criticisms of rhetorical training chime with those found elsewhere (e.g. Seneca the Elder, *Controversiae* 1, preface 6–10; Quintilian 2.10.1–15; Tacitus, *Dialogue on Orators* 1, 28–9, 31, 35), but their primary purpose here is to characterize Encolpius as a *scholasticus*, 'egghead': a stock figure of ridicule.

3. *pirates standing . . . virgins during a plague*: The hypothetical scenarios in the rhetorical exercises given to students really were as outrageous as Encolpius' list implies. Highlights are collected in Seneca the Elder's *Controversiae*.

4. *just so much poppycock*: Sullivan's translation captures Encolpius' scorn, but loses the food metaphor in the Latin. A more literal version would be 'sprinkled with poppy seed and sesame', the first of many occasions in which narrative is envisaged as food.

5. *Sophocles or Euripides . . . Demosthenes*: Sophocles and Euripides are two of the greatest Greek tragedians (5th–4th century BC). Pindar is conventionally counted among the nine lyric poets (the others being Bacchylides, Sappho, Anacreon, Alcaeus, Stesichorus, Alcman, Ibycus and Simonides). Sullivan noted that

Corinna is sometimes added to the list, which would give us the required total of nine, but it is also possible that Encolpius made an error. The lyric poets flourished 8th–5th centuries BC and 'shrank away' from the epic poetry of Homer by composing in lyric metres rather than hexameters. Plato and Demosthenes (both 4th century BC) were equally renowned for stylistic innovations in their respective fields, philosophy and oratory.

6. *from Asia to Athens*: The 'Asiatic' style of oratory was exuberant and florid, in contrast to the restraint and simplicity of the 'Attic' style, whose followers emulated the Greek orators of the 5th and 4th century BC. These are, of course, political terms, and to accuse an orator of being 'Asiatic' was a clichéd means of one-upmanship. The irony here is that Encolpius is using precisely the kind of the over-emotional rhetoric that he is criticizing.

7. *Thucydides or Hyperides*: Thucydides was the renowned 5th-century historian of the Peloponnesian War; Hyperides a great 4th-century orator. They make an uneasy pairing, as Thucydides' prose style might be thought too convoluted to be a good model for an orator; once again, Encolpius' criticisms reflect badly on him.

8. *the unscrupulous Egyptians*: Uncertain what technique in Egyptian art is intended.

9. *Cicero says . . . schools"*: From *Pro Caelio* (*In Defense of Caelius*), 41.

10. *spongers in drama*: The parasite, who sponged off the wealthy, was a stock figure in ancient comedy.

11. *the manner of Lucilius*: i.e. fast and furious improvisation. Lucilius (*c.* 180–102 BC) was the earliest and most savage of the Roman satirists; he boasted that he could improvise 200 verses an hour standing on one foot, an approach that earned the disapproval of Horace (*Satires* 1.10).

12. *Humiliating invitations to drunken dinners*: Ironic criticism given Agamemnon's later behaviour at Trimalchio's feast.

13. *Lacedaemonian colony*: Possibly Tarentum in Italy, which was once a Spartan (i.e. Lacedaemonian) colony.

14. *home of the Sirens*: Traditionally thought to be near Naples. These mythical creatures, part woman, part bird, lured sailors to their deaths with the irresistible sweetness of their songs (*Odyssey* 12). See also ch. 127.

15. *Pierian spring*: Pieria was a region of Greece said to be the home of the Muses, the deities who presided over the arts and sciences. To 'drink from the Pierian spring' thus means to become inspired by the Muses.

Adventures with Ascyltus and Giton

1. *where our lodging was*: The precise setting of this scene is unknown. We later learn that the town is an important trading port and, given that it is not far from Trimalchio's villa, is likely to be one of the towns on the Bay of Naples. Sullivan took it to be Puteoli, modern Pozzuoli; this is possible, but not certain.

2. *aphrodisiac*: The Latin is *satyrion*, 'satyr-plant'; on which see Pliny, *Natural History* 26.10. The pun on its title prompts the question: is the novel itself an aphrodisiac? Greek romances were thought by some to put readers in an erotic mood, but *Satyri_on* is arguably as much an emetic as an aphrodisiac.

3. *my little friend*: The word that Sullivan translated as 'little friend' is *frater*, which means 'brother'. It is unusual to find *frater* used to denote an erotic relationship.

4. *Lucretia . . . Tarquin*: Lucretia, an exemplary wife to Collatinus, was raped by Tarquin, son of the king of Rome; this led to her suicide and the end of Rome's monarchy (Livy 1.57–9; Ovid, *Fasti* 2.685–852).

5. *It was*: There are significant lacunae in the text before this chapter and the following episode with Quartilla. As Sullivan noted, it is possible that both of these scenes are misplaced, that they came from an earlier part of the novel. We can deduce that the young men stole a cloak and, through Encolpius' folly, they lost it and the gold that they had also stolen.

6. *free of that loathsome suspicion*: It would appear that Ascyltus has accused Encolpius of filching their money.

7. *Cynics*: Followers of the philosopher Diogenes, who first practised in the 4th century BC and whose movement enjoyed a revival in the early Empire. 'Cynic' means 'dog-like': they preached that happiness lay not in material possessions but in satisfying needs through the most natural and basic means, i.e. through living like dogs.

Quartilla's Brothel

1. *Priapus*: Roman deity whose huge and permanent erection threatened sexual assault (statues of Priapus were put up in Roman gardens to ward off trespassers with the threat of penetration) and a frequent character in mime and other comic drama. His anger towards Encolpius drives much of the action, in a parodic take on the anger of Poseidon in the *Odyssey* and Juno in the

Aeneid (see further Introduction, p. xvi; chs 101, 133, 139; and Fragment IV). Encolpius' disruption here of the ritual in honour of Priapus is one reason for the god's anger.

2. *their theatrical laughter*: The Latin, *mimico risu,* makes it clear that the reference is more pointed than the generic 'theatrical'. The scene is envisaged as a kind of mime, was a popular but relatively unsophisticated and often obscene entertainment, to which episodes in the *Satyricon* are frequently compared.

3. *the women*: As Sullivan explained:

> The text at this point becomes extremely fragmentary. It is quite likely that we have two collections of fragments or two recensions to deal with. The sequence of events is very confused and it is, for instance, unlikely that two *cinaedi* ('pansies' as I have translated) enter to harass Encolpius, particularly as they behave in much the same way and between each incident the atmosphere is one of jovial friendliness. It would be difficult and confusing in a translation such as this to reallocate the fragments, so I have translated them in the received order. The plot, such as it is, although jerky and repetitious, is fairly clear.

4. *a male prostitute*: Literally, 'a *cinaedus*, or pansy': see the next note. It is not clear whether this is the same man who had appeared in ch. 21.

5. *Pansy boys . . . come out to play*: Written in Sotadean metre, said to have been invented by Sotades of Maroneia in Thrace, who wrote scandalous verse in the third century BC, and having strong associations with obscenity. Encolpius' address to his penis in ch. 132 is also in Sotadean metre. Sullivan's translation well captures the derogatory sense of *cinaedi*: no one called himself a *cinaedus*; it was a term of abuse for a man who liked to be penetrated (it was this that was censured, not male–male relations per se).

6. *cropped the Delian way*: i.e. to be castrated. The island of Delos was renowned for its poultry farming. Cockerels were castrated to make their meat tender and the implication is that the *cinaedi* have been similarly excised.

7. *a night-cap*: There is a pun in the Latin: *embasicoetas* (here 'night-cap') means both an obscene drinking-vessel and also a *cinaedus*

8. *the ceremony*: What follows is a parody of the Roman marriage ceremony with a veil, torches and decorated bridal suite. The bride is Pannychis, whose name means 'All Night'.

Trimalchio's Feast

1. *drinking his health*: In Roman toasts, a small amount of wine was poured on the ground as an offering to the gods.

2. *couriers with lots of medals*: Trimalchio is described in terms reminiscent of the Emperor Nero (Suetonius, *Nero* 30); the first of many such parallels.

3. *painted on the wall*: A *trompe l'œil* image, a painting so realistic that it creates a 'trick of eye', fooled the viewer on first glance into believing it is real. These were common in Roman times, e.g. a large dog in the vestibule of the House of the Tragic Poet in Pompeii.

4. *a mural*: The mural depicts an extraordinarily self-aggrandizing allegory of Trimalchio's rise from slave to successful business-man. Presiding over Trimalchio's success are Mercury (god of trade – and thieves), Minerva (representing learning and craft), Fortuna ('Fortune' whose presence recurs), and the Fates (whose spinning determined the length of a man's life). Typically only funerary art featured autobiographical narrative; the mural pre-figures Trimalchio's 'funeral' at the end of this episode.

5. *the master's first beard was preserved*: The preservation of the hair cut from a young man's first beard was a common Roman practice: the hair symbolized the transition from boyhood to manhood. Trimalchio keeps his in a gold box, which may be a pointed reference to the Emperor Nero who was said to have done this (Suetonius, *Nero* 12).

6. *The Iliad, the Odyssey . . . Laenas*: The *Iliad* and the *Odyssey* are the epic poems of Homer. Trimalchio's paintings of them next to that of his own life-story cast him too as an epic hero, and they also illustrate his pretensions to be a learned man, as a cultured Roman would know the Greek classics. Laenas was presumably a local magistrate who sponsored a gladiatorial show; the juxta-position of themes here further emphasizes Trimalchio's lack of taste.

7. *rods and axes*: Known as fasces, bundles of rods and axes were symbols of political power. Trimalchio was a *sevir Augustalis*, a minor public office held by six men, often ex-slaves, whose job was to oversee the local cult honouring the deified Emperor Augustus. If displaying the fasces is over-the-top for a *sevir*, then displaying the bronze beak of a ship completely oversteps the mark: it is a symbol of a commander's victory in a naval battle.

8. *C. POMPEIUS TRIMALCHIO*: As a slave, Trimalchio would have had just one name, but as a freedman he has assumed the typical Roman three-part name. 'C' is the initial used for his first name, Gaius.

9. *PRIEST OF THE AUGUSTAN COLLEGE*: i.e. a *sevir* (see note 7).

10. *OUT TO DINNER*: The announcement that Trimalchio will be dining out in December advertises that from now (the summer) until then, he will entertaining at home; i.e. it trumpets his generosity.

11. *Right foot first*: The left was thought by some Romans to be unlucky. This, and marking out unlucky and lucky days, are signs of Trimalchio's superstitious nature.

12. *we took our places*: At a typical Roman dinner party the guests reclined on three large couches with tables in the middle. Guests were seated at the couches according to their distinction. Here the rhetoric teacher Agamemnon is favoured with a position on the highest couch, and Encolpius and Ascyltus, as his followers, on the middle couch, alongside Habinnas, who, as *praetor* (leading Roman magistrate), has a place of honour. Usually, the host would recline next to the *praetor*, but Trimalchio has placed his wife there, while he takes the position at the very top of the upper table, above all of his guests.

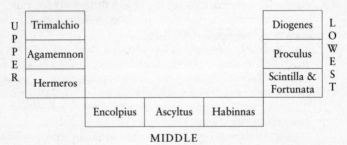

13. *like a musical comedy*: Literally, 'like a pantomime dancer'. The Roman pantomime was a drama performed through mime and dance.

14. *The sight of him drew an astonished laugh*: Trimalchio's closely shaved head is a sign of the freedman, but also of the *stupidus* (the fool) from mime. His napkin bears the purple stripe worn by senators, and his rings (gilt and gold studded with iron) come

daringly close to the gold rings that were the sole privilege of members of the Roman equestrian class. His gold armlet might be another allusion to the Emperor Nero (Suetonius, *Nero* 6).

15. *my game*: Sullivan conjectured that this was probably *latrunculi*, a game somewhere between draughts and chess; the object was to trap an opponent's piece between two of one's own and thus take it.

16. *FALERNIAN ... OPIMIUS*: Consul in 121 BC, but wine of this vintage would be undrinkable (and was not bottled in glass at this early date). Trimalchio has either been conned with a false label or is conning his guests.

17. *a silver skeleton*: The skeleton was a common spectacle at dinner parties; it reminded diners to 'Eat, drink and be merry for tomorrow we die.'

18. *some appropriate dainty*: Each of the foods placed over the signs of the Zodiac is either connected with the sign in question, e.g. above the Twins are testicles and kidneys (which come in pairs), or involves some wordplay, e.g. above Aries are placed chickpeas (*cicer arietinum*).

19. *The Asafoetida Man*: Asafoetida was an aromatic plant, but we know nothing about a mime of this title.

20. *the sauce of all order*: The Latin (*ius cenae*) conveys another of Trimalchio's excruciating puns: 'the order (i.e. rules) of the dinner' and 'the sauce for dinner'. Sullivan's translation draws on both meanings.

21. *Pegasus ... Marsyas*: The winged horse of classical mythology, born from the blood of the beheaded gorgon Medusa, and a satyr (part goat, part man), whom Apollo had flayed alive after he challenged the god to a music contest and lost.

22. *Carve 'er, Carver*: Another pun: the Latin *Carpe* is both the vocative case of the name Carpus and the imperative of the verb *carpere* 'to seize' or 'to 'pluck'.

23. *"Is this like the Ulysses you know?"*: Quotation from Virgil, *Aeneid* 2.44, where Laocoon is warning his fellow Trojans that appearances are deceptive where Ulysses is concerned.

24. *display some culture*: Culture (*paideia*) was the mark of every distinguished Roman. Trimalchio, like Eumolpus, often shows his erudition to be confused.

25. *twelve gods*: Jupiter, Juno, Ceres, Venus, Diana, Apollo, Neptune, Mercury, Vulcan, Mars, Minerva and Vesta.

26. *find their own feed ... chain-gang*: Trimalchio's explanations of

how astrological signs influence character largely rely on obvi-
ous symbolism. For a further gloss: 'those who find their own
feed' refers to independent people, whom popular astrology
associated with the Bull; and 'runaways' are born under the Vir-
gin, because myth has it that the constellation Virgo was once
the girl Astraea, who 'ran away' from the earth after the Golden
Age, and they are 'candidates for the chain-gang' probably
because Virgo was near one of the 'knots' (*nodi*) of the zodiac
(i.e. one of its crucial points), and because in visual representa-
tions her feet appeared to be tied by this knot.

27. *Hipparchus and Aratus*: Hipparchus (*c.* 190–120 BC) and Ara-
tus (*c.* 315–*c.* 240 BC), renowned Greek astronomers.

28. *the liberated sort*: More of Trimalchio's puns: *Liber* means 'free'
and is one of the names of the god Bacchus or Dionysus (*Liber*
and *Liber Pater*). So when the slave boy Dionysus is asked by
Trimalchio to be Liber (i.e. an aspect of Bacchus), the boy under-
stands him to say 'now be free' and so puts on the cap of a
freedman. Trimalchio quips that he is 'the liberated sort'; liter-
ally, that he has a *liber pater*. This can mean that he is the son of
Bacchus (i.e. a heavy drinker) and that he has a free man for a
father, highly unlikely for a freedman.

29. *morra*: Each player simultaneously thrusts out his hand, with zero
to five digits displayed, and guesses aloud what the total number
of fingers and thumbs displayed by the pair or group will be.

30. *beast fighters*: The *bestiarii*, who fought wild animals in the
arena, were often criminals condemned to death, and therefore
were not always trained in combat as gladiators were.

31. *in Thracian armour*: Different categories of gladiator were called
by different names. 'Thracians' were lightly armed and fought
with a helmet, curved sword and small shield.

32. *Tarracina and Tarentum*: Tarracina is a town midway between
Rome and Naples; Tarentum is at the top of the heel of Italy.
They are over 300 km (200 miles) apart, so Trimalchio's estate
covers a large swathe of southern Italy.

33. *Hercules . . . Ulysses . . . Cyclops*: Trimalchio's knowledge of myth-
ology (like that of Calvisius Sabinus who may be satirized here: see
Introduction) is laughably distorted. The hero Hercules did per-
form twelve labours, but they were not related by Homer; the
Cyclops Polyphemus did not harm Ulysses, rather he put out its
sole eye.

34. *the Sibyl at Cumae*: Prophetess at Cumae (near Naples), who
was granted immortality by Apollo, but forgot also to ask for
eternal youth. Old age shrivelled her so much that she could fit

inside a bottle. She features in Virgil's *Aeneid*, not Homer's *Odyssey* as Trimalchio implies. 'What do you want, Sibyl?' and her reply are given in Greek – the only Greek in the *Satyricon*.

35. *Corinthian plate*: A luxury item. Trimalchio confuses the story that Corinthian bronze was discovered by the Roman general Lucius Mummius during his destruction of Corinth in the Achaean War of 146 BC with the myth of the Trojan War, and further confuses Mummius with the Carthaginian general Hannibal.

36. *the Emperor*: According to similar anecdotes in Pliny (*Natural History* 36.195) and Cassius Dio (57.21), this is Tiberius.

37. *Cassandra killed ... Trojan Horse*: Trimalchio's mythology is hopelessly confused. Cassandra had no children; she was the Trojan priestess who became Agamemnon's concubine and was killed by his wife Clytemnestra. It was Medea who killed her sons, to exact revenge on her unfaithful partner, Jason. Daedalus was a distinguished artist, but he was not responsible for the construction of the Trojan horse; he did build a wooden cow in which Minos' wife, Pasiphae, hid and satisfied her unnatural lust for a bull (which led to the birth of the Minotaur). Nor did Niobe hide inside the Trojan horse; the Greek warriors did. She is known for suffering grief, after her boasting led to the deaths of her children.

38. *Hermeros and Petraites*: Other references to these gladiators have been found from the 1st century AD. Trimalchio's jarring juxtaposition of the contemporary with the mythological here recalls his murals in ch. 29.

39. *the Cordax*: An indecent choral dance.

40. '*Madeia, Perimadeia*': We do not know what is being referred to here, or what meaning is intended.

41. *the slave Mithridates crucified*: Crucifixion was a common punishment for criminals and slaves.

42. *a job at Baiae*: Swanky resort on the Bay of Naples; not too tough a 'demotion' (if at all) to be relocated there.

43. *Atellan farces*: Improvised comic dramas featuring crude low-life stereotypes.

44. *the boy tumbled down*: A possible allusion to entertainments hosted by Nero, when an actor playing the mythological character Icarus fell and sprinkled the emperor with his blood (Suetonius, *Nero* 12).

45. *Mopsus of Thrace*: Either a reference that eludes us, or Trimalchio is once again confused and means Orpheus of Thrace, a famous singer.

46. *Cicero and Publilius*: Publilius Syrus was a writer of mimes and

a contemporary of the great orator Cicero; they make an odd pairing.

47.   *read out the presents*: According to Suetonius, giving punning gifts was a favourite game of the Emperor Augustus (*Augustus* 35). Like most translators, where it is too hard to render the pun in English, Sullivan has provided a reasonable substitute; I explain the 'jokes' below.

48.   *Rich man's prison*: The Latin *argentum sceleratum* means 'tainted silver' and puns on the Greek word for 'ham', σκέλος (*skelos*): the gift comprises a leg of ham and a silver vinegar dish.

49.   *Pillow*: The Latin *cervical*, 'neck-piece', certainly leads one to expect a cushion, but a scrag-end of neck meat is offered instead.

50.   *Old man's wit and a sour stick*: Serisapia probably means 'late learning' but also has connotations of 'dry' from the Greek ξηρός (*xeros*), and the Latin *sapo*, a preparation used in drying hair, and *sapor*, 'taste': this leads to a gift of dry salt biscuits. *Contumelia*, 'outrageous insult', puns on the words for 'apple and stick' (*contus cum malo*): the gift is an apple on a stick.

51.   *Lick and spit*: In the Latin, *porri et persica*, 'leeks and peaches': the gifts are a whip and a knife, probably playing on *persica* and *sica*, 'knife', or *persecare*, 'to cut through', and maybe *porrum sectivum*, a particular type of leek, and the verb *secare*, 'to cut'.

52.   *Flies and a fly-trap*: In the Latin, 'sparrows and fly-paper', *passeres et muscarium*: these are gifts of raisins and Attic honey, and it involves a play on *passeres* and *uvam passam* (raisins) and on the stickiness of honey.

53.   *Dinner-clothes and city-suit*: The Latin *cenatoria et forensia* can imply this but can also have the more general meaning 'dinner things and forum things', and this ambiguity is played on in the gifts of a piece of meat and writing tablets.

54.   *Head and foot*: The Latin *canale et pedale* means 'something for a dog and something for the foot', hence the gifts of a hare and a slipper. Sullivan changed the joke to pun on hair/hare.

55.   *Lights and letters*: The Latin *muraena et littera* means a 'lamprey [a type of fish] and a letter'. The gifts are (1) a mouse (*murem*) with a frog attached to it (*cum rana alligata*), with punning wordplay on *muraena/murem . . . rana*, and (2) a bundle of beets (*fascemque betae*) with a pun on the Greek letter beta.

56.   *a Roman citizen, not a subject with taxes to pay*: Roman citizens, unlike their subjects, did not pay taxes. It was a possible, if unlikely, tax dodge for a non-citizen voluntarily to become the slave of a Roman, with the intention of being freed as a Roman citizen in due course (it was often possible for a slave to buy his freedom).

57. *Saturnalia*: A five-day festival in December during which masters and slaves played at reversing their roles; a period of allowed licence.

58. *liberation tax*: When a slave was manumitted, a tax of 5 per cent of his or her value was payable to the public treasury, either by the master or the slave. Hermeros is being sarcastic: Giton has not paid his tax, i.e. he is still a slave.

59. *Something we all have ... smaller*: Sullivan suggested that the most plausible answers to this riddle (or riddles) are the shadow or the penis; others have proposed the foot, the eye and hair. Petronius' riddles, like his other interpretative puzzles, do not work as we might expect them to.

60. *Diomede and Ganymede ... Achilles*: Another mythological mess. Diomede was a Greek warrior who fought at Troy and Ganymede a Trojan boy who was abducted by Zeus; Helen of Sparta's brothers were Castor and Pollux. The Trojan prince Paris stole Helen (not her brother-in-law Agamemnon); the doe was substituted for Iphigeneia, Agamemnon's daughter (not for Helen), who was to be sacrificed by him at Aulis so that the Greek fleet could set sail for Troy, and Diana herself was said to have made the substitution. The Trojans fought the Greeks, not the Tarentines. Agamemnon did win, but only after the death of Achilles, and Iphigeneia was promised to Achilles before the war (and her sacrifice), not after it. Ajax went mad through dishonour when the armour of Achilles was awarded not to him but to Ulysses (see next note).

61. *Ajax, slashing at the calf*: A parody of the myth in which Ajax, in a fit of madness, slaughtered cattle under the delusion that he was murdering his fellow warriors (Sophocles, *Ajax*).

62. *the coffered ceiling began rumbling*: Nero's banquet hall in his Domus Aurea was said to have such a ceiling, from which petals and perfumes showered down upon his guests (Suetonius, *Nero* 31).

63. *the household deities*: The Lares, household gods responsible for the well-being of the household. Trimalchio's gods have appropriately commercial names.

64. *Apelles*: Famous tragic actor of the time of Emperor Caligula (reigned AD 37–41).

65. *Habinnas' entry*: An evocation of Alcibiades' late and drunken entrance to Agathon's dinner party in Plato's *Symposium* (212 D–E).

66. *the praetor's place of honour*: This was the seat at the lower end of the middle couch, usually next to that of the host; see also note 12.

67. *a ninth-day dinner*: It was the custom in Roman funerary rites to have a special dinner on the ninth day after interment (*Cena Novendialis*).

68. *one-tenth per cent to Mercury*: Trimalchio has pledged to give a small portion of his profits to Mercury and has made the offering in the form of a gold bracelet.

69. *The first tables've deserted*: In the Latin, *secundae mensae* means both 'dessert' and (more literally) 'second tables'. Trimalchio delivers another terrible pun.

70. *'Meantime . . . fleet'*: From Virgil, *Aeneid* 5.1.

71. *Daedalus*: The inventor who, according to myth, built the labyrinth on Crete to house the Minotaur, and designed wings to enable him and his son Icarus to escape from the island.

72. *rubbed it on our feet*: A fashion introduced to Nero's court by Otho, who became emperor not long after Nero's death (Pliny, *Natural History* 13.22).

73. *the Greens*: One of the teams of charioteers that raced in the Circus; the others were the Reds, the Whites and the Blues.

74. *the tragedian Ephesus*: We have no further record of this tragic actor.

75. *wearing five gold rings*: Wearing gold rings was a privilege of those of equestrian rank.

76. *POMPEIUS . . . MAECENATIANUS*: Slaves usually adopted the family names of their masters, so 'Pompeius' suggests that Trimalchio once belonged to the family of the Pompeii. Maecenatianus suggests Trimalchio was a freedman of Maecenas, adviser of the Emperor Augustus, an unlikely boast.

77. *modern labyrinth*: The original labyrinth was built on Crete for King Minos the Minotaur. This mythological thread is picked up in ch. 79 when Giton leads the others out of the labyrinth by marking their way, as myth tells us Ariadne had done in order to help Theseus.

78. *Menecrates*: Probably the harpist named Menecrates who was favoured by Nero (Suetonius, *Nero* 30).

79. *a cock crowed . . . to his right hand*: A crowing cock was regarded as an ill omen and Trimalchio's reactions reveal his superstitious character: he has wine sprinkled under the table (usually water would have been used) and on a lamp (a flickering lamp was a good omen), and also moves his ring from his left hand to his right, thought to protect against bad luck (Pliny, *Natural History* 28.57).

80. *Cassandra*: The priestess who prophesied the fall of Troy but

was believed by nobody. Calling Fortunata 'Cassandra' is to call
her a nagging pessimist.

81. *co-heir with the Emperor*: It was common practice for wealthy
individuals to name the emperor as one of their heirs; partly to
curry favour, and partly to reduce the risk of the emperor ignor-
ing the will and confiscating the estate.

82. *a senator's fortune*: A colloquial way of saying 'one million ses-
terces'. In order to qualify for senatorial rank, an individual had
to have property worth at least this.

83. *Apulia*: A region in south-east Italy.

84. *Scaurus*: Possibly the famous Pompeian fish-sauce manufacturer,
Aulus Umbricius Scaurus.

85. *Pretend I'm dead ... nice*: Trimalchio's staging of his own
funeral has real-life parallels. Seneca tells us that Pacuvius
enacted his own funeral procession every day after dinner (*Let-
ters*, 12.8), and Turannius arranged for his household to mourn
him as if he were dead (*On the Shortness of Life*, 20.3).

Encolpius is Jilted and Robbed

1. *another pair of Theban brothers*: Eteocles and Polyneices, sons
of Oedipus who fought over the kingdom of Thebes, but Encol-
pius and Ascyltus are 'brothers' in a rather different sense,
fighting over a different kind of 'territory', i.e. Giton.

2. *The mime ... faces appear*: As Sullivan commented, this verse
seems to have been introduced from somewhere else in the novel
and is 'singularly inappropriate' here. However, in *Satyricon*,
appropriateness is always hard to determine.

3. *Poor Tantalus ... eat*: Tantalus was subject to eternal punish-
ment in Tartarus for the atrocious crimes of killing his son and
serving him to the gods to eat. He was made to stand in a river
that always evaded his lips and beneath fruit that always evaded
his grasp (hence 'tantalize').

Eumolpus in the Art Gallery

1. *Zeuxis ... Protogenes ... Apelles*: Three of the most important
painters of classical Greece. Encolpius makes puns on their
names impossible fully to capture in translation. Zeuxis means
'yoked' and is still 'unburdened' (cf. 'unaffected') by the ravages
of time; Protogenes means 'firstborn' (i.e. to be brought into life)
and his sketches are lifelike; there is a play upon Apelles and

appellant ('they call'). 'The Goddess on One Knee' causes Encolpius to go down on one knee before her.

2.   *the Idaean youth*: Ganymede, the Trojan prince who was raped by Jupiter in the form of an eagle, and taken to become his cup-bearer on Mt Olympus.

3.   *Hylas*: Beloved by the hero Hercules. While the pair were journeying with the Argonauts, Hylas went to get water from a pool and was pulled in by an amorous nymph and drowned.

4.   *Apollo cursed his murderous hands*: Apollo loved a Spartan prince called Hyacinth but accidently killed him with a discus. Encolpius sees in the paintings reflections of his own love affair with, and loss of, a boy (Giton).

5.   *Lycurgus*: He must have featured in earlier episodes, now lost to us: from chs 81 and 117, it seems that Encolpius stayed with Lycurgus and then for some reason murdered him.

6.   *Pergamum*: The most important city in the Roman province of Asia.

7.   *Democritus . . . Eudoxus . . . Chrysippus*: Eumolpus is showing off his knowledge, but reveals ignorance or confusion instead. Democritus of Abdera (*c.* 460–370 BC) was more renowned for his work on atoms and for his ethical ideas than for his contributions to botany and geology. Eudoxus of Cnidos (*c.* 408–355 BC) was an astronomer, but far from growing old on a mountain, he was politically active in his later years. Chrysippus (*c.* 280–207 BC) was a famous Stoic philosopher, but he was said to have taken hellebore (a well-known purgative) as a cure for mental illness, not to facilitate his work (he wrote more than seventy-five books).

8.   *Lysippus . . . Myron*: Important and celebrated sculptors of classical Greece. However, Eumolpus' knowledge and critical judgement are suspect here too. Lysippus of Sicyon (*fl.* 328 BC) was said to have sculpted 1,500 works and to have died a wealthy man. Myron of Eleutherae (*fl.* 480–455 BC) was renowned for casting realistic bronze sculptures; his cow, celebrated in epigrams, was said to have been so lifelike that calves tried to suckle from her. However, he failed to capture the souls of his subjects.

9.   *Phidias*: Celebrated sculptor of the Parthenon temple, in the 5th century BC.

10. *the Fall of Troy*: On this poem, see Introduction, pp. xix–xx.

11. *Phrygians . . . Ida*: By the time of the Roman empire Phrygians had long been identified with Trojans. *Calchas*: The priest of Apollo who predicted that Troy would fall after ten years.

Delian: The god Apollo, who was born and worshipped on the island of Delos. *Ida*: Mountain near Troy.

12. *in the gods' vail . . . Sinon*: i.e. as a gift to the gods. *Danaans*: Another term for Greeks. *Sinon*: Greek who pretended to be a deserter and persuaded the Trojans to take the horse inside the walls of Troy.

13. *Laocoön*: The deaths of the Trojan priest Laocoon and his two sons were the subject of a celebrated statue group, now in the Vatican Museum, Rome.

14. *Tenedos*: Small island off the coast of Troy.

Reconciliation with Giton

1. *What's legitimate*: Eumolpus is speaking.

2. *Ulysses had once clung to the ram*: In Book 9 of Homer's *Odyssey*, Ulysses escaped from the blinded Cyclops' cave by clinging to the stomach of a ram.

Aboard Ship with Lichas and Tryphaena

1. *Thunderstruck*: Lichas and Tryphaena must have encountered Encolpius in lost episodes: Encolpius appears to have wronged Lichas by seducing his wife Hedyle, as well as having had sex with the prostitute Tryphaena and then stealing Giton, who was her slave.

2. *Hannibal*: The general who led Carthage in the war against Rome in 218–201 BC (The Second Punic War), Hannibal became stereotyped as cruel and deceitful.

3. *trick did work nicely once*: Cleopatra, Queen of Egypt, was said to have had herself delivered to Julius Caesar wrapped in a carpet (Plutarch, *Caesar* 49).

4. *Epicurus*: Athenian philosopher (340–270 BC), founder of Epicureanism, which promoted living a tranquil life, free from religious fears and superstitions. The irony here is that even as Eumolpus praises Epicurus' rejection of such 'nonsense', the dreams of Lichas and Tryphaena do actually foreshadow events that will happen later in the episode.

5. *with Spartan disdain*: Citizens of the Greek city of Sparta were renowned for their physical endurance.

6. *Ulysses' nurse after twenty years*: Eurycleia recognized the scar on her master's leg (*Odyssey* 19.473ff.). In a parodic twist, Encolpius' identifying mark is his penis.

7. *the colonnade of Hercules*: A missing part of the work; the location is usually taken to be Baiae, the resort on the Bay of Naples.

8. *Did a salamander burn your eyebrows off?*: The salamander, a lizard-like amphibian, was thought to secrete a substance that had scorching properties.

9. *No maddened Medea*: Medea fled from Colchis with her lover Jason and managed to delay her father's pursuit of their ship by chopping up her brother, Absyrtus, and throwing his body parts overboard, knowing her father would stop to gather them up.

10. *There was once a lady of Ephesus*: Ephesus was a large Greek city in the Roman province of Asia Minor (near what is now Selcuk in Turkey). 'The Widow of Ephesus', perhaps the most famous episode in the *Satyricon,* is thought to be one of the 'Milesian Tales', popular and salacious short stories composed by Aristides of Miletus in the second century BC and adapted into Latin by Lucius Cornelius Sisenna. However, none of the original tales survives, and we know little about them.

11. *Believe you . . . know*: A near quotation from *Aeneid* 4.34, spoken by Anna to her sister Dido.

12. *Would you . . . passion*: Quoted from *Aeneid* 4.38, again spoken by Anna to Dido.

13. *'If you had*: While the manuscripts attribute this speech to Tryphaena's maid, Sullivan conjectured that it more suitably belongs to Encolpius, jealously complaining about Giton's behaviour with Tryphaena.

14. *sacred robe and the goddess's rattle*: Sacred objects belonging to the Egyptian goddess Isis which, in a lost episode, Encolpius stole from the ship.

The Journey to Croton

1. *Croton*: Town on the coast of the toe of Italy (modern Crotone), its glory days in the fifth century BC were long over by the time of the Roman Empire.

2. *fortune-hunters*: Legacy-hunting is a common topic of Roman satire, e.g. Horace, *Satires* 2.5.

3. *the robe I'd stolen*: Further references to lost episodes. We can conjecture that the robe is the robe of Isis that Encolpius had stolen from Lichas' ship.

4. *"I hate . . . off"*: A well-known quotation from Horace, *Odes* 3.1.1.

5. *the Civil War*: Eumolpus delivers a terrible poem on the series of conflicts that took place in the first century BC and ended when

Octavian (Augustus Caesar) established stability in 31 BC, inaugurating the Roman Empire and ending the Roman Republic. For an interpretation of the poem, see Introduction, pp. xix–xx. Petronius was imitating and possibly parodying Lucan's epic poem *Civil War or Pharsalia*, and Sullivan rendered this with a brilliant imitation of the *Cantos* of Ezra Pound (see 'Note on the Text and Translation').

6. *Taurus . . . sells dear*: Taurus is a mountainous region of southern Anatolia, in what is now southern Turkey. *Ammon*: The Egyptian god often identified with Jupiter. *his tooth sells dear*: Refers to the expensiveness of ivory; the 'tooth' is from an elephant, the 'monster' (22).

7. *oysters . . . birds*: Oysters from the Lucrine Lake near Baiae were particularly valued. *The Phasian Lake emptied of birds*: the river Phasis flows into the Black Sea; the birds are pheasants.

8. *Cato is defeated*: Cato the Younger (95–46 BC) was a defender of Roman Republicanism, staunch moralist and opponent of Julius Caesar. He was defeated in the elections for the praetorship and then the consulship by the combined opposition of Julius Caesar and Pompey. He is a major figure in Lucan's *Civil War*.

9. *Usura*: Not personified in the original; *usura* means usury, i.e. charging exorbitant interest rates on debts.

10. *furor militaris . . . the sword*: Not in the Latin here, but paraphrases line 60: *furor et bellum ferroque excita libido*, 'madness and war and desire pricked by the sword'.

11. *three captains . . . Enyo*: Crassus, Pompey and Julius Caesar, who formed the power pact known as the First Triumvirate (60 BC), were killed: Crassus died fighting the Parthians in 53 BC; Pompey was executed in Egypt in 48 BC; Caesar was assassinated at Rome in 44 BC. *Enyo*: Greek war deity (Roman Bellona).

12. *The scene*: The action takes place in the Phlegrean Fields, a volcanic area from where Aeneas descended into the Underworld in *Aeneid* 6 (modern Solfatara at Pozzuoli near Naples).

13. *Dis*: Lord of the Underworld (also known as Pluto (Greek Hades)).

14. *Tisiphone . . . Sulla's sword*: Tisiphone is one of the Furies, avengers of murder. *Sulla*: Roman general who slaughtered hundreds of supporters of Marius in 82 BC (thirty years before the Civil War), in order to become dictator at Rome.

15. *Cocytus*: One of the rivers in the Underworld.

16. *Philippi . . . Actium*: The Battle of Philippi (42 BC) saw Octavian and Mark Antony defeat Brutus and Cassius; although the battlefield is in Macedonia, on the border with Thrace, Roman

writers often conflated it with the Battle of Pharsalus in Thessaly (where Caesar vanquished Pompey in 48 BC) and hence, the 'double slaughter'. *Spanish and Libyan dead*: The Battle of Munda in Spain (45 BC). *Nile's barriers groaning*: Refers to Caesar's battles in Egypt in 48 and 47 BC. *Actium*: The Battle of Actium (31 BC) saw Antony and Cleopatra decisively defeated by Octavian, whom the god Apollo was said to have aided (173).

17. *Charon*: Transported dead souls across the river Styx in the Underworld.

18. *fraternal bolts*: Lightning hurled by Dis' brother, Jupiter.

19. *Hyperion . . . Cynthia*: The original has 'Titan' instead of 'Hyperion'; in this context, both mean the sun. *Cynthia*: The moon.

20. *Etna*: A volcano in Sicily.

21. *He abandons the Gallic*: Caesar fought in Gaul 58–49 BC, and on his return, crossed the Rubicon, the small river separating Gaul from Italy, and began the civil war. Eumolpus substitutes the Alps (220) for the river.

22. *a Greek divinity*: Hercules, hero and son of Zeus, was said to have been the first to have crossed the Alps, after killing the monster Geryon in Spain.

23. *Saturnian land*: Italy, where Saturn fled after Jupiter ousted him and assumed sovereignty.

24. *raven, Delphicus ales*: A bird special to Apollo who had a shrine at Delphi.

25. *Hercules, Amphitryonides*: Hercules, whose mortal father was Amphityron, had travelled to the Caucasus to rescue Prometheus, who was chained to a mountain there.

26. *doomed race of Giants*: The Giants attempted to overthrow the Olympian gods; 'doomed' because Jupiter triumphed over them.

27. *Palatine*: An important hill of Rome and later the site of the imperial residence.

28. *Quirites*: The formal name for Roman citizens.

29. *Auster*: The South Wind.

30. *both consuls . . . the pirates*: Gaius Claudius Marcellus and Lucius Cornelius Lentulus Crus were 'both consuls' in 49 BC and supporters of Pompey. *Terror of the Pontus*: Pompey had beaten Mithridates, king of Pontus, in 63 BC. *Hydaspes*: The river in India where Alexander the Great had success in battle; transferring Alexander's victory to Pompey is deliberate or confused hyperbole. *Wrecked the pirates*: In 67 BC Pompey cleared the Mediterranean of pirates.

31. *Erebus*: The god of darkness.

32. *Erinys, Bellona ... Megaera*: A Fury, the goddess of war and another Fury.

33. *Dione ... Cyllene born*: Venus is sometimes referred to by her mother's name, Dione. *Pallas*: Pallas Athene is the Greek name for Minerva, goddess of skill in battle. *Romulus*: The mythical founder of Rome and the son of Mars, i.e. 'Mavortius'. *Phoebus and Phoebus' sister*: Apollo and Diana. *Mercury, on Cyllene born*: The original does not refer to the god by name, but by his birthplace, Cyllene, a mountain in Arcadia.

34. *Pompey ... Hercules Tirynthius*: Pompey is compared to Hercules, who was born in Tiryns; as Hercules saved the Greeks, so Pompey saved the Romans.

35. *Marcellus*: It would be odd, given the naming of the consul Marcellus (362) and his co-consul Lentulus (362 and 437), if he were not the same Marcellus. However, more appropriate in context is his brother Marcus Claudius Marcellus, consul in 51 BC, who proposed to the senate that Caesar be removed from his military command in Gaul. Perhaps Eumolpus is muddled.

36. *Curio ... son of heaven*: Curio Scribonius was tribune in 50 BC and a supporter of Caesar. *Lentulus*: Consul and one of those who agitated for civil war. *son of heaven*: Julius Caesar who was deified after his death.

37. *Epidamnus*: The Greek name for Dyrrachium in Epirus, Pompey's base after he fled from Rome.

38. *dye Thessalian bays*: The massacre at the Battle of Pharsalus, staining the waters with blood.

The Seductions of Circe

1. *While all this ... deserves*: Sullivan conjectured that this fragment might be out of place here. It is possible that in the original it came later in the episode.

2. *as Praxiteles imagined Diana's*: Praxiteles, a fourth-century-BC Greek sculptor, was famous for works such as the Aphrodite of Cnidos. He made at least one statue of Artemis (Roman Diana).

3. *Parian marble*: Marble from the island of Paros was renowned for its whiteness.

4. *Doris*: Encolpius' relationship with Doris must have been related in an earlier (lost) episode.

5. *Two horns ... a swan*: Jupiter was said to have metamorphosed into different forms before raping mortal women: a bull for Europa, a swan for Leda and a shower of gold for Danaë.

6. *girl-friend*: The word *soror* literally means sister.

7. *Circe ... Polyaenus*: Circe, daughter of Helios, the Sun, is the sorceress in Homer's *Odyssey* who turned Ulysses' crew into pigs and became his lover for a year. The irony is, of course, that the impotent Encolpius is neither hero nor lover.

8. *When Jove and his wifely love united*: Another allusion to lovers in Homer: Hera's seduction of her husband Zeus (*Iliad* 14.346–51).

9. *an honourable Platonic way*: Literally, 'with Socratic trustworthiness' (*Socratica fide*), which refers to the failure of the gorgeous politician and general Alcibiades to seduce his teacher, Socrates (Plato, *Symposium* 217–19); said to be the origin of 'Platonic love' meaning 'non-sexual love'.

10. *my body that once made me an Achilles*: In the *Iliad* the Greek warrior Achilles is a paradigm of physical strength and virility.

11. *a letter*: This and Encolpius' reply are comic versions of the letters exchanged by lovers in the Greek romance novels, where they declare a couple's fidelity and chastity, but this exchange concerns Encolpius' sexual impotence.

12. *bringing a little old woman with her*: In ch. 132 we learn her name is Proselenus.

13. *Metamorphosed Daphne*: The nymph Daphne was changed into a laurel tree to prevent her rape by the god Apollo.

14. *Procne turned urban swallow*: Procne's husband, Tereus, raped her sister Philomela. In revenge, Procne killed their son and served him up to be eaten by Tereus. Realizing the hideous deception, Tereus pursued the sisters, but all three were turned into birds: Tereus a hoopoe, Philomela a nightingale and Procne a swallow. (In some versions the birds for the sisters are reversed.)

15. *Her sheer*: In the manuscripts (Codex 1) this paragraph is preceded with the words *Encolpius de Endymione puero* ('Encolpius speaking about a boy Endymion') that are likely to be an intrusion. Müller puts the phrase in brackets to indicate its probable spuriousness and Sullivan omits it altogether. If we were to accept the phrase, then what follows would be '*His* sheer physical beauty ...'

16. *Three times ... deeper bite*: The address is in Sotadean metre: see p. 174 note 5.

17. *Turning away ... poppyhead*: A pastiche of lines from Virgil. The first two lines are taken from *Aeneid* 469–70 and are used to imagine Encolpius' penis reacting to him in the way that Dido's

ghost responded to Aeneas, her lover who had broken her heart by abandoning her. However, where the *Aeneid* continues by comparing Dido to unmoving flint and marble, we get instead half a line from *Eclogues* 5.16 and half from *Aeneid* 9.436, which provide very different images for comparisons: those of a weeping willow and a drooping poppyhead.

18. *Cato*: Literally *Catones*, 'Catos'. Refers to Marcus Porcius Cato (234–149 BC), also known as 'Cato the Censor', a statesman renowned for his strict morality, and his great-grandson, also Marcus Porcius Cato, or 'Cato the Younger', who was a politician and a follower of Stoic philosophy. More generally, any moralist.

19. *Epicurus*: Epicurus did indeed promote the pursuit of pleasure, but not the sort celebrated here because sexual desire was considered as much a torment as a pleasure – a view repeatedly reinforced by behaviour in the *Satyricon*.

20. *the hostile deity*: i.e. Priapus, whose parents were Bacchus and Venus, also known as Dione.

21. *Dryads*: Nymphs who lived in the woods.

22. *when I robbed the temples*: Events now lost: perhaps Encolpius had robbed the temples of Priapus, which would explain the god's hostility.

23. *Hyrcanian tigers*: Hyrcania was a region south of the Caspian Sea known in antiquity for having an abundant tiger population.

24. *Proteus*: The 'old man of the sea', a water god who had the ability to assume any shape he wanted (hence our adjective 'protean').

25. *Hecale ... Callimachus*: Hecale, an old and impoverished woman who gave hospitality to the hero Theseus, was the subject of a short narrative poem, now lost, by the Alexandrian poet and scholar Callimachus (c. 305–240 BC). He is referred to in the Latin text as Battiades (Battus was the mythical founder of his native city, Cyrene).

26. *Stymphalian birds ... Harpies*: The Stymphalians were man-eating birds which terrorized the Stymphalian lake in Arcadia until Hercules drove them away. The Harpies were monstrous bird-women, 'Snatchers', sent to punish the prophet Phineus by snatching away some of his food and fouling the rest; myth has it that they were killed by the Argonauts.

27. *Danaë*: The daughter of Acrisius, King of Argos, who shut her up in a tower because it was prophesied that a son of hers would kill his grandfather. Zeus turned himself into a shower of golden

rain (see ch. 126) and fell through her window; she gave birth to Perseus who eventually did cause the death of Acrisius.

28. *Cato ... a lawyer of note*: Probably a reference to the eminent legal expert Cato, the son of Cato the Censor (though the Censor was a practised orator in the courts). The Latin text gives the names of the other 'lawyers of note': Servius and Labeo (Servius Sulpicius Lemonia Rufus (*c.* 106–43 BC) and Marcus Antistius Labeo (*c.* 54 BC–AD 10/11) were both distinguished legal experts).

29. *her life*: Sullivan noted that the order of the fragments in chs 138–9 'seems seriously dislocated', but he followed the manuscript tradition, 'leaving it to the reader to work out a more satisfactory order of events'.

30. *Ariadne or Leda ... Helen or Venus*: Famous mythical beauties: Ariadne was the daughter of King Minos of Crete, lover of Theseus and wife of Dionysus; Leda was seduced by Zeus in the form of a swan and became the mother of Helen of Sparta, the most beautiful woman in the world; Venus was the Roman goddess of love and desire.

31. *Paris*: Judge of a beauty competition between Juno, Minerva and Venus; all three offered bribes and Paris chose that offered by Venus: Helen of Sparta.

32. *Others have been hounded ... Hellespont*: Encolpius lists examples of divine hostility against a mortal, apparently a reflection of his own situation with Priapus. Juno's jealous hatred of Hercules, who was Zeus' child with a mortal woman, led to his twelve labours, one of which involved him taking the sky off the shoulders of Atlas and propping it up for a short time. Laomedon, king of Troy, cheated Apollo and Neptune out of their payment for helping him rebuild the city walls (hence he is 'Impious'), and Neptune punished him by sending a sea-monster to ravage Troy. Pelias somehow slighted Juno and incurred her wrath, and later was murdered at the hands of his daughters, under the influence of Medea. The allusion to Telephus possibly refers to a version of the myth in which Telephus' injury (by Achilles) was caused by a god. As told in the *Odyssey*, Ulysses incurred the anger of Neptune when he blinded his son, the Cyclops Polyphemus. Nereus was a sea deity who lived in the Aegean and was the father of the Nereids.

Eumolpus and the Extortionists

1. *Mercury*: The Roman god Mercury (identified with the Greek god Hermes) was said to guide the dead to the Underworld.

2. *Protesilaus*: The first Greek hero killed in the Trojan War, Protesilaus was allowed to return from the Underworld for a brief visit to his grieving wife, Laodameia. Encolpius raises his tunic to reveal his own 'resurrection'.

3. *Gorgias*: The name of this legacy-hunter recalls that of the famous orator and sophist (*c.* 485–*c.* 380 BC). Sophists were notorious for arguing weak cases strongly for their own financial gain. Petronius' Gorgias, seeing money to be made, argues for cannibalism!

4. *Saguntines . . . Petelians . . . Numantia*: Saguntum and Numantia were cities in Spain: captured by the Carthaginian general Hannibal in 219 BC, and by the Roman general Scipio Aemilianus in 133 BC, respectively, both after eight-month sieges. Petelia, a town near Croton in southern Italy, was besieged and captured by Himilco, one of Hannibal's deputies, in 216 BC. The historians give more sober accounts of these sieges (Livy, *History of Rome* 21.14–15, 23.30; Silius Italicus, *Punica* 12.431–2; Appian, *Roman History* 6.96-7).

5. *children*: The translation attributed to Oscar Wilde (see Introduction) uses the forged Latin text by François Nodot (1692) to provide an ending to the novel, depicting the sacrifice of Eumolpus:

> 'In fine, seeing it is merely the idea of cannibalism that can cause disgust, you must fight with all your heart to banish this repugnance from your minds, to the end you may receive the enormous legacies I put you down for.'
>
> The insolent extravagances Eumolpus reeled off with such reckless inconsequence as made the fortune hunters begin to distrust his promises. Instantly they began to scrutinize more closely our words and actions, and everything they saw only increasing their suspicions, they soon set us down for a gang of common cheats and swindlers. Hereupon such as had gone to more than ordinary expense for our entertainment, resolved to have at us and take their just revenge.
>
> But now Chrysis, who was in all their secrets, warned me of what the Crotonians' intentions towards us were. This news scared me so terribly I fled with Giton, leaving Eumolpus to his fate; and a few days later I learned that the Crotonians, furious at the old fox having lived sumptuously at their expense for so long, had massacred him in the Massilian fashion. To show you what this means I must tell you that whenever the Massilians were visited by the Plague, one of the poorer inhabitants would volunteer himself as the expiatory victim, on condition of being maintained a full year at

the public cost and fed on choice food. Later on, the unhappy man, bedecked with festal wreaths and sacred robes, was carried in procession through the whole city, and made the butt of general execration, to the end that all the calamities of the State might be concentrated on his devoted head. This done, he was hurled headlong from a rock.

(*The Satyricon of Petronius Arbiter in the translation attributed to Oscar Wilde with an introduction, notes and bibliography,* 2 vols (Chicago: 1927), pp. 354–6)

THE FRAGMENTS AND THE POEMS

This is a mixed collection, containing quotations from Petronius and poems, some obviously Petronian, others more doubtfully attributed. Several of the concerns of the poems (Epicurean ideas, love, sex) reflect those of the *Satyricon* and it is an enjoyable frustration for the reader to attempt an imaginative reconstruction of its lost parts.

Sullivan followed the numbering in Müller's edition, but also included XVII–XVIII and XXXI–LVII, which were thought by Müller not to be by Petronius.

Abbreviations

AL	Bücheler, F. and A. Riese, eds., *Anthologia Latina* (Amsterdam: 1893, repr. 1973)
Bücheler	Bücheler, F., *Petronii Arbitri Satirarum Reliquae adiectus est Liber Priapeorum,* (Berlin: 1862)
Helm	Helm, R., *Fabius Planciades Fulgentius* (Lepizig: 1898)
GL	Lindemann, J. F., ed., *Corpus Grammaticorum Latinorum* (Leipzig: 1831)

I

auri sacra fames: 'Sacred hunger for gold' or 'accursed hunger for gold' (in the Virgilian context, clearly the latter). The ambiguity of *sacra* is presumably why the scholar Servius feels the need to gloss the phrase.

III

Canidia: A sorceress.

IV

Arbiter: i.e. Petronius; see Introduction.

VI

Albucia: Does not appear in the parts of the novel that have survived.

VII

So . . . desires: The incident takes place in ch. 20 of the novel. It has been suggested that Fulgentius may be confusing the drinking of myrrh as an aphrodisiac with the 'myrrhine cup', a drinking cup made of myrrhine. The sentences in brackets are the additions of a later commentator.

VIII

Cerberus: The mythical dog with three (or more) heads that guarded the entrance to the Underworld.

XVI

Neapolitan tunnel: Provides a short cut to Puteoli and Baiae from Naples.

XVII and XVIII

These two fragments are omitted in Müller's edition, but preserved in that of Bücheler. It is unlikely that these fragments are from Petronius. XVII makes little sense.

XIX

such verses: By this, the writer means verses in a particular metre: catalectic iambic dimeter. No verses in this metre survive in *Satyricon*. *Memphis*: An important city in Egypt.

XX

Anacreon: Greek lyric poet of the sixth century BC.
Petronius used it: i.e. Anacreontic metre.

XXIV

'*he who . . . smell*': Also found in Martial (2.12.4), so either it has been misattributed to Petronius or, more likely, both authors are quoting a common saying.

XXV

Nicagorus: Probably Nicagoras, an Athenian sophist who lived during the third century AD and who wrote biographies of famous men.

XXVI

Apollo's tortoise: Apollo had a special relationship with the tortoise because he played the lyre, an instrument made out of its shell.

XXVII

This poem is a quintessentially Epicurean account of religion (comparable to that given in Lucretius, *On the Nature of Things* 5.1161–240) and sounds like something Eumolpus might say.

Athos: Mountain in northern Greece, now famous for its monastery.
Phoebus: The sun
Pales: Roman deity of shepherds and flocks who was worshipped in a festival called the Parilia (or Palilia) on 21 April.

XXVIII

His Majesty: King Midas supported Pan, rather than Apollo, in a lyre-playing contest and was punished by Apollo with the gift of ass's ears. Midas kept his ears a secret from all but his hairdresser who thought it was safe to blurt it out into the open air. The reeds, however, kept whispering the secret and gave Midas away (see also Ovid, *Metamorphoses* 11.183–93).

XXIX

the vagrant senses lie: An exposition of the Epicurean theory of sense perception. Epicureans believed that physical objects continually emit thin layers of atoms that travel through the air and come into contact with our sense organs. As far as sight is concerned, the further the images travel through the air the more they can become distorted. See Lucretius, *On the Nature of Things* 4.353ff., which also discusses the optical illusion of the tower.

XXX

This poem, which presents the Epicurean doctrine that dreams are memories replayed (see Lucretius, *On the Nature of Things* 4.962–1036), would, as Sullivan suggested, fit appropriately into ch. 104 as another of Eumolpus' pompous poems.

XLV

India bore me: Spoken by a parrot.
purple as Tyre: The ancient Phoenician city of Tyre was a centre for the production of purple dye.
myrmidon: i.e. faithful follower (as the Myrmidons were loyal to Achilles).

XLVIII

Phoebus' sister . . . Delia: Diana, sister of Apollo.

LI

Anti-semitism was rife in Petronius' day, but without a context for this unpleasant poem (rendered less so in Sullivan's translation) it is hard to know quite how the stereotypes are being employed. The poem appears to satirize men who give the appearance of being Jewish but do not circumcise themselves, this being, for Romans, a prime marker of Jewish identity (see ch. 102).

LV

Frequently translated, most famously by Ben Jonson ('Doing a filthy pleasure is . . .'). For this and other versions, see *Arion* 2: 1 (Spring 1963), pp. 82–4.

LVII

Almost certainly a medieval poem, this story has no obvious ancient precedents but finds an odd echo in the hermaphrodite whom Ascyltus abducts in *Fellini-Satyricon*.

THE STORY OF PENGUIN CLASSICS

Before 1946 ... 'Classics' are mainly the domain of academics and students; readable editions for everyone else are almost unheard of. This all changes when a little-known classicist, E. V. Rieu, presents Penguin founder Allen Lane with the translation of Homer's *Odyssey* that he has been working on in his spare time.

1946 Penguin Classics debuts with *The Odyssey*, which promptly sells three million copies. Suddenly, classics are no longer for the privileged few.

1950s Rieu, now series editor, turns to professional writers for the best modern, readable translations, including Dorothy L. Sayers's *Inferno* and Robert Graves's unexpurgated *Twelve Caesars*.

1960s The Classics are given the distinctive black covers that have remained a constant throughout the life of the series. Rieu retires in 1964, hailing the Penguin Classics list as 'the greatest educative force of the twentieth century.'

1970s A new generation of translators swells the Penguin Classics ranks, introducing readers of English to classics of world literature from more than twenty languages. The list grows to encompass more history, philosophy, science, religion and politics.

1980s The Penguin American Library launches with titles such as *Uncle Tom's Cabin*, and joins forces with Penguin Classics to provide the most comprehensive library of world literature available from any paperback publisher.

1990s The launch of Penguin Audiobooks brings the classics to a listening audience for the first time, and in 1999 the worldwide launch of the Penguin Classics website extends their reach to the global online community.

The 21st Century Penguin Classics are completely redesigned for the first time in nearly twenty years. This world-famous series now consists of more than 1300 titles, making the widest range of the best books ever written available to millions – and constantly redefining what makes a 'classic'.

The Odyssey continues ...

The best books ever written

P E N G U I N CLASSICS

SINCE 1946

Find out more at www.penguinclassics.com